In Search of April Raintree

In Search of April Raintree

Beatrice Culleton

PEGUIS PUBLISHERS
WINNIPEG • CANADA

First published by Pemmican Publications, Winnipeg, 1983
Ten printings to 1991

95 96 97 5 4 3

*All characters in this novel are fictional and any resemblance to any
person, living or dead, is purely coincidental.*

Canadian Cataloguing in Publication Data

Culleton, Beatrice, 1949–

In search of April Raintree
First published: Winnipeg: Pemmican Publications, 1983.
ISBN 1-895411-46-7

I. Title.

PS8555.U475I5 1992   C813'.54   C92-098126-7
PR9199.3.C84I5 1992

Printed and bound in Canada by Kromar Printing Ltd.

Peguis Publishers Ltd.
318 McDermot Avenue
Winnipeg MB
Canada R3A 0A2
Toll Free 1-800-667-9673

In memory of my sisters,
Vivian and Kathy

ACKNOWLEDGEMENTS

I WOULD like to acknowledge my appreciation to the many people who made this book possible. Special thanks to Murray Sinclair, LL.B., for his advice and assistance, and to the staff at Pemmican Publications who worked with me.

I extend my appreciation to Mom and Dad, whose experiences gave me insight; to Edward, my brother; to my foster families, who shared their homes with me. Especially, I would like to thank my own family—Bill, Billy, and Debbie— for their encouragement and support in writing this novel.

(Excerpt from a letter)

Dear Beatrice,

I read your manuscript over twice and I am very excited. You are a fine writer and I hope this book will be the first of many.

...You have written an important story, one that should be read by all Canadians, Indian and White.

In the past few years there has been much controversy regarding Native children and the question of foster homes and adoption. Reems of papers and reports have been written. How many of those papers were written by people who have lived through such an experience?

...It is a powerful story because, with gentleness, it deals with the sickness in our society and our people. It is the kind of writing that will begin the healing of our people and help a dominant society understand and feel the lives of a people it almost destroyed.

Thank you for sharing your story with me.

My love and best wishes,
Maria Campbell

1

MEMORIES. SOME memories are elusive, fleeting, like a butterfly that touches down and is free until it is caught. Others are haunting. You'd rather forget them but they won't be forgotten. And some are always there. No matter where you are, they are there, too. I always felt most of my memories were better avoided but now I think it's best to go back in my life before I go forward. Last month, April 18th, I celebrated my twenty-fourth birthday. That's still young but I feel so old.

My father, Henry Raintree, was of mixed blood, a little of this, a little of that and a whole lot of Indian. My sister, Cheryl, who was 18 months younger than me, had inherited his looks: black hair, dark brown eyes which

9

turned black when angry, and brown skin. There was no doubt they were both of Indian ancestry. My mother, Alice, on the other hand, was part Irish and part Ojibway. Like her, I had pale skin, not that it made any difference when we were living as a family. We lived in Norway House, a small northern Manitoba town, before my father contracted tuberculosis. Then we moved to Winnipeg. I used to hear him talk about T.B. and how it had caused him to lose everything he had worked for. Both my Mom and Dad always took this medicine and I always thought it was because of T.B. Although we moved from one run-down house to another, I remember only one, on Jarvis Avenue. And of course, we were always on welfare. I knew that from the way my Dad used to talk. Sometime he would put himself down and sometimes he counted the days till he could walk down to the place where they gave out cheques and food stamps.

It seemed to me that after the welfare cheque days, came the medicine days. That was when my parents would take a lot of medicine and it always changed them. Mom, who was usually quiet and calm would talk and laugh in a loud obnoxious way, and Dad, who already talked and laughed a lot, just got clumsier. The times they took the medicine the most were the times when many other grown-ups would come over and drink it with them. To avoid these people, I would take Cheryl into our tiny bedroom, close the door and put my box of old rusted toys in front of the door. Beside the aunties and uncles out there, there were strange men and they would start yelling and sometimes they would fight, right in our small house. I would lay in my cot, listening to them knocking things over and bumping into walls. Sometimes they would crash into our door and I would grow even more petrified, even though I knew Mom and Dad were out there with them. It always took a long time before I could get to sleep.

There were days when they came with their own children. I didn't much like these children either, for they

reminiscent of 'Once were Warriors'...

were sullen and cranky and wouldn't talk or play with us or else they were aggressive bullies who only wanted to fight us. Usually, their faces were dirty, their noses were runny and I was sure they had done 'it' in their pants because they smelled terrible. If they had to stay the night, I remember I would put our blankets on the floor for them, stubbornly refusing to share our cot with them. Once Mom had let a little girl sleep with us and during the night she wet the bed. It had been a long time before the smell went away.

My mother didn't always drink that medicine, not as much as my father did. That's when she would clean the house, bake, do the laundry and sewing. If she was really happy, she would sing us songs and at night she would rock Cheryl to sleep. But that was one kind of happiness that didn't come often enough for me. To prolong that mood in her, I would help her with everything, chattering away in desperation, lest my own silences would push her back into her normal remoteness. My first cause for vanity was that out of all the houses of the people we knew, my mother kept the cleanest house. Except for those mornings-after. She would tell her friends that it was because she was raised in a residential school and then worked as a housekeeper for the priest in her home town.

Cheryl and I always woke up before our parents so I would tend to Cheryl's needs. I would feed her whatever was available, then wash and dress her in clean clothes. Weather permitting, we would then go off to the park, which was a long walk, especially on hot summer days. Our daily routine was dictated by our hunger pangs and by daylight. Darkness brought out the boogeymen and Dad told us what they did to little children. I liked all of Dad's stories, even the scary ones because I knew that Cheryl and I were always safe in the house.

It was very rare when Mom would go downtown to the department stores where they had ride-on stairs. Mom didn't like going shopping. I guess it was because sometimes people were rude to her. When that happened, Mom would get a hurt look in her eyes and act apologetic. One day, I didn't notice any of that because that day I saw my first black person. I was sure he was a boogeyman and wondered how come he wandered around so easily, as if nothing was wrong. I watched him and he stopped at the watch counter. Since Mom and Cheryl were nearby and there were a lot of other people close enough, I went over to him. My voice was very shaky but I asked: "Mr. Boogeyman, what do you do with the children you catch?"

"What's that?" his voice seemed to rumble from deep within him and when he turned to look at me, I thought he had the kindest eyes I'd ever seen. Maybe, though, they changed at night. No, he couldn't be bad.

"Nothing," I said and walked back to my mother's side.

When winter came, we didn't go to the park anymore. There was plenty to do with the snow around our house. Sometimes Mom would come out and help us build our snowmen and our houses. One December, we all went downtown to watch the Santa Claus parade. That was such a thrilling, magical day for me. After that, we went to visit an aunt and uncle where Cheryl and I had a glorious old time, feasting on cake, fruit and hot chocolate. Then we walked home. Dad threw snowballs at Mom for a bit before he carried sleepy-eyed Cheryl in his arms. I was enchanted by all the colored Christmas lights and the decorations in the store windows. I think that was the best day ever, because Mom and Dad laughed for real.

Not long after that, many people came to our house to drink the 'medicine' and in the beginning they all sounded cheerful and happy. But later they started their yelling and even the women were angrily shouting. One woman was loudly wailing and it sounded like she'd gotten smacked a few times.

In the middle of the night when everything had been quiet for a while, I got up to go to the toilet. There were people sprawled all over the place, sleeping and snoring.

One man, though, who was half sitting up against a wall, grumbled and shifted and I saw that his pants were open. I knew that I should hurry but I just stood there watching and he played around with his thing. Then he peed right in my direction. That made me move back out of the room. I went through the kitchen and there was my Dad sleeping on the bare floor, still in his clothes. I wondered why, so I went to their bedroom. When I put the light switch on, I saw my mother. She was bare-naked and kissing a strange man. I guess she realized that someone was in the room and she sat up while trying to hide her nakedness. She looked scared but when she saw that it was only me, she hissed at me, "Get out of here!"

I forgot about having to go to the toilet and went back to my bed. I tried to figure everything out but I couldn't.

A few days later, I was sitting on my Dad's lap and Mom was doing the laundry. A woman came to visit but then it became an argument. She was shouting terrible names and she began to push my mother around. Meanwhile Dad just watched them and laughed, and even egged them on. To me this was all so confusing. I just knew that Mom shouldn't have kissed someone else; my Dad shouldn't have slept on the floor; that old man shouldn't have played with himself and then peed on the floor; and right now, Dad ought to be trying to protect Mom, not finding the whole thing amusing. I squirmed off Dad's lap, walked over to that woman and kicked her as hard as I could, yelling for her to leave Mom alone. I heard Dad laughing even louder. But it worked because the strange woman left.

That winter, I noticed that my Mom was getting fatter and fatter. When winter was finished, my Mom got so sick from being fat she had to go away to the hospital. One of our aunties came to stay with us. She and Dad would sit around joking and drinking their medicine. I used to wonder how come they all drank this medicine yet no one ever got better. Another thing, they couldn't all be sick like Mom and Dad, could they? So one evening while Dad and

Auntie Eva were busy playing cards, I picked up his glass and took a quick swallow before he could stop me. Ugh! It burned my mouth and my throat and made me cough and choke. I spit it out as fast as I could. It was purely awful and I was even more puzzled as to why they all seemed to enjoy taking it. I felt so sorry for them and I was real glad I wasn't sick.

When my mother came back, she wasn't as fat as when she left. The snow was all gone, too. We celebrated my sixth birthday and one of my presents was a book. I took my book with me everywhere. There was talk of my going to school in the fall. I didn't know what reading and printing were like, but I was very curious about it. I looked forward to school. I promised Cheryl I would teach her reading and printing as soon as I knew how. But for the time being, I would pretend to read to Cheryl and as I turned the pages of my book like Mom did, I would make up stories to match the pictures in the book.

A few weeks later, we came home from a day's ramblings to find a real live baby in Mom's arms. Mom was rocking it and singing a soft melody to it. I asked her, "Where did it come from?"

"The hospital. She was very sick. She's your new little sister, Anna."

"Will she have to take that medicine? It tastes awful," I said, pitying the baby for being sick.

"No, she drinks milk. The nurse came this morning and helped me prepare some," Mom answered. I knew from the way she talked that she hadn't taken any medicine so far. I hoped that from now on, she wouldn't have to take it any more. I studied the baby for a while. It was so tiny and wrinkled. I decided I'd much rather play with Cheryl.

That summer, Cheryl and I spent whole days at the park. I would make us sandwiches of bread and lard so we wouldn't have to walk back home in the middle of the day. That's when it seemed the hottest. We played on the swings and slides and in the sandbox as long as they weren't being used by the other children. We would build sandcastles and install caterpillars and ladybugs in them. If the other children were there we would stay apart from them and watch the man mow the park grass, enjoying the smell of the fresh-cut lawns and the sound from the motor of the lawn-mower. Sometimes the droning noise lulled Cheryl to sleep and I would sit by her, to wait for her to wake up.

There were two different groups of children that went to the park. One group was the brown-skinned children who looked like Cheryl in most ways. Some of them even came over to our house with their parents. But they were dirty-looking and they dressed in real raggedy clothes. I didn't care to play with them at all. The other group was white-skinned and I used to envy them, especially the girls with blond hair and blue eyes. They seemed so clean and fresh, and reminded me of flowers I had seen. Some of them were freckled but they didn't seem to mind. To me, I imagined they were very rich and lived in big, beautiful houses and there was so much that I wondered about them. But they didn't care to play with Cheryl and me. They called us names and bullied us.

We were ignored completely only when both groups were at the park. Then they were busy yelling names at each other. I always thought that the white-skinned group had the upper hand in name calling. Of course, I didn't know what 'Jew' or the other names meant. Cheryl was too young to realize anything and she was usually happy-go-lucky.

Our free, idle days with our family came to an end one summer afternoon. We came home and there were some cars in front of our house. One had flashing red lights on it and I knew it was a police car. When we entered the house, Mom was sitting at the table, openly weeping, right in front of all these strange people. There were empty medicine bottles on the small counter and the table but I couldn't figure out why the four people were there. A nice-smelling woman knelt down to talk to me.

"My name is Mrs. Grey. I bet you're April, aren't you? And this little girl must be Cheryl." She put her hand on Cheryl's head in a friendly gesture, but I didn't trust her.

I nodded that we were April and Cheryl but I kept my eyes on my mother. Finally, I asked, "Why is Mom crying? Did you hurt her?"

"No, dear, your mother is ill and she won't be able to take care of you anymore. Would you like to go for a car ride?" the woman asked.

My eyes lit up with interest. We'd been in a taxi a few times, and it had been a lot of fun. But then I thought of Baby Anna. I looked around for her. "Where's Anna?"

"Anna's sick," the woman answered. "She's gone to the hospital. Don't worry, we'll take you for a ride to a nice clean place. You and Cheryl, okay?"

That was not okay. I wanted to stay. "We can stay with Daddy. He will take care of us. You can go away now," I said. It was all settled.

But Mrs. Grey said in a gentle voice, "I'm afraid not, honey. We have to take you and Cheryl with us. Maybe if your Mommy and Daddy get well enough, you can come to live with them again."

The man who was with Mrs. Grey had gone to our bedroom to get all our things. He came back with a box. I was more worried and I looked from the woman to the man, then over to one policeman who was looking around, then to the other who was writing in a notepad. I finally looked back at my Mom for reassurance. She didn't look at me but I said in a very definite manner, "No, we'd better stay here."

I was hoping Dad would walk in and he would make them all go away. He would make everything right.

The man with the box leaned over and whispered something to my mother. She forced herself to stop sobbing, slowly got up and came over to us. I could see that she was struggling to maintain control.

"April, I want you and Cheryl to go with these people.

It will only be for a little while. Right now, Daddy and me, well, we can't take care of you. You'll be all right. You be good girls, for me. I'm sorry . . ."

She couldn't say anymore because she started crying again. I didn't like to see her this way, especially in front of these people. She hugged us and that's when I started crying, too. I kind of knew that she was really saying goodbye to us but I was determined that we were not going to be taken away. I clung to my Mom as tight as I could. They wouldn't be able to pull me away from her and then they would leave. I expected Mom to do the same. But she didn't. She pushed me away. Into their grasping hands. I couldn't believe it. Frantically, I screamed, "Mommy, please don't make us go. Please, Mommy. We want to stay with you. Please don't make us go. Oh, Mom, don't!"

I tried hard to put everything into my voice, sure that they would all come to their senses and leave us be. There were a lot of grown-up things I didn't understand that day. My mother should have fought with her life to keep us with her. Instead, she handed us over. It didn't make any sense to me.

The car door slammed shut on us.

"Please, don't make us go," I said in a subdued, quiet voice, knowing at the same time that I was wasting my time. I gripped Cheryl's hand and we set off into the unknown. We were both crying and ignored the soothing voices from the strangers in front.

How could Mom do this to us? What was going to happen to us? Well, at least I still had Cheryl. I thought this to myself over and over again. Cheryl kept crying, although I'm not sure she really knew why. She loved car rides but if I was crying, I'm sure she felt she ought to be crying too.

We were taken to an orphanage. When we got there, Cheryl and I were hungry and exhausted. Inside the large building, all the walls were painted dismal green. The sounds we made echoed down the long, high-ceilinged corridors. Then this person came out of a room to greet us.

She was dressed in black, from head to foot, except for some stiff white cardboard around her neck and face. She had chains dangling around her waist and she said her name was Mother Superior and she had been expecting us. My eyes widened in fear. It was even worse than I had imagined. We were being handed over to the boogeyman for sure! When Mrs. Grey and the man said goodbye and turned to leave, I wanted to go with them but I was too scared to ask. Mother Superior took us into another room at the far end of the corridor. Here, another woman dressed the same way, undressed us and bathed us. She looked through our hair for bugs, she told us. I thought that was pretty silly because I knew that bugs lived in trees and grass, not in people's hair. Of course, I didn't say anything, even when she started cutting off my long hair.

I was thinking that this was like the hen my mother had gotten once. She plucked it clean and later we ate it. I sat there, wondering if that was now to be our fate, wondering how I could put a stop to this. Then the woman told me she was finished and I was relieved to find that I still had some hair left. I watched her cut Cheryl's hair and reasoned that if she was taking the trouble to cut straight then we had nothing to fear. Between yawns, Cheryl complained that she was hungry so afterward, we were taken to a large kitchen and fed some of the day's leftovers. When we finished eating, we were taken to the infirmary and put to bed. It felt as if we were all alone in that pitch black space. During the night, Cheryl groped her way to my bed and crawled in with me.

That was the last night we'd share the same bed or be really close, for a long time. The next day, Cheryl was placed with a group of four-year-olds and under. I found out from the other children that the women were called nuns and that they were very strict, at least the ones who tended to my group. I'd seen the ones who looked after the younger children smile and laugh but whenever I saw Mother Superior, she always seemed so unruffled, always dignified and emotionless. But the ones who took turns looking after us gave us constant orders and that made my head spin. One would want us to hurry with this and that, and another would scold us for hurrying. Like at mealtime, I was told, "Don't gulp your food down like a little animal."

Eventually, I figured out what the different nuns wanted and avoided many scoldings. My parents had never strapped us and I never had to think about whether I was bad or good. I feared being ridiculed in front of the other children, I feared getting the strap, I feared even a harsh word. When I was quietly playing with some toy, and somebody else wanted it, I simply handed it over. I longed to go over to Cheryl and talk and play with her but I never dared cross that invisible boundary.

Most of my misery, however, was caused by the separation from my parents. I was positive that they would come for Cheryl and me. I constantly watched the doorways and looked out front room windows, always watching, always waiting, in expectation of their appearance. Sure enough, one day I saw my Dad out there, looking up at the building. I waved to him and wondered why he didn't come to the door, why he just stood there, looking sad. I turned from the window, saw that the attending nun was busy scolding a boy, so I left the room and went to look for Cheryl. I found her down the hall in another room. I looked in to see where the nun was and saw that her back was turned to Cheryl and the door. I tiptoed in, took hold of Cheryl's hand, whispering for her to stay quiet. I led Cheryl down to the front doors but we couldn't open them. They were locked. I didn't know of any other doors except for the ones which led to the play-yard at the back but it was all fenced in. I left Cheryl there and raced back to the nearest empty room, facing the front. I tried to call to Dad but he couldn't hear me through the thick windows. He couldn't even see me. He was looking down at the ground and he was turning away.

"No, no, Daddy, don't go away! Please don't leave us here! Please, Daddy!" I pounded the window with my fists, trying desperately to get his attention but he kept walking further and further away. When I couldn't see him anymore, I just sank to the floor in defeat, warm tears blurring my vision. I sat there and sobbed for we had been so close to going home again.

"WHAT ARE YOU DOING IN HERE?" the nun from my room asked, making me jump. "Don't you know what a fright you gave me, disappearing like that? You get back into the playroom. And quit that snivelling." Then she asked why Cheryl was at the front and what did I intend on doing. I wouldn't tell her anything so she gave me the strap and some warnings. That strap didn't hurt nearly as much as watching helplessly as my Dad walked away.

A few days later, I woke up feeling ill. My head hurt, my body ached, and I felt dizzy. When I sat at the breakfast table and saw the already unappetizing porridge, I knew that I wouldn't be able to eat it. I tried to explain to the nun at our table but she merely looked down at me and said in a crisp voice, "You will eat your breakfast."

I made the attempt but every swallow I forced down pushed its way back up. Tears had come to my eyes and I finally begged, "Could I please be excused?"

The nun responded in exasperation. "You will stay right there until you are finished. Do you understand?"

To my horror, I threw up just then. Instead of getting heck, though, I was taken to the infirmary room. I was bathed and put to bed and by then I was feverish. When I slept, I dreamt I was somewhere near home but I couldn't find our house. I was very hot and I walked and walked but our house was no longer where it should have been. I woke up and called for Mom and Dad.

The next time I went to sleep, I dreamed my parents were on the other side of a large bottomless hole and I had to edge my way slowly and carefully around the hole to get over to them. But when I got there, they were back over where I had started from. At last, I dreamt that I was finally running towards them and there was nothing around that could stop me. They even had Cheryl with them. I felt such relief, such happiness! Just as I was about to jump into their outstretched arms, I glanced up at their faces again. The faces had changed. They weren't my parents. They were the two social workers who had taken us away in the first place. Meanwhile, my temperature was rising and the nurse decided I'd better be taken to hospital.

My dreams continued in the hospital. I was always on the verge of reuniting with my parents but that was always thwarted by something beyond my control. When I was awake, a new kind of terror came to me. I guess it was delirious imaginings, but I would see this huge, white, doughy thing, kind of like a dumpling, and it would come at me, nearer and nearer and nearer. It would always stop just in front of me and I felt that if it ever touched me it would engulf me and that would be the end of me. Sometimes, its huge bulk would whizz around my head, back and forth in front of me. I was always scared it would bang into me but I couldn't duck it or anything. It didn't matter if my eyes were open or closed; I could see it there, and it seemed to know I was scared of it. I remained in the hospital for about a week before the fever broke and the dreams became less intense.

2

I WAS GLAD to get back to the orphanage because I was looking forward to seeing Cheryl. A new social worker had been assigned to me. Her name was Mrs. Semple. She told me she would find a home for Cheryl and me together. Maybe she said she would try but I didn't understand that. When I found Cheryl was no longer at the orphanage, I thought she had already gone to our new home. I wondered how come I wasn't sent there too. But the day soon arrived when Mrs. Semple came for me. I was really excited but I pretended nonchalance. I figured if they knew how much I wanted to move with Cheryl, they might take me to another place or else leave me at the orphanage. So Mrs. Semple was now taking me to the Dion family.

When we arrived, I jumped out of the car, looking for Cheryl and wondering why she wasn't outside waiting for me. The front door was opened to us by a pleasant-looking lady.

I walked in, looked around and asked, "Where's Cheryl?"

Mrs. Semple realized then that I had misunderstood her and she tried her best to explain to me but I wouldn't hear her. She assured me, "Don't worry about Cheryl. She'll be well taken care of in her new home."

"But I can take care of Cheryl," I said indignantly. "I want my sister."

"April, you'll be going to school now. So, don't make a fuss." Mrs. Semple had a hint of exasperation in her voice.

"Why don't you come into the kitchen, April? I've got some milk and cookies waiting for you," Mrs. Dion, my new foster mother, spoke up. For some reason she reminded me of my mother. Obediently, I followed her and sat at the table. The two women went back into the living room, leaving me there, alone. My eyes were stinging as I took a bite of an oatmeal cookie. The tears spilled over and rolled down my cheeks. I was so sad, so lonely, so confused. Why was all this happening?

St. Albert was a small French Catholic town south of Winnipeg. The Dion's lived on the outskirts not far from the Red River. It was September 9, 1955, when I moved there and the three Dion children were into their fourth day at school. Usually, they came home for lunch but on this day, it had been raining quite heavily and they had been allowed to take their lunches to school. It was mid-morning when I arrived and I spent most of that day moping around the house, fretting over Cheryl.

In the afternoon, Mrs. Dion turned the television set on for me. I'd never seen one before and I sat in front of it transfixed. I was still sitting there when the Dion children came home. The oldest was Guy who was twelve. Then there was Nicole, whose room I would be sharing. She was ten and the youngest was seven-year-old Pierre. They were all friendly and polite and only Pierre asked about my hair which was still ridiculously short. Of course, I was very shy and I couldn't look them in the eye. They reminded me of the rich white kids in the park, so I was amazed at their friendliness.

I had come on Friday. So the next day, I got up at eight with everybody else, had breakfast, then waited for Nicole to finish her Saturday chores. Meanwhile, Guy swept out the garage, washed the car, and collected all the garbage. When they were finished, we all went to the vegetable garden to do some weeding. Pierre and I carried the boxes of weeds over to a pile which was to be burned. We stopped for lunch which Mrs. Dion brought outside for us. When we finished, some other kids came over and we all played dodge ball. By the end of that day, I had forgotten how lonely I was.

The next day, when we got up, Mrs. Dion came into our bedroom and got out a real nice dress for me from the closet. She told me it had been Nicole's. I saw that there were some more nice clothes for me and I was very happy. I thought now I was rich, too, just like those other white kids.

We went to Mass that morning. I didn't like it. I was fidgetty from having to stay still for so long. But after Mass, we had a nice big Sunday dinner. When the dishes were done, we all piled into the car to go on one of Mr. Dion's excursions to find plants to bring back to his gardens. On these trips, Mr. Dion would tell us about the trees and the plants and the wildlife that lived in the forests. Of course, I didn't learn much on that first trip. I was excited about the venture and explored things by myself.

Monday was my first day of school. Mrs. Dion came with me that day while the others rode on their bikes. I was scared and excited at the same time. When I was introduced to the rest of the class, I was so shy, I couldn't look at any of the other children. All I knew was that there must have been at least a hundred kids in that classroom. By the end of that first week, a few of the girls had deemed me acceptable enough to take possession of me. That is, they made it clear to the others that they were going to show me the ropes. At recess times, I played jump rope with them, along with hopscotch and other such games. Although I found them bossy, even haughty, I was very grateful for their acceptance.

I learned that I had been baptized a Roman Catholic when I was a baby. Therefore, I had to study catechism to prepare for my First Communion in the springtime. Since the majority of the students were also Catholics, we had catechism classes every day at school. Every evening, I was obliged to learn my prayers in French, so when they were said at church, I would be able to say them, too. I memorized all the Acts, and there were a lot of them: the Act of Love, the Act of Charity, the Act of Faith, the Act of Penance. I was allowed to learn the prayer for the confession in English because later I would be telling the priest my sins in English. I also learned the answers to all the questions in my manual and there were a lot of things in it which puzzled me. My parents had done a lot of mortal sins because they had never gone to Mass on Sundays. That meant they were going to hell. I didn't think that I'd want to go to heaven so much, after all. Another thing was that the Church was infallible, never to be questioned. Yet, I couldn't help it, nor could I ask anyone else about it or they would know that I, April Raintree, had sinned!

By October, all the vegetables and crabapples had been canned and Mr. Dion had made his last trips to get transplants for his gardens. I had settled in at school, and I had found that this home could be as safe and secure as the tiny one on Jarvis Avenue. Sometimes, when it was windy, cold and grey outside, I even enjoyed the cozy feeling of being with a family. At the same time yearning to be with my own.

Back then, there were a lot of good shows on television.

It made one yearn for adventure. And also for pets just like the ones on T.V. First there was Tornado, Zorro's black stallion. Then there was Rin Tin Tin, a big German shepherd. And, of course, Lassie. I wanted them all. When I grew up, I would have German shepherds and collies, black stallions and white stallions and palominos too! I spent many church hours thinking what it was going to be like.

By November, my hair had grown long enough that the other children in school who had teased me, stopped. Mrs. Dion told me I could grow it long if I wanted to. But even better than that, she told me that I would be going to visit Cheryl and my parents at the Children's Aid office. I circled the date on the calendar, then waited with impatience and excitement. When the day finally came and Mrs. Semple came to pick me up, I suddenly remembered those horrible dreams. I was very quiet on the trip to Winnipeg. What if something happened? What if Mom and Dad got too sick and couldn't come? What if Cheryl couldn't come?

"Why the glum face, April? Aren't you glad you'll be seeing your parents and sister again?" Mrs. Semple asked me.

"Oh yes!" I almost shouted, fearful that Mrs. Semple would turn the car around and it would end up being me who didn't make it.

I was the first one there and I was taken to one of the small sitting rooms down the hall. Mrs. Semple showed me some books and toys with which I could occupy myself while I waited. Then she left, shutting the door behind her. I chose to sit on the edge of the chair and stared real hard at the closed door, wishing with all my might that the next time it opened, there would be Dad, Mom and Cheryl. I could see movements going back and forth through the thick-frosted windows. What if they all went to the wrong room? Maybe I should wait in the front waiting room. Better yet, maybe I should wait downstairs at the front entrance. I settled for opening the door a crack and peering out. When I saw someone approaching, I shut the door quickly and went back to the chair. The door opened and in walked Cheryl, followed by her worker, Miss Turner. When Cheryl saw me, her face lit up and she screamed, "Apple! Apple!"

I was just as happy to see her and for a moment forgot my fears that Mom and Dad might not make it.

"Hi Cheryl. I got a present for you. Mrs. Dion gave it to me to give to you." I presented the gift to her and she tore off all the wrapping and held up a black and white teddy bear.

"Has he got a name, Apple?"

I nodded and said, "Andy Pandy. Do you like that name?"

"Uh-huh. I like Andy Pandy. I don't got a present for you Apple. But you could have this." Cheryl put her hand in her pocket and pulled it out, her chubby little fist clutching something. She opened up her hand and offered me a brass button which had obviously come off her coat.

Miss Turner and I both laughed, then I said, "It's not my birthday, Cheryl. Don't you remember having a cake for your birthday?"

"I had lots of cake," Cheryl answered, moving the arms of Andy Pandy.

"Why don't you girls take off your coats. I'll be back as soon as your mother and father come."

I helped Cheryl take her coat off, then took my own off. While I asked Cheryl questions, I kept my eyes on the door.

"What's your new home like? Mrs. Semple told me you live with the MacAdams. Are they nice?"

"Oh, yes. We have lots of good things to eat. There's lots of other boys and girls there. And I got my own bed. At night, Mrs. MacAdams reads us stories. But no one reads good stories like you Apple. Cindy always reads the same story. You used to read me lots of different stories."

"I'm going to school now and I'm learning to read and

print for real. Pretty soon, I'm going to have a confirmation. Right now I have to learn a lot of prayers in French."

"What's French?"

"French is, well, it's not English. We talk in English. And the Dions talk in English a lot but they probably think in French. Do you go to Mass on Sundays, Cheryl?"

"Yes. I don't like going to Mass, Apple. We got to behave and not play. Mrs. MacAdams said so. Cindy was bad in church so Mrs. MacAdams made her sit in a corner and she couldn't have dessert. But I took her some cake to eat when she was sitting there."

I was laughing when the door opened again and this time Mom and Dad entered. I was into my mother's arms while Dad picked Cheryl up and twirled her around the room. Then I noticed the tears in Mom's eyes.

"Oh, Mommy, did I hurt you?" I remembered that she was sick.

"No April, I'm just so happy to see you again."

"See what we brought you?" Dad said, after he had hugged me. He had brought some doughnuts and milk and some candies for us to take home.

"See what Apple got me?" Cheryl said, holding up her teddy bear. "His name is Andy Pandy. He's going to be my friend now."

"So you're five years old. Happy Birthday, Cheryl. My baby girl is growing up fast. And we brought you a present, too," Dad said to her. He nudged Mom to open her purse and brought out a tiny leather purse with beadwork on it. Cheryl was delighted. Then she asked, "Could we come home now?"

We all became suddenly silent and I looked at each one of them, hopefully. But Mom said very softly, "I'm sorry my babies, but we can't take you back yet. Soon maybe."

To change the subject, Dad said to me, "So, April, you're in Grade One now, eh? How do you like your school?"

I realized he wasn't all that interested but I told him

anyways. I didn't tell him how much I liked the Dions and I liked living there because I felt that would hurt their feelings. Besides, going back home with them was my first choice. We had our snack and talked some more. Cheryl talked the most because she liked to talk. Too soon, though, Cheryl's worker returned to say it was time to leave. As I was getting my coat on, I felt total despair. I didn't want to leave Mom, Dad and Cheryl again. I kissed and hugged my Mom, then my Dad. I pleaded with him. "Please take us home with you. Please Daddy?"

"April, we just can't do that. We want to but we can't."

"Why not, Daddy?"

"Look, you're making your mother cry and you're going to make Cheryl cry. If it was up to us, you would never have left home. But this isn't up to us and you can't come home with us. I'm sorry."

I felt defeated. My shoulders slumped inside my heavy coat. I walked out of the room, my head down. I didn't want anyone to see that my eyes were wet. Then I remembered I hadn't even said goodbye to Cheryl. I ran back and kissed and hugged her, and shot one last pleading glance at our parents. I knew it was of no use. I had to wait a bit for Mrs. Semple. By then, the rest of my family had left. As we were going down to the road, I saw my parents up ahead. Dad had his arm around Mom's shoulders. I wondered if they still lived in the house on Jarvis. They looked so much like they loved each other. It gave me a good feeling to see them like that. At least they were together. They had each other. As we passed them, I waved to them, excited that I was seeing them in such a short time. They both smiled and waved back to me.

As we drove further and further away from them and I could no longer see them from the rear window, I became sad again. I just wanted to cry but I couldn't, not in front of Mrs. Semple. I figured that if I did cry, she wouldn't let me see them again. I answered 'yes' or 'no' whenever Mrs. Semple asked me something because I knew my voice would give me away. When we got to the Dions, Mrs. Semple explained to Mrs. Dion that I would be moody for a while because of the family visit but not to coddle me or I would carry on like this after every family visit. I didn't much like Mrs. Semple for saying that. How would she feel? I went off to my bedroom and was glad that Nicole wasn't there. I felt the same as when I first came there.

A little later, Mrs. Dion came into my room and asked me in a gentle, coddling voice, "April, do you want to come out for supper? It'll be ready in a few minutes."

"I'm not hungry," I said listlessly.

"I know how you must feel. But if you eat something, you'll feel much better. How about if I brought a plate in for you? Nicole can do her homework in the kitchen tonight." Mrs. Dion patted me on the arm and left.

I ate all the food on my plate that night, knowing it would make Mrs. Dion happy. When I finished, I took my plate and glass into the kitchen. The Dions were all sitting at the table having their meal. I felt shy and timid again. I felt like an outsider. I felt that I didn't belong to this family. They were being nice to me, that's all. And I did have my own real family. I wondered again how long it would be before I could go home.

"Are you feeling any better, April," Mrs. Dion later came in to ask me.

"Yes," I replied. I had been half lying and sitting so I sat up properly on the edge of the bed. Mrs. Dion sat next to me. I asked, "Mrs. Dion, why can't I be with my Mom and Dad?"

"You poor angel. It must be so hard on you." Mrs. Dion put her arm around my shoulders.

"I want to be with my Mom and Dad. I want to be with Cheryl." I tried hard not to cry but I felt so sorry for myself that the sobs and tears broke loose. Mrs. Dion hugged me to her and rocked me back and forth. She tried to explain. "Honey, sometimes we can't have everything we want. Believe me, living here with us is what's best for you right now. I know it's hard to understand that. You just have to trust God's wisdom."

"Mom and Dad say they're sick. They say that when they're better, then we can go home to them. But they used to take a lot of medicine before and it never made them any better. So, will they ever get better, will they? They never will take us home with them, will they?"

"Honey, that medicine that your Mom and Dad take does make them feel better but not for long and not in the right way. Someday you'll understand that. For now, just keep loving them and praying for them. And try to be happy with us. We all care for you very much, April."

"I know. It's just that . . . I belong to my Mom and Dad."

"That's true, April." Mrs. Dion gave me a big hug and then stood up. "Come and join us for the Rosary now. Tonight we'll say it for your family."

I did feel a whole lot better but I wondered about the mysterious medicine.

My first Christmas with the Dions was the most memorable because it was celebrated so differently than when I was with my family. We went to bed right after supper but of course we couldn't sleep for a long time. Then Mrs. Dion came to wake us up so we could go to the Midnight Mass. As we walked to church, it was snowing but it wasn't cold. The snow shone like a million sparkling diamonds. The Mass seemed endless that night but relief was provided by the choir singing Christmas hymns. After it was over, we went back home and gathered in the living room to open all the presents. That's what stood out for me, all those presents. I got a set of books, puzzles, games, a doll, and I couldn't decide which present to play with first. In the kitchen, Mrs. Dion had set out the best dishes, and all the baking she had been doing was displayed. By the time we had eaten it was almost four in the morning.

It wasn't that long after Christmas that I received the very first letter from Cheryl. I was amazed that she could print and she wasn't even in school or anything. There were spelling mistakes and some of the letters were reversed but I could make out exactly what she meant.

January 5, 1956

Dear Apple,

How ar you? Mrs. Madams tole me to ast that. I got lots a presnts. A dol and sum books of my very own an sum puzles an gams to play with Cindy an Jeff an Fern an some craons an a colring book. Wen they is at scool I colr an lok at my boks. I am lerning to reed an print an count an Mrs. Madams says I is fast lerner. I wish I was going to scool. Jeff is bad boy. I is good. I is good girl like Dady tole me. I mis you, Apple. I mis Momy an Dady.

luv,

Cheryl Raintree

p.s. I had to ast how to spel sum werds.

I had never written a letter but I sure learned how to write one that day! Nicole helped me write it and I made sure that my letter was a little bit longer than hers.

Our next family visit came in February. Until then, I had begun to get the feel of being part of the Dion family. Like all our future visits with our parents, the pattern would be the same. From the day I was told about the coming visits, I would become excited and the excitement would mount until the day of the visit. Then when I actually saw our parents and Cheryl, it was a constant high for those few hours. As soon as a social worker came to tell either Cheryl or me it was time to go, I turned instantly despondent and I would stay that way for maybe a week or more. But for those few hours, I was with my real Mom and Dad and I was with my real sister. I loved them and they loved me. And there were no questions of ties or loyalties. Just family.

I loved the Dions because they took care of me and they were nice to me. They were deserving of my love because I had nothing else to give them. But Mom and Dad were different. It didn't matter that they were sick and couldn't give us anything. I thought then that I would always love them, no matter what. Cheryl and I did ask them when we would go back with them—we would always ask them that—and they would promise us that as soon as they got better, we would all be together again. So, I had hope and I knew it wouldn't be long before we once again had our own home.

The next big event for me was my birthday. Mrs. Dion gave a small birthday party and some of the girls in my class came to it. I got a present and a card from Cheryl. After that was my First Communion. I felt more grown-up because from then on I was able to receive Communion. I bragged about this to my parents at our summer visit but they didn't seem at all interested. Then I remembered they had never gone to Mass and realized they probably knew they would go to hell. I wanted to tell them that if they went to confession and then went to Mass every Sunday, they too would go to heaven, but I felt awkward about the whole thing so I didn't say any more on religion. Cheryl had been going to kindergarten and she told us that she could read and print while most of her classmates were still learning their ABC's. She was still very funny and she always made Mom, Dad and me laugh. Most of the time, she had no intentions of being comical. I sure did a lot of wishing, once I was back with the Dions.

It was after that family visit when I received another letter from Cheryl.

August 20, 1956

Dear Apple,

How ar you? Mrs. Madams got our scool thins. I is so cited to go to scool for reel. I wil be in Grad 1. Apple on Sunday I wuz bad. I did not meen to be. I wanted to see the litle peeple who lives in the radio. I culd see the lits on. The radio fel on the flor. The lites wont even werk an thos peeple is ded. I am skared. Mr. Madams is mad. He ast who brok it. I wuz to skared. I didnt say nothin. Dont tell Momy and Dady. Pleese Apple. I am so skared.

luv,
Cheryl

I felt so sorry for Cheryl. I used to feel scared like that at the orphanage. I knew what it felt like. I also knew that there weren't any people who lived in radios. I'd seen Mr. Dion fix their radio. Poor Cheryl. She was scared she'd killed some people and she was scared she'd get heck. Mrs. Dion had told us that telling the truth was always easier and better than telling lies. I wrote to Cheryl and told her to go to Mr. MacAdams and explain how she broke the radio. I told her to write me and tell me what happened afterward. Her response came on August 30th.

Dear Apple,
How ar you? Mr. Madams sed you wuz good to tel me what to do. He even laft after I tole him. He sed to me the peeples werds cum frum waves in the air or sumthin. I dont no. Now I is cited agin bout going to scool. 1 week to wat. I try to be good. I promis.

luv,
Cheryl

I felt warm and happy that I had been able to help Cheryl. I was glad that Mr. MacAdams was the kind who could laugh at something like that. Not that I knew of any other kind because Mr. Dion was just as understanding and my Dad, well, I really couldn't remember when we had broken anything in the house. Of course, we never had much to break. One of the good things about having nothing, I guess.

I don't remember the exact day when I began to call my foster parents "Maman" and "Papa". I just copied their children and nobody made any comments about it. I was still very shy and if anyone had made note, I would have stopped. It did make me feel more comfortable in their home.

At the beginning of the winter when I was in Grade Two, my classroom was overcrowded. I was among six students who were placed in the Grade Three class. With Nicole's help and patience, I was able to adapt very quickly to the higher grade. When I passed with a good average, all the Dions were very proud of me and they made a little celebration. For an eight-year-old, I had a very large head for a while.

That summer and the following summer, we all went to a Catholic camp at Albert Beach on Lake Winnipeg. Those two weeks were filled with wonderment for me. At home, all the neighborhood kids would gather to play baseball, mostly in the evenings. When there weren't many kids around, we'd play badminton. If it were raining, we'd find something to do indoors. There was always lots to do.

In winter, we'd go tobagganing down the slopes of the Red River. Sometimes, a man from a farm on the outskirts would come with a team of horses and hayrack and give the kids of the town a hayride. At the end, Mrs. Dion or some other mother would give us all cookies and hot chocolate. At Christmas time, we would go around carolling even those of us who couldn't sing. And for me, there were my regular family visits. They always made me happy and sad at the same time.

Mrs. Dion had always been a happy, cheerful person and as long as I had been there, she had never been sick in bed. I must have been the last to sense the change in her. Mostly, I was told that Maman was very tired and Nicole urged me to help with the chores a little more. When Maman took to her bed, I offered to do as much as I could. At the end of November, Papa coaxed her to see a doctor. She was supposed to be going to the hospital for a week to have some tests done but her stay was prolonged to another week, then another.

I remember that Christmas was my saddest. Maman came home and stayed for New Year's. Everyone was very sad but made a pretense of being happy. When I saw Maman, I wanted to cry. She looked so different. She used to joke about being too fat. She wasn't really—just pleasantly plump—but now . . . she was skinny, and to me she looked grey. Any movement, even breathing, seemed to be such a strain for her. Yet, she led us all in forced cheerfulness.

I'd lay in bed at night, worrying about her. I'd say my prayers over and over, pleading with God to make her better. I must have overheard Papa and Grandmère Dion saying in French that Maman was dying because my prayers to God changed to 'please don't let Maman die.' I would think of Niclole, Guy and Pierre. It would be so awful for them not to have a real mother. Finally, I would cry myself to sleep.

One night, I sat up in bed and was wondering what had woken me. After a while, I put my robe on and went to the kitchen for a glass of milk. I was on my way back to my bedroom when I heard a noise in the living room. Because of the bright moonlight, I could see everything clearly. There in his rocker was Papa, with his arms on the armrests, and his back very straight. I knew he wasn't sleeping, that he was very, very sad. I went in without turning on any lights and sat on the stool beside him. I wanted to comfort him but I didn't know what to say. I put my hand on his and said softly, "Maman says it's okay to cry sometimes. Maman says it makes you feel better."

I saw tears, glistening in the moonlight, run down his face.

"Maman says we have to trust in God's wisdom."

I heard him restrain a sob and felt him patting me on my hand. I knew then I should leave him alone. I returned to my room and said another prayer for Papa.

In January, Mrs. Semple told me that I would be moving. At first, I thought I was finally going home. I was both happy and excited to be going home at last and very sad that I was going there only because Maman Dion was so sick and maybe dying. But my happiness was short-lived because Mrs. Semple began telling me about the farm which would be my new foster home. I was permitted a last visit with Maman in the hospital. She smiled when I walked into her hospital room and after asking me about school and other things, she said, "April, I wanted to say good-bye to you. We're all very sorry to see you go, but the final decision was theirs. You understand that, don't you?"

I nodded slowly, trying hard to smile courageously. I couldn't talk because of the lump in my throat.

She continued, "I wanted to say some things to you before you . . . Papa told me how you gave him comfort. We all love you very much, April. When life seems unbearable, remember there's always a reason. April, you're a very special person. Always remember that. Mrs. Semple says that the home you're going to is a fine home. I'm sure you'll be happy there."

"I love you, Maman." It was the first time I had ever said those words. To me, they were precious words to be used on very special people. When I saw how much she appreciated hearing those words, I was glad I had said them.

There were tears all around when I said goodbye to the rest of the Dion family. I had promised to write and always keep in touch with them. I left them with the hope of either coming back to live with them or returning to my own home.

3

I WAS TAKEN to a small farming community further south of Winnipeg on the outskirts of Aubigny, to the DeRosier farm. It was a Friday afternoon when we arrived. While Mrs. Semple talked with Mrs. DeRosier, I studied my new foster mother with great disappointment. She was a tall woman with lots of make-up and badly dyed hair. If she had been a beauty once, the only thing left of it now was the vanity. Her voice was harsh and grating. The more I watched her, the more positive I became that she was putting on an act for Mrs. Semple's benefit. I wondered why Mrs. Semple couldn't figure that out but then I thought it was okay as long as Mrs. DeRosier gave me a good home.

After my social worker's departure, Mrs. DeRosier turned to me. I looked up at her with curiosity. She went to the kitchen drawer, took out a strap and laid it on the table near me. She told me the routine I would be following but in such a way that it made me think she had made this speech many times before.

"The school bus comes at eight. You will get up at six, go to the hen house and bring back the eggs. While I prepare breakfast, you will wash the eggs. After breakfast you will do the dishes. After school, you'll have more chores to do, then you will help me prepare supper. After you do the supper dishes, you will go to your room and stay there. You'll also keep yourself and your room clean. I know you half-breeds, you love to wallow in filth. You step out of line once, only once, and that strap will do the rest of the talking. You don't get any second chances. And if you don't believe that I'll use it, ask Raymond and Gilbert. And on that subject, you will only talk to them in front of us. I won't stand for any hanky-panky going on behind our backs. Is that clear? Also, you are not permitted the use of the phone. If you want letters mailed, I'll see to it. You do any complaining to your worker, watch out. Now, I'll show you where your room is." *threats... orders*

I was left alone in a small room at the back of the house. It was cold, smelled mouldy and felt damp. There wasn't even a closet, just nails sticking out all over the walls. The Dions had given me a new set of suitcases and I opened one up and started hanging a few things on the nails. I stopped and sat on the bed. The mattress was soft and warped. Self-pity was not good for one's spirits, Maman Dion had told me, but right now, I felt sorry for myself. Mrs. DeRosier had said, " . . . you half-breeds". I wasn't a half-breed, just a foster child, that's all. To me, half-breed was almost the same as Indian. No, this wasn't going to be a home like the Dions'. Maybe if there were other children, they might be nice. Most people I'd met when I had stayed at the Dions had been nice enough. With this thought, I finished hanging up my clothes, looking forward to the arrival of Raymond and Gilbert, who I thought must be at school.

I was waiting at the kitchen table in order to meet them. Mrs. DeRosier was in the kitchen too, but she only glared at me as if to warn me to stay quiet. I saw the school bus from the kitchen window and thought how nice it would be taking a bus from now on. Four kids got off, two older boys around thirteen or fourteen and a girl and a younger boy. I was hoping that they would like me. They all walked in but the two older boys walked by without looking at me and I heard them going up the stairs. The younger boy and the girl eyed me contemptuously. The boy said to Mrs. DeRosier, "Is that the half-breed girl we're getting? She doesn't look like the last squaw we had."

The girl giggled at his comment.

"April, you may as well start earning your keep right now. Here, I want you to peel these potatoes." Mrs. DeRosier got out a large basket of potatoes and put them down in front of me. I was sure that the two children must be Mrs. DeRosier's very own. They made themselves sandwiches, making an unnecessary mess in the process. When I finished peeling the potatoes, Mrs. DeRosier told me to clean up their mess. Mr. DeRosier came in at suppertime and it became apparant to me that Mrs. DeRosier towered over him not only in size but also in forcefulness of personality. He and the two boys who had changed into work clothes, sat on one side, Mrs. DeRosier was at the head and Maggie and Ricky and I sat on the other side. The only talking at the table was done by the mother and her two children. I had finished my milk and reached for the pitcher to pour myself another glass.

"You're not allowed more than one glass." Maggie said in a whiny voice. I froze, my hand still on the handle, waiting for Mrs. DeRosier to confirm that statement or say it was all right. I wondered if I should give in to this girl, then realized I had no choice because Mrs. DeRosier simply remained silent. Slowly, I withdrew my hand from the pitcher and looked over at the mother and daughter. Maggie had a smug look on her face. I wanted to take that pitcher of milk and dump it all over her head. At other meals she would make a show of having two glasses of milk herself.

When Ricky finished eating, he burped and left the table without excusing himself either way. The other two boys had also finished eating but remained seated until Mr. DeRosier got up to leave. Then they followed him outside. Mrs. DeRosier put the leftovers away and indicated I was to start on the dishes. While I washed and wiped them, Maggie sat at the table and watched. I wondered why this family was so different from the Dions, especially those three. So much malice, so much tension. It seemed to me that it was a lot easier being nice, after all, the DeRosiers were Catholics, too. How I wished that my own parents would rescue me and right this minute would be a good time. I finished wiping the last pot and put it away. I started for my bedroom, relieved to get away from Maggie's watchful eyes.

"You're not finished," Maggie said in a bossy tone. "You didn't even sweep the floor. I heard you half-breeds were dirty but now I can see that it's true."

"You didn't do anything yet. Why don't you sweep the floor?"

"Because it's not my job. My job is only to see that you do yours. So get the broom!" Maggie hissed at me.

I stood there for a minute, looking down at Maggie. She was still sitting, very composed, very sure of how far she could go. Helpless fury built up inside of me but I was alone here, unsure of what my rights were, if I even had any. So I went to get the broom. After sweeping the floor, I went to my room. I had nothing to do but think. Was it only this morning I had felt loved and cherished? Now, I had been told I would have to earn my keep. I knew that Children's Aid paid for my keep. And I didn't like that word 'half-breed' one bit! It took me a while to get over all these new things I didn't like so I could get ready for bed and say my prayers.

Praying could bring me comfort, Maman Dion had told me. I had memorized the Lord's Prayer in French and English but I had never really thought about the meaning of each sentence. Now, I said it slowly.

"Our Father, who art in Heaven, hallowed be Thy Name. Thy Kingdom come, Thy will be done, on earth as it is in heaven. Give us this day our daily Bread. Forgive us our tresspasses, as we forgive those who tresspass against us. And lead us not into temptation, but deliver us from evil, Amen."

I would have to forgive these people their trespasses and no doubt there would be many. 'But, hold on there, God,' I thought. 'I don't have any trespasses for them to forgive. So how come I'm going to have to forgive theirs?' I looked for the answers in the talks and the Bible readings at the Dions. I remembered the saints and the martyrs. They had been tested. Maybe I was being tested. Maybe what I had to do while I was here was turn the other cheek. When I went to sleep, I was feeling very saintly.

Saturday morning, Mr. DeRosier rapped at my door, telling me I was supposed to go for the eggs. It had been windy all night and I had not slept well in my chilly room. I sleepily got dressed and went to the kitchen. No one was there but I saw a pail by the doorway and supposed I was to use that. It was still dark outside and it took me a while to find the chicken house. There were deep drifts of snow which had been whipped up by the wind overnight. Another thing I decided was that I didn't like winter anymore. Not as long as I lived on this farm. I gathered the eggs, got nasty pecks from the hens that were too stubborn or too protective. As I floundered through the snowdrifts, my mouth watered at the thought of breakfast, but when I entered the house, no one seemed to be up. I was still cold and very hungry but I didn't dare touch anything. I washed the eggs and found that a few had broken and many were cracked. I worried while I waited for Mrs. DeRosier. A few hours later, she came down in her housecoat and she looked a whole lot worse without her make-up.

She started to put some coffee on to perk and noticed the eggs still drying in the trays.

"What the hell did you do with these eggs? They're all cracked. I can't sell them that way!" I jumped up when she screamed. She picked up a few of them and threw them down on the floor in front of where I was sitting. She went on ranting and raving, not wanting my explanations. Finally, she told me to clean up the mess and she started breakfast.

When everyone had eaten, she and her two children got ready to go to town. She left me instructions to wash the floors and clean the bathroom after I finished the breakfast dishes. I thought to myself that if Ricky had been a girl, I would have been just like Cinderella. When I finished my assigned chores, I washed out my own room, trying to rid it of the musty smell. I had a few hours to myself before they came back, but when they did, Maggie, with her boots on, walked all over the kitchen floor and I had to wash it over again.

On Sunday morning, we all went to Mass. After the services, while Mr. DeRosier and the two older boys waited in the car, Mrs. DeRosier chatted with some neighbours. I was by her side and she explained my presence, adding that I was a lovely little child and we all got along very well. She wallowed in their compliments on what a generous, good-hearted woman she was to take poor unfortunate children like myself into her home. I just stood there meekly, too scared to say different.

I had looked forward to Monday because I would be going to school on a bus. There were a lot of kids on the bus already and being too shy to walk further I took the first empty seat near the front. I could hear the DeRosier kids tell their friends that I was a half-breed and that they had to clean me up when I came to their house. They said I even had lice in my hair and told the others that they should keep away from me. They whispered and giggled and once in a while, they would call me names. I sat all alone in that seat, all the way to school, staring straight ahead, my face burning with humiliation. Fortunately for me, no one on the school bus was in my classroom. By the end of the first day, I had made one friend, Jennifer. Unfortunately for me, I had to board that school bus again to go back to the farm. I had decided that I wasn't going to let them see that their taunts really hurt me.

The months went by very slowly. The kids on the bus tired of picking on me, mostly, I guess, because I wouldn't react. My tenth birthday passed without celebration. One evening in May, Mrs. DeRosier told me I wouldn't be going to school the next day because of a family visit. That was my first happy moment since I had arrived. She drove me in to Winnipeg, complaining all the way that these visits would disrupt the routine she had set for me.

I was waiting, alone, in the reception area when Cheryl came in, bubbling with enthusiasm.

"Hi April, I got a present for you. Can we go to a visiting room now Miss Turner?" she asked her worker. After we were left alone in one of the small cubicle-sized rooms, Cheryl turned to me and handed me a gift-wrapped package.

"Happy Birthday, April. It's a book."

"You're not supposed to tell me what it is, Cheryl. Half the fun is trying to guess what it is while I unwrap it," I grinned at her and shook my head.

"A book about Louis Riel?" I said and crinkled my nose in distaste. I knew all about Riel. He was a rebel who had been hanged for treason. Worse, he had been a crazy half-breed. I had learned about his folly in history. Also, I had read about the Indians and the various methods of tortures they had put the missionaries through. No wonder they were known as savages. So, anything to do with Indians, I despised. And here I was supposed to be part-Indian. I remember how relieved I was that no one in my class knew of my heritage when we were going through that period in Canadian history.

"He's a Métis, like us," Cheryl said proudly. "Mrs. MacAdams says we should be proud of our heritage. You know what that means? It means we're part Indian and part white. I wish we were whole Indians."

I just about fell off my chair when I heard that. There were a few Indians or part-Indian kids in my class who couldn't hide what they were like I did. They knew their places. But here was my very own sister, with brilliant grades, saying such idiotic things. Well, I didn't want to argue with her so I didn't voice my opinion. She continued talking which was usual for her.

"Mrs. MacAdams is a Métis you know, but Mr. MacAdams isn't. He teaches somewhere. Not at my school. They got a lot of books on Indian tribes and how they used to live a long time ago." Cheryl paused for a breather, then continued in a sombre tone.

"Mrs. MacAdams gave them to me to read because no one at school would talk to me or play with me. They call me names and things or else they make like I'm not there at all. This one girl and her friends would follow me home and make fun of me so I slapped that girl. So her Mom called Mrs. MacAdams. And Mrs. MacAdams says that all the bad stuff was 'cause I'm different from them. She told me I would have to earn their respect. How come they don't have to go around earning respect? Anyways, I don't even know what respect is exactly. I just wanted to be friends with them."

I knew what Cheryl was talking about from my own experience on the school bus. Yet, I couldn't share that with her. I suppose it was my vanity. She had admitted to me that some people didn't like her because she was different, but I simply couldn't return that kind of honesty. So, I told her about the DeRosiers, and how much I missed the

Dions. Telling her how the DeRosiers were mean to me was easy because they probably didn't like anyone and it wasn't only me.

"Why don't you give those two kids a good whack?" Cheryl asked.

"Are you kidding? Mrs. DeRosier would kill me." I replied as I leafed through the pages of my new book. "Besides, you can't go around whacking people you don't like."

"Well, that's what I do," Cheryl retorted off-handedly.

"And what if the kids are bigger and stronger than you?"

"Then I pretend not to hear them," Cheryl answered with a mischievious smile. We both laughed over that and then we talked of more light-hearted things.

I got to wondering about the present my Mom and Dad would be bringing me. Those precious hours together slipped away and Cheryl's good mood faded, too.

"Maybe they're not going to come," she said as she paced back and forth. She was puzzled and hurt and she was fighting back tears.

Miss Turner came in to tell me Mrs. DeRosier was there to pick me up. Cheryl begged for just a little more time. I sat back down and Cheryl came to me and knelt before me. She looked up at me with her large, questioning eyes, now glistening.

"They're not coming?" she asked softly.

"Maybe they got mixed up on the days or something." I knelt down to face her on the same level. "Cheryl, no matter what we'll always have each other." I hugged her close, knowing that what I said was small comfort to her. She started to cry and that made me cry, too. Miss Turner came and poked her head in saying I really had to go. Cheryl and I started putting on our jackets. She looked so pitiful when I left her alone in the visiting room.

Mrs. DeRosier had been told that my parents had not come for the visit. That evening, at suppertime, she told her own children they were fortunate in having a parent like her as my parents were too busy boozing it up to even come to visit me. I sat silently, not believing a word of what she said and pretending the insult of my parents didn't even bother me. She was forever putting my parents down so I was getting used to her remarks. But inside, I despised her more than I would despise my own parents, even if all the things she said about them were true.

Later that night, I lay in my bed, unable to go to sleep and unable to say my prayers. I couldn't forget that look on Cheryl's face when I had to leave her. I felt anger towards my mother and father because they were responsible. They were responsible for me being in this foster home. While I was at it, I turned on Our Holy Father in Heaven.

'Oh God, why did you let me be born? Why? Why was I ever born? Why do you let these bad things happen to Cheryl and me? You're supposed to be loving, protective and just. But you're full of crap, God! You're just full of crap and I hate you. You hear me? I hate you!' That's how angry I was. I started crying and when I had cried my heart out, I then felt sorry for saying those things. At last, I was able to say my prayers and ask God to help me be strong and good.

For the rest of that month, the DeRosier kids taunted me about having drunkards for parents. It was new ammunition for them to use against me and it bothered me a lot. One Saturday morning, they started in on me again and finally I made my feeble defense. "They're not drunkards! They're sick. That's all. Sick."

"Sick? Boy, what a dummy you are. But then half-breeds and Indians are pretty stupid, aren't they?" Maggie said maliciously.

"Yeah. Your parents didn't know how to take care of you. They just know how to booze it up," Rick added. And then they started mimicking drunken people and talking to each other with slurred speech, laughing at intervals.

47

"NO!" I screamed.

I ran out of the house, across the grain fields, running as hard and as fast as I could. They had acted and sounded just like my parents and their friends, I remembered. I could run all I wanted but I couldn't run away from the truth. When I reached the edge of the woods, my side was aching. I stopped and sat down, my back against a pine tree. I was panting and sobbing very hard. By the time I caught my breath, I could picture my parents.

'So. That's why you never got any better. Liars! That's what you are! All those promises of getting well. All those lies about taking medicine. Liars! You told us, 'Soon, April; soon, Cheryl. We'll take you back home as soon as we get better.' Well, you lied to us. You never intended to get better. You never cared about us. You made Cheryl cry and you don't even care. And because of you, I'm stuck here. I hate you both for lying to us. I hope I never see you again.'

I got up and started walking back to the house because I still had floors to wash. I stopped and thought, 'No. Why should I? They can beat me if they want to. I don't care. I just don't care anymore. To hell with them! To hell with my parents! To hell with everyone, except Cheryl. Even the Dions didn't answer my letters. They lied too. They didn't really care for me. But that's okay because I don't care either!'

I turned back into the woods and made my way through the heavy underbrush. I don't know how far I walked before I came upon a small clearing which bordered the Red River. The sunlight filtered through the towering trees, warming even the shady spots. The area was alive with the sounds of birds, squirrels and bugs. But I felt at peace, the tensions from the past months were lifted. I knew I felt this was because I was all cried out and I had decided that for now, I didn't care about anything.

I wasn't really thinking about anything when I noticed my arms and hands. They were tanned a deep, golden

48

brown. A lot of pure white people tanned just like this. Poor Cheryl. She would never be able to disguise her brown skin as just a tan. People would always know that she was part Indian. It seemed to me that what I'd read and what I'd heard indicated that Métis and Indians were inclined to be alcoholics. That's because they were a weak people. Oh, they were put down more than anyone else, but then, didn't they deserve it? Anyways, I could pass for a pure white person. I could say I was part French and part Irish. If I had to, I could even change the spelling of my name. Raintree looked like one of those Indian names but if I changed the spelling to Raintry, that could pass for Irish. And when I grew up, I wouldn't be poor; I'd be rich. Being a half-breed meant being poor and dirty. It meant being weak and having to drink. It meant being ugly and stupid. It meant living off white people. And giving your children to white people to look after. It meant having to take all the crap white people gave. Well, I wasn't going to live like a half-breed. When I got free of this place, when I got free from being a foster child, then I would live just like a real white person.

Then the question came to my mind. What about Cheryl? How was I going to pass for a white person when I had a Métis sister? Especially when she was so proud of what she was? I loved her. I could never cut myself off from her completely. And she wouldn't go along with what I planned. I would never even be able to tell her what I planned. I sat there thinking for a long time but the problem wouldn't be resolved. Well, I had a long time to figure that one out. For sure, she would never turn out to be like the rest of the Métis people. She and maybe Mrs. MacAdams were special people. Cheryl was already a whole lot smarter than all the rest of the kids in her class. I sighed, stood up and stretched. I felt I was ready to face whatever the DeRosiers had in store for me. One day I would be free of them. One day. . .

Over the summer holidays, Maggie was going to Vancouver to visit her grandmother. I looked forward to the day when she would be leaving because she, more than Ricky, made my life miserable. She had started coming into my room whenever she felt like it, saying it was her house and she could go wherever she pleased. One night, she was looking at my suitcases thoughtfully and then she said, "I'm going to borrow your suitcases for my trip."

I looked up at her and said, "You can't take them with you. What if I had to move while you're gone?"

"Move? My mother's not going to let you move from here. C'mon Ape, I've got to start packing tonight," she said in what was supposed to be a sweet coaxing voice. I knew very well that her mother would let her have her way but I still felt stubborn.

"Look, you owe it to me. You live in my house and eat our food. You're just lucky I don't tell Mother about your selfishness." With that, she dumped all the things in my suitcases on the floor and took them with her.

When she came back from the trip, she kept my suitcases. I asked to have them back several times but she would ignore me. One day, I entered my bedroom and my suitcases were there. They had been scratched up as if Maggie had deliberately tried to cut into them with a knife. Inside, there was dried red fingernail polish poured to form the words, "Ape, the bitch." I was angry but there was nothing I could do about it. I couldn't even show them to my social worker because it would be her word against mine. I thought that would be the end of it, but it wasn't.

That same night, during supper, Maggie said, "Mother, Ape let me use her suitcases and I forgot to give them back right away. So you know what she did today? She went up to my room, threw my stuff around and stole some of my money and my jewelry. I wasn't going to say anything about it but it makes me mad that she can just come into my room and do that."

I couldn't believe what she'd said and I looked over at her with complete astonishment. I practically growled at her,

"You bloody liar!"

Mrs. DeRosier slammed her fork and knife onto the table, stood up and came over to where I was sitting. She slapped me across the side of the head, took a vise-grip of my arms and yanked me out of my chair to shake me seemingly, all at the same time. And she was screaming.

"Don't you ever talk to my daughter in that tone of voice again! Who the hell do you think you are? We take you in because your parents don't want you, we give you food and shelter and this is how you pay us back?"

Then she asked Maggie, "Is your room still in the same condition that April left it in?"

"Yes, it is, Mother," said Maggie in an injured tone of voice.

"April, you march up there right now. We're going to see what you did. And then you're going to get the strapping of your life."

I'd never seen Maggie's room before because the upstairs was off limits to me. Her room was beautiful. The fancy furniture all matched and was white with gold trimming. Her bed even had a canopy over it. The wall-paper was of pink and yellow roses. But right now, books, papers, and clothing littered the deep pile rug.

"You must be a sick girl, April, to do this kind of thing. What did Maggie ever do to you?" Mrs. DeRosier asked.

All the while, I was being shaken about like a rag doll. She marched me back down to my room and started to look through my things. In one of the pockets of my coat, she found some money and some earrings. Maggie was standing at the doorway with a smug look of satisfaction on her face. While Mrs. DeRosier went for the strap, Maggie said softly, "That's what you get for bugging me, April Raintree."

The beating I got that night was one of the worst but I wouldn't cry. That seemed to infuriate Mrs. DeRosier all the more. I was sure that after that, Mrs. DeRosier would have me moved. I thought the beating would have been worth it after all. I waited for things to start happening but over the next few weeks, nothing more was said about the incident.

At the end of the summer, Cheryl and I had another visit. When we got to the Children's Aid office, we were told that our parents were not expected to come. I felt guilty about the resolutions I had made a few months back. To make up for it, I told Cheryl how our family life had been when we were all together. That is, I told her the good things. I told her how Mom used to rock her to sleep and sing songs to us; how Dad always laughed and joked and played with us for hours, telling us lots of stories; how we would all go out to visit our aunts and uncles or that they would come over to our house; how Dad would bring out his fiddle and play while everyone danced jigs. I wondered if it was right to tell her only the good things. Maybe I was lying by not telling her about the drinking and the fights and the dirty children. But then, Cheryl didn't need to know that just yet. I wanted Cheryl to be happy.

At our next family visit in October, only Dad came. He explained that he had been up north and couldn't get back for our visits. Mom, he said, was sick. Cheryl accepted the explanations with ease. She was, as usual, affectionate with him. But I knew the truth about them. I was aloof but polite. I had thought once of telling him about what a bad place the DeRosier farm was. But now I didn't bother. He wouldn't care. He'd pretend to care but he wouldn't do anything about it. I didn't have much to say to him. As children, that would be the last time Cheryl and I would see him.

Winter and spring passed. Life with the DeRosiers was the same: miserable. I had become bitterly passive and I now said fewer prayers. I was sure that God had heard me say I hated him and He never heard me ask for his forgiveness. Three more visits were arranged but our parents never showed up. Each time, Cheryl would end up crying. She was beginning to change. Before she had been outgoing, always talking and normally cheerful. At the last two visits, I tried my hardest to bring out her laughter but was rewarded only with sad smiles.

By the end of June, I had passed Grade Six with a low B average, and that was because English, French and Math were easy for me. I felt torn in different directions and often changed my mind regarding my parents. Sometimes, I would think of the life I would have been leading if we were all together. So what if we were poor and lived in slums. Being together would be a million times better than living on this horrible farm. Other times, I would remind myself that my parents were weak alcoholics who had made their choice. And then I would loathe them. Or I would think of the Dions and all their religious teachings. What was the sense of praying to a God who didn't care about me either? On Cheryl, it was still the question of how I was going to live as a white person with her around. I had seven more years of probably being stuck with the DeRosiers and if not, then in some other foster home. Seven years of not having control of my own life.

Most of the kids in my class were excited about the summer holidays. Some were going away on trips. Me, I was just going to be alone, unloved, with nothing to look forward to. For seven more years . . . Did I ever feel sorry for myself.

4

IN JULY, Mrs. DeRosier had her husband move an old musty-smelling dresser from one of the outbuildings into my room. It had a cracked, spotted mirror on it and the thing looked like it was about to fall apart. But I was grateful to have something to put my things in and wondered why the small kindness. Later, Mrs. DeRosier went out and bought an old cot from an auction and had it put in my room. Since it was in worse condition than the one I already had, my curiosity was really piqued. I suspected that Maggie knew the reason but I knew better than to ask her. She and Ricky had stopped calling my parents drunkards. I knew it was my lack of reactions which made them ignore me for the most part. Now, they were constantly at each other to their mother's mortification. And to my amusement.

I was weeding in the garden the morning the car drove into the farmyard. I glanced at it, not really caring who it was. I glanced again, surprised to see Miss Turner get out. My face had a grin from ear to ear when I saw Cheryl getting out on the other side. I dropped my garden tool and ran over to her.

"Cheryl, what are you doing here? Oh, I'm so happy to see you."

Mrs. DeRosier had her phoney smile showing and she said to me in a pleasant tone, "I wanted this to be a surprise for you, April. Your sister has come to live with us. We all thought this would be a good idea, because your parents haven't come to see you." She then took Miss Turner into the house for a cup of coffee.

I turned to Cheryl and asked her why she had moved from the MacAdams. I knew that she had liked them a lot and that they were real nice people.

"They asked me last month if I would like to move with you. I asked why you couldn't move there because you didn't like it here but they just said they didn't have the room. I told them that I liked them but that I'd rather be with you. So here I am." Cheryl shrugged and grinned, as if she had pulled off a brilliant plan.

From the day she arrived, I changed. I was more alert and openly defiant towards the DeRosiers, sending them silent warnings to leave my sister alone. We did all the chores together and while we did them, we talked and joked around. While we did the outside work, Maggie would put her bathing suit on to tan herself. She would lay on a blanket wherever we happened to be working. The first time she tried to order Cheryl to go in and get her a glass of lemonade, Cheryl said, "Get it yourself."

We were weeding in the garden and I was further away from Maggie and behind Cheryl. I stood up and eyed Maggie with such loathing that Maggie got up and went off to get her own drink.

"You lazy half-breeds," was her comment as she stalked off.

I bent down to resume my weeding and Cheryl turned to me and said, "See? That's all there is to it. They got no guts."

Before Cheryl had come, the DeRosier's dog, Rebel, had always followed the foster boys around, down to the barns or out to the fields. Now, he stuck close to Cheryl's side. When I took Cheryl down to my favorite spot by the river, the big yellow mongrel came with us. Cheryl told me the MacAdams had taken her to see this movie, "Old Yeller", and Rebel looked like Yeller. She'd tell me all about the television shows that she'd seen. Since I'd moved to the DeRosiers' I wasn't even allowed to go into the living room, except to clean it. Our privacy at the river was protected for us by nature. A few times, the DeRosier kids had tried to follow me before. Maggie found the underbrush too scratchy and too difficult and she had given up. Ricky had come down with a bad case of poison ivy the first time. The second time, there had been too many mosquitoes for his liking.

When school started in September, the DeRosier kids had the other kids on the bus picking on Cheryl and me. Cheryl was easy to goad and she'd get into verbal exchanges of insults. It was impossible for me to get it across to her that that was exactly what they wanted from her. At home, there was a constant testing of wills between the DeRosiers and Cheryl and me. I grew tired of feeling I always had to be on guard. I preferred the passive state I'd been in before Cheryl had come. I was worried that Cheryl would get into physical fights when I wasn't around. Fist fights were for people who couldn't keep their self-control. Furthermore, they were undignified. Because Cheryl hadn't made any friends in her own class, she often sat with Jennifer and me at lunchtimes. We had different recess periods. I guess she managed to keep out of fights because I never heard of any.

When our report cards came out before Christmas, Cheryl had maintained her high grades, despite the DeRosiers. My own average jumped considerably. Knowing the DeRosier kids had done poorly by their mother's reaction, Cheryl and I were both vain about our marks. It was about the only thing we could rib them about, especially Maggie and we took full advantage. We'd say things like, "Hey Maggie, you told us that half-breeds were stupid. Well, if we're stupid, you must lack brains altogether." It was the only time I'd refer to myself as a half-breed—to spite them.

It was after Christmas that Cheryl got into trouble at school. She told me all about it at lunchtime. That morning, her teacher had been reading to the class how the Indians scalped, tortured and massacred brave white explorers and missionaries. Cheryl's anger began to build. All of a sudden, she had loudly exclaimed, "This is all a bunch of lies!"

"I'm going to pretend I didn't hear that," the teacher had said calmly.

"Then I'll say it again. I'm not going to learn this garbage about the Indian people," Cheryl had said louder, feeling she couldn't back down.

Everyone else had looked at her as the teacher came and stood by her desk. "They're not lies; this is history. These things happened whether you like it or not."

"If this is history, how come so many Indian tribes were wiped out? How come they haven't got their land anymore? How come their food supplies were wiped out? Lies! Lies! Lies! Your history books don't say how the white people destroyed the Indian way of life. That's all you white people can do is teach a bunch of lies to cover your own tracks!"

The teacher had marched her down to the principal's office. Cheryl had been scared but she was also stubborn. She believed she was right and she intended to stand up for her beliefs, no matter what they dished out.

Her teacher had explained Cheryl's disruptive attitude and then left the principal's office.

"So what's this business of upsetting your history class? Learned men wrote these books and you have the gall to say they're wrong?" the principal had boomed in his loudest voice.

"They are wrong. Because it was written by white men who had a lot to cover up. And I'm not going to learn a bunch of lies," Cheryl had said, more scared than ever before.

The man then pulled a strap from his drawer and said, "Now, I don't want to have to strap you but I will. You'll go back to your classroom, apologize to your teacher and to the class and there will be no more of this nonsense. All right?"

Cheryl had shaken her head defiantly. "No. I won't apologize to anyone because I'm right." Then she had put out her hand, knowing he would give her the strap. He did. Each time he hit her, her resolve had grown stronger and stronger. When he stopped to ask if she was going to come to her senses, she had answered, "Giving me the strap isn't going to change the fact that your history books are full of lies."

Seeing he wasn't going to get anywhere, he put his strap away and phoned Mrs. DeRosier. She had arrived in about half an hour and was angry. She told the principal she had nothing but trouble with Cheryl. He left her alone with Cheryl in his office.

"You're going to do exactly as they wish or else I'll call your worker, have you moved and then I'll make sure you never see April again. Now, are you going to co-operate?"

Cheryl nodded meekly. The fight had gone out of her.

Before Mrs. DeRosier left, she had turned and warned Cheryl, "I'm not through with you yet, Cheryl Raintree."

When Cheryl told me all this, I swelled with pride. My kid sister was spunky. She had guts. More than I would ever have. But Mrs. DeRosier's warning bothered me. No doubt, Cheryl was in for a beating and somehow I had to do something. For the rest of the day, I was nervous but Cheryl didn't seem worried at all.

That night when we sat down to supper, Mrs. DeRosier said, "Cheryl, since you already got the strap at school, I'm not going to give you another strapping. Instead, you won't have supper tonight and when we're finished, you will do dishes all alone. Now, go to your room and wait till we finish eating."

I was surprised to find that was going to be Cheryl's only punishment. I told Mrs. DeRosier that I wasn't hungry, since Cheryl had to miss supper.

"Very well, you can go to your room and stay there for the rest of the night."

With that, she followed me to my room and commanded Cheryl to follow her to the kitchen. When Cheryl came back a few hours later, I looked up and was shocked. Cheryl's long hair had been her pride and glory. *Had* been her pride and glory. There was hardly any left and it was cut in stubbles. As she told me what happened, my anger mounted.

After she had finished telling me about it, Cheryl added, "And she made me sweep all my hair from the floor and then do the dishes. But I didn't cry, April. Not once."

Still, I wasn't going to let that old hag get away with that without voicing my opinion! My fury outweighed my normal fear of Mrs. DeRosier. I stormed into the kitchen, saw Mrs. DeRosier there, and demanded, "Why did you scalp my sister?"

Instead of answering me, Mrs. DeRosier slapped me.

I ignored the sting from the slap and yelled, "You had no right to do that!"

"No two-bit little half-breed is going to yell at me like that!" Mrs. DeRosier screamed back. Out came the scissors, again. I actually pushed her hand away from my hair. I think we would have had a fight except that she used the threat of separating Cheryl and me for good. So, in the end, I, also, went back to our room minus my own crowning glory. I was still breathing hard when I walked in. Cheryl looked at me and did a double-take. Her eyes, like saucers, remained on my hair. Her mouth opened and closed a few times but she remained speechless. She had heard the commotion in the kitchen but Mrs. DeRosier's threat had kept her back. I looked in the mirror. My new hair-do looked worse than Cheryl's. There I was, the big, protective sister going out to avenge the humiliation of my little sister and I came back, myself properly humbled. It all seemed ridiculously funny and I started to laugh. Cheryl joined in. It was good to be able to laugh defeat in the face. Heck, our hair would grow back.

The next morning, though, the DeRosier kids told the others that we had tried to dye our hair and that's why our hair had been cut. We were jeered and laughed at. At lunchtime, I confided in Jennifer and she went to the Home Economics room and got some scissors. In the washroom, she cut Cheryl's hair and mine, so that it looked better. The aggravation over this incident gradually died down. The DeRosier kids were back to fighting with each other, although I sometimes had the feeling they were conspiring against Cheryl and me.

Left to ourselves in our room, Cheryl and I did our homework and read a lot. Sometimes, she would read my geography book and day-dream. But mostly, she'd read about animals and adventure stories. I was into Nancy Drew books and other mystery books, and occasionally I would read some of Cheryl's animal books. So far, I had not read the book on Louis Riel. Whenever Cheryl wanted to talk about him, I would change the subject. I guess she got the hint because she began staying away from such topics.

On Saturdays, Mrs. DeRosier would take her eggs in, do her visiting and her shopping and usually her kids would go with her. Mr. DeRosier, Raymond and Gilbert went to work at the barns or in the springtime they would work the fields all day. Cheryl and I would have Saturdays to ourselves. Since I was good at doing the floors, I'd let Cheryl go rambling outside with Rebel. One Saturday morning, in the springtime, Ricky and Maggie didn't go to town with their mother. Later that day, Cheryl and I knew why.

Cheryl was outside looking for Rebel. I was cleaning the kitchen. Ricky had already gotten ahold of Rebel and he brought the dog close to the house for Maggie to watch. Then, making sure Cheryl didn't see him, he slipped out to the pasture where the bull was kept. When he saw Cheryl nearing the pasture, he climbed back through the fence as if he had just come through the pasture. He yelled to Cheryl that Rebel had been hurt and that the dog was on the other side of the pasture. He said he was going for help.

Thinking that Ricky had just come across the pasture, Cheryl climbed through the fence and started running. She didn't notice the bull raising its head to watch her. She didn't see it start moving towards her. Her mind was only on Rebel.

As I saw this through the kitchen window, I flew out the door, saw Maggie giggling to herself, and ran horrifed toward the pasture. The bull was now charging across the field, straight at Cheryl. I called Rebel and raced toward Cheryl. I climbed though the fence and yelled to Cheryl to run.

Cheryl heard the pounding of the bull's hoofbeats and at the same time she heard me. She stopped to look around and when she saw the bull, she froze in terror. I was screaming all the while for her to run and at the last minute, she did move. The bull narrowly missed her. It slowed to stop and turned around. Cheryl heard Rebel barking but she didn't know that he had streaked behind her and was now preoccupying the bull. I was running towards her and when I reached her, I grabbed her hand

and we ran back to the safety of the fence. We turned to see how Rebel was doing. The dog was prancing around the bull, easily avoiding the short charges. Cheryl called him and he came happily loping back to her.

Ricky and Maggie had stopped laughing and they glared defiantly at me as I walked up to them. Without saying a thing, I hauled back and punched Maggie right in the face. Her nose started bleeding as she landed on the ground. Ricky jumped on me from behind and his weight knocked me off-balance. Cheryl, who was still shaking, walked over to him and kicked him hard. I motioned for Cheryl to leave things to me. Ricky and Maggie fought back and screamed bloody murder. I was silent as I ploughed into them. The fury in me wouldn't let their punches and their scratches hurt me. When my anger had evaporated, I stepped back and looked at them with contempt. They were bloody and crying. As I turned to ask Cheryl if she was all right, I noticed Mr. DeRosier and the two foster boys in the distance. The boys who were standing just behind him had big grins on their faces, the first time I had ever seen that. The expression of Mr. DeRosier's face was unreadable. He didn't say or do anything. He just turned and continued towards the garage.

At suppertime, Ricky and Maggie came down after everyone else was seated. Maggie wore a sleeveless dress to show off all the bruises and scratches she had received. Ricky had also dressed for the occasion. As they expected, their mother noticed their appearances right away.

"What happened? Did you two get into a fight?"

Maggie turned the tears on so Ricky explained. "April and Cheryl were teasing the bull this morning and we tried to make them stop so they beat us up."

Before Mrs. DeRosier could turn on us, Mr. DeRosier spoke up in a quiet voice. "Now try telling the truth for a change. The tractor broke down this morning. I came back for some parts. You didn't see me, did you, Maggie and Ricky? But I saw you. And what you tried to do. You're both darn lucky I didn't have time to get to you first.''

"Are you calling my children liars?" Mrs. DeRosier asked him angrily.

"They're worse than liars! What they did this morning could have gotten Cheryl killed. What the hell's the matter with you? You three make me sick!" He slammed his fist on the table and silenced Mrs. DeRosier from saying any more. After a minute, he got up and stormed out of the house. Raymond and Gilbert looked lost. Even though they had barely begun to eat, they got up and left after him.

The rest of us finished our meal in silence. Mrs. DeRosier told Cheryl and me to go to our room when we finished the dishes. I knew she wasn't going to let this go by without doing something but I kept this worry to myself.

On Monday, Mrs. DeRosier kept Maggie home from school. When we got off the bus that evening, Maggie was in her good clothes and it looked as if they had gone somewhere. She looked gleeful and triumphant. She whispered to Ricky and they went into the living room, laughing.

At the beginning of the summer holidays, about a month after the incident, I was in the house one morning, when I noticed a car enter the driveway and saw that it was Miss Turner. Then it hit me. Miss Turner was here to take Cheryl away. Of course, that's what their secret had been. That's why we had never been punished. I panicked. I couldn't be separated from Cheryl again! I just couldn't! But what could I do to stop it? Nothing! Nothing, except run away with Cheryl! But where could we go? Cheryl was outside somewhere. I didn't stop to think what we would take. I just ran out the kitchen door and looked around the farmyard. I saw Cheryl coming towards the house. Ricky and Maggie were still upstairs, sleeping. I heard Mrs. DeRosier calling for Cheryl from the other side of the house. I ran towards Cheryl and urged her to duck behind a building.

"Cheryl, Miss Turner is here. I'm sure she's come to take you away." I was shaking. I was glad to see that Cheryl had her jacket on.

"April, I don't want to go away from you. They told me I'd never see you again."

"I know, Cheryl. We are going to run away. Right now."

I looked around the corner of the building. There was nobody in sight. We ran across the open grain field as fast as we could, trying to keep low. When we were into the safety of the woods, I said, "We're going to Winnipeg. I'm sure I know the way there. We'll just follow along the roads through the fields. When we get there, I'll try to find the Dions. I'm sure they'll help us. I know Mrs. Semple. She'll just believe whatever DeRosier tells her. Okay?"

Cheryl nodded, and we started on our journey. I had no idea how far it was or how long it would take. We followed along side Highway 200, the same way we went to Winnipeg by car. We walked all that day, ducking low in the tall grasses in the ditch whenever we saw or heard a car. Sometimes, we walked through nearby woods. Once, we saw a car moving slowly and when it came closer we saw that it was an RCMP car. I knew they were looking for us, and that we'd have to be more careful. It grew dark and the darker it got, the harder it was for us to walk through the weeds. We waited until it was pitch black and returned to the road. Cheryl began complaining that she was hungry and tired and wanted to stop and rest.

I urged her on, saying that we had a better chance to make it if we continued through the night. In the middle of the night, Cheryl insisted she just couldn't go on anymore. I knew how she felt because I was dead tired myself. We left the road and found ourselves in a field. Cheryl fell asleep, her head resting on my lap. I sat for a while to guard her, but I soon lay back and fell asleep, too.

I was awakened by somebody who prodded at me. The

sun was shinning down on us and when I remembered where we were, I felt exposed. I blinked and was dismayed to find a police officer standing over me. Cheryl was already sitting up and she was still rubbing her eyes.

We were told to get into the car and I sat there, glumly. The Mountie talked to us but we ignored him and didn't say anything. I was so disappointed that I couldn't think of anything except that we had been caught. I wondered if running away was a crime. We couldn't possibly go to jail, just because we wanted to stay together. I was surprised when we got to Winnipeg after all. But we were taken straight to a police station. We were told to sit in the waiting area. After a while, the officer came back and gave us milk and cinnamon buns. I was wondering why we were waiting there.

"We almost made it, didn't we?" Cheryl said. "If I hadn't gone to sleep, we would have made it."

"I went to sleep, too, Cheryl. Don't worry, we'll explain everything to them." I had read about the RCMP. I knew they were good guys and that they would listen to us. I began to wish that I had talked to the Mountie in the car, after all.

We never did get another chance to talk to the Mounties. Mrs. Semple came in first and she gave us a disapproving look.

"I never expected this of you, April. Mrs. DeRosier is worried sick. Don't you know how much she cares for you? You girls put a scare into all of us. You should be ashamed of yourselves. Do you know what could happen when you hitchhike? Why you . . . could have been hurt."

"We didn't hitchhike. We walked," Cheryl said, sullenly.

"Don't try to tell me that you walked all that way. You girls have had a very bad influence on each other." She turned to stare at Cheryl. "And you, young lady, I won't be surprised if you land in reform school."

"Why should she land in reform school?" I said,

bitterly. "I'm the one who talked her into running away. I didn't want us to be separated again."

"And I suppose you're the one who attacked Maggie?" Mrs. Semple asked.

"I beat her up. And Ricky, too. They tried to kill Cheryl."

After I said it, I realized it must have sounded ridiculous. Nothing was coming out right. I had wanted to explain everything out in a very sensible manner. Instead, here I was sounding almost hysterical.

"You have too much imagination and not enough common sense," Mrs. Semple said. "Mrs DeRosier brought her poor daughter in and showed us what happened. Now they have no reason to lie about who did what. It was a very vicious act, Cheryl. Especially when Maggie refused to defend herself. Futhermore, Mrs. DeRosier brought a report from school to back her claim that you are a troublemaker. April, it's touching that you want to cover up for your sister. But if we don't do something now, she'll end up in a reform school."

"I'm not covering up! I'm telling the truth!" I shook my head in disbelief. How come they couldn't see through Mrs. DeRosier and Maggie? How could I convince them of our honesty? Then I remembered Mr. DeRosier and the boys. He had spoken up for us once. If he knew about this, surely he would speak up again.

"Did you talk to Mr. DeRosier and Raymond and Gilbert?" I asked excitedly.

Mrs. Semple eyed me suspiciously and said, "April, you're a beautiful girl. I advise you to keep your charms to yourself. Mrs. DeRosier told us that you've been flirting with them."

Of course. The old hag had that covered too. After that, I just didn't know what to say. Then Mrs. Semple gave us a little speech about what she called the native girl' syndrome.

". . . and you girls are headed in that direction. It starts out with the fighting, the running away, the lies. Next come the accusations that everyone in the world is against you. There are the sullen uncooperative silences, the feeling sorry for yourselves. And when you go on your own, you get pregnant right away or you can't find or keep jobs. So you'll start with alcohol and drugs. From there, you get into shoplifting and prostitution and in and out of jails. You'll live with men who abuse you. And on it goes. You'll end up like your parents, living off society. In both your cases, it would be a pity because Miss Turner and I knew you both when you were little. And you both were remarkable youngsters. Now, you're going the same route as many other native girls. If you don't smarten up, you'll end up in the same place they do. Skid row!''

I thought if those other native girls had the same kind of people surrounding them as we did, I wouldn't blame them one bit. Much of the speech didn't make sense to me anyway. I'd never heard the terms shoplifting, prostitution and I didn't even know what drugs were. I'd been into drug stores and they sold all sorts of useful things. So far, I hadn't had a crush on a boy, well, not a major crush. And what the heck was skid row? All I knew for sure was that somewhere in that speech, she had insulted our parents and I could see that it rankled Cheryl. I held her hand.

I thought of once more trying to reason with Mrs. Semple but then Miss Turner walked in. Mrs. Semple went over to her and they talked for a few minutes. Then they came to us and told us we were going to the Children's Aid office.

There we sat alone in one room while they discussed our futures in another. I was still angry and felt like a criminal. We hadn't done anything wrong. Well, maybe I shouldn't have laid such a beating on those two brats. But it was Cheryl who was getting all the blame. Between the two of us, she was the more innocent. It was unjust.

''Cheryl?'' I said quietly.

''What?''

"I'm sorry."

"You're not the one who should be sorry. All of them are the ones who are doing wrong. They're the ones who ought to be sorry," Cheryl said, vehemently. After a few minutes, she said, "I guess I'm going that syndrome route, huh?"

"Of course not. Why do you say that?"

Cheryl smiled. "I just kind of accused everyone of being against us, didn't I?" We both laughed.

It was a while before Mrs. Semple and Miss Turner came back into the room. Mrs. Semple said to me, "April, we've decided it's in your best interest for you to return to the DeRosiers. You never got into any trouble until Cheryl came to live with you."

"No, don't send her back there. They're mean people. Mrs. DeRosier said we'd never see each other again," Cheryl shouted.

"Cheryl, we've arranged for you to go to the Steindalls. If you give them a chance, you'll be happy there. And don't you worry. There'll be visits between you and April," Miss Turner said.

"Please don't send April back to the DeRosiers. They'll do something bad to her. I just know it. Why can't she come with me?"

"Because you're not good for each other. Now, I don't want any more nonsense, Cheryl. April, if you can talk any sense into your sister, you'd better try," Miss Turner said to me.

"I want to talk to Cheryl alone," I said. The two women looked at each other, shrugged and left the room.

I knelt before Cheryl and said, "Cheryl, we can't fight them. I know I'll be okay with the DeRosiers. I don't want you to worry about me, okay? And I don't want to have to worry about you. I want you to be good at the Steindalls. I want you to keep your grades up. This won't last forever. When we're old enough, we'll be free. We'll live together. We're going to make it. Do you understand me? *We are going to make it.* We are not going to become what they expect of us." I sat back on my heels and looked her in the eyes. She nodded and smiled through her tears.

"Okay, April, I'll try to be good."

5

ON THE RIDE back to the DeRosier farm, I went over what I had said to Cheryl. Those were big words said on the spur of the moment. I had this idea that anyone who went to reform school was doomed for life. I didn't want Cheryl to have to go there and end up in one either. I could let the DeRosier's suck out my dignity for now and I could pretend they had me where they wanted me. But my future would belong to me. I had said to Cheryl that we would live together but that was a long way off. Maybe things would change and I wouldn't have to live up to that statement. Or maybe if I became so rich and important, people wouldn't care that I had a proud Métis for a sister. As we approached Aubigny, my thoughts returned to my present predicament. Just what was in store for me? It was easy to think to myself that I didn't care but living it was different.

I'd often thought to myself that those three DeRosiers were crazy. That night when I did the dishes and they all sat behind me, silently staring at me, I was sure of it. Earlier that day, when I had returned with Mrs. Semple, Mrs. DeRosier had made a big fuss over me. It had made me sick and I hadn't been able to hide my hostility towards her. For that whole summer, they wouldn't talk to me except to give me curt orders. Ricky and Maggie made no comments about Cheryl and I thought this plan of theirs of giving me the silent treatment must be hardest on Maggie because she was such a verbal person.

The only companion I had was Rebel, who had now adopted me as his new friend. When I could sneak off, I'd go down to my spot at the riverbank, taking Rebel with me.

By the end of the summer, I didn't have anything good to tell him. "You know, Rebel, I think you're going to be my only friend around here for a long, long time. When I first came here, I hated you because you were their dog. Now I think of you as Cheryl's dog. You saved her life, you know. You must miss her as much as I do. But now, I don't have to worry about protecting her from them any more. Doesn't help me from being jumpy, though. If it's not the hot stuffy air in my room keeping me from sleep, it's staying awake, listening for sounds. I'm so scared they'll do something during the nights. They're crazy, Rebel. I don't trust them one bit. I wish you could sleep in my room."

Rebel would give a low whine and wag his tail to indicate he was still listening, whenever I had one of these talks with him.

"You want to hear the latest? That old hag gave me a box of school clothes. You should see them, Rebel. All 'gramma' stuff. And she told me that from now on I won't be able to use the sewing stuff. I'm going to look worse than a Hutterite. I guess I shouldn't say that. They look all right to each other. But me, I'm going to have to go to school in those things. I don't know what I'm going to do. I'm glad they built that new high school. That means Ricky and Maggie won't be in my school. And I hope Ricky doesn't fail or he could end up being in my class next year. This year, I'm going to ask Jennifer if she can mail my letters for me and if I can have letters for me mailed to her place. I'm positive that old DeRosier has been throwing all my letters away. Cheryl said she wrote to me and I wrote to her but neither of us got any letters at all. I sure hate it here, Rebel. Except for you. Oh yeah, and you want to know what else that old hag came up with? Now, if I want my clothes washed, I'll have to do all the laundry and ironing. But if she thinks that's going to keep me from doing good in school, she's wrong. You know, Rebel, you and me, we talk the same language. We both whine." I smiled and scratched him behind the ears. Cheryl had said he liked that. Then I got up to walk back.

I started Grade Eight as the laughing stock of the school and from the first day on the bus, I was often called, "Gramma Squaw". I renewed my friendship with Jennifer but I could see that even she was embarrassed to be seen with me. One day, we were in the washroom, and she made fun of the way I was dressed. I expected that from the others, although when they would call me "Gramma Squaw", it was more painful than I'd expected and each time a lump would come to my throat. But when Jennifer teased me, I did start crying. She immediately became contrite and sympathetic and that made me cry even more.

"April, don't cry," she said. "I'm sorry. I didn't mean it. Hey listen, I'll bring you some of my stuff and you could keep it in your locker, okay?"

I was wiping my eyes when our Home Economics teacher walked in to see what was taking us so long.

"What's going on? What's the matter, April?"

Jennifer explained, "Mrs. DeRosier's making her wear

these kinds of clothes and she won't let April use the sewing things at home to make them look better."

"Would it help if I transferred you from the cooking class to the sewing class right now?," the teacher asked me.

Her kindness made me want to cry all over again but I kept my self-control and simply nodded.

Between the chores I was assigned and all my homework, there wasn't much time to alter my clothing. Whenever I could the first things I'd do would be to shorten my skirts as they hung down almost to my ankles. I'd still have to wear the black, ugly shoes to school but once I'd get to school, I would change into a pair that Jennifer had brought from home. I told her about my postal problems and she had checked with her mother and they agreed to be my go-between. The first letter I wrote was to the Dions. It would have been to Cheryl but I still didn't know where she was. In November my letter to the Dions was returned. They had moved from St. Albert.

Before Christmas, I had a visit with Cheryl. She was full of enthusiasm about her new foster home. Mostly, it was because the Steindalls had horses.

"Mr. Steindall gives lessons most nights and when he's not busy, he's been teaching me how to ride. We went on a sleigh ride last week. Oh, April, it's so much fun. It's easy being good there. The kids at school are all right. They don't make fun of me or anything. And some of the girls who like horses made friends with me but that's only 'cause they figure I'll invite them over and they'll get to ride. Mr. Steindall gave me my own horse to ride. His name is Fastbuck. I got to help clean their stalls and feed them but I like doing all that."

She went on telling me all the good things that were now happening to her and I hardly said anything. What could I say? That I was lonely and miserable and my foster mother dressed me funny? I envied Cheryl. I envied her having her own horse to ride. I envied that she could feel so much excitement. I knew I should have been so happy for her but comparing our lives, I simply envied her. I even envied the fact that she was so smart at school. Before we parted company, I got her address and told her Jennifer's.

In early February, I received my first letter through this new courier system. I had sent her a letter in January.

Dear April,

How are you? Mrs. Steindall says we will have our next visit in April or May. I can't wait. We had to make speeches in front of the class and I made mine on buffalo hunting. Mr. Darnell, my teacher, said I was an exceptional Métis, 'cause most would have avoided such subjects. That made me so proud that I just had to send you what I wrote. Tell me what you think of it.

Have a Happy Valentine's Day. I've enclosed a homemade card. Do you like it? I'm going to ask Mrs. Steindall if you could at least come to see me here for the summer holidays. I want to show you my horse. (Not really mine.) Would you like that? I told them about the DeRosiers but I don't think they believed me. That's the only thing I don't like about them. I got your letter. I feel so sorry for you, April. I wish there was something I could do to help you. I'm glad you got a friend like Jennifer. I'm glad too that Rebel's keeping you company. I sure do miss him. He was a good ol' dog. They have an Irish red setter here. Nice looking but what a nervous wreck. She follows me all over the place. I thought of all these funny things to tell you so you would laugh when you read this letter but once I started writing, all those funny things disappeared. Sorry about that.

Well, I'll close off for now and I'll be seeing you in the springtime. Write back soon.

Love,
Cheryl

Buffalo hunting! That was almost as bad as giving me a

book on Riel. I looked at the card. Cheryl had drawn a picture of a horse, a girl and a red setter. Meant to be her setting. How lucky could one get.

Then I chided myself, 'Now, April, you should be happy for her. Isn't that what you wanted? Didn't you want her to be safe and sound? Yeah, sure, but can't I even be a little bit jealous?'

Great, now I was talking to myself. Dutifully I started reading her speech. I had to be impressed, it was so well written and it was so obvious she had pride because she was writing about her people.

...The Métis hunters, equipped with buffalo guns, used one method known as 'running the buffalo'. This was perhaps the most dangerous way but definitely the most exciting. Men on horseback would ride through the stampeding herd, shooting prime animals. Once a shot was fired, the hunter had to pour some more powder from his buffalo horn into the muzzle of the gun, spit in one of the lead balls which he carried in his mouth, hit the gun butt on his saddle to shake down the powder and ball. All this was done as he raced his horse among the stampeding buffalo. If a horse stepped into a gopher hole or if the rider became dismounted for any other reasons, his hours as a buffalo hunter were probably numbered to mere seconds. Perhaps a bull would turn on him or a stray shot could bring him down. Or he may have loaded his rifle too fast or not properly enough and it could explode and blow his hand off. The hunt required steady nerves, much skill and expertise in horsemanship and marksmanship. . .

For a very brief moment I was caught up in her excitement. Then I wondered how she ever had the courage to stand up in front of her class and give the speech. I would never have the courage.

Grade Nine became the very worst school year I'd ever have. A lot of the kids in my class had started pairing off and going steady. I'd never been interested in boys except as friends. When I was younger, I had thought different ones were cute but that was the end of it. As long as I lived with the DeRosiers, I knew that I would have to give up any ideas about special friendships with boys and the easiest thing to do was simply not to look.

But then a new family moved into Aubigny and with it came a boy who was in Grade Eleven, the same class Maggie was in. While I secretly worshipped him from afar, Maggie talked about him every night at the supper table. Mrs. DeRosier even went so far as to invite his family over for a Sunday dinner. The boy was named Peter. I guess he liked me because after that Sunday dinner, he would stop and talk to me at school. Being seen with him brought me more friends. I loved school

Until the other kids' attitudes changed, Maggie had not been openly hostile towards me. I knew she felt that way because of Peter's friendship with me and not with her. It had even made me smug and more sure of myself. As soon as the whispering started behind my back, I knew that she and Ricky were behind it. Whatever they were saying spread throughout the school quickly. Kids were looking at me and snickering. I'd pass by a group of boys and they'd whistle. I started getting notes on my desk that said things like, "If you want a really good time, meet me at such and such a place." Some of the notes had obscenities in them and the comments I got from the boys were also obscene.

First Peter stopped talking to me and then Jennifer began avoiding me. This confused me even more. Jennifer was the kind of girl who would stick by a friend no matter what. I asked her, "What is going on, Jenny?"

Jennifer had looked around quickly because there were other kids watching us and obviously talking about me. "April, I have to go."

She slipped me a note that said she'd still post my letters for me but that was all. I became so angry and hurt my first impulse was to tell her to just forget it. But she was my only connection with Cheryl and I had to accept things the way they were. Again I was a loner and now I didn't have a single friend at school.

I was glad I still had Jennifer as a go-between on letters because in January I got another fat envelope from Cheryl. At lunchtime, I looked around to make sure Maggie and Ricky weren't around. If they ever found out that Cheryl and I were exchanging letters, I felt sure they would put an end to it. I was rather disappointed when I opened the letter and found most of it was a speech on the Métis.

January 26, 1964

Dear April,

How are you? I just know you're waiting for my next speech with anticipation. Well, here it is. Actually, it's not really a speech. I'm just caught up in this stuff. I don't think . . . Scratch that, it's a silly expression. I think my fellow-classmates might not be able to hack another speech on Métis people. I was going to deliver this speech but now I've decided I will keep it among my papers on the history of the Métis people. I think it's important that we know our own history. It's rather a short history compared to other races but it's interesting as I've already stated and I wouldn't have minded one bit living in those days. Mrs. MacAdams used to have so many good books on the subject of natives. I've been babysitting lately and next time we go to Winnipeg, I'm going to spend all I've got on books. I wish I could afford to buy every book there is. Sally says I'm soon going to need glasses. I doubt it. I'd hate to have to wear glasses. Wouldn't you? It's un-Indian.

Oh, I made the volleyball team. We'll be going around to different places and playing other schools. Rita, one of the girls in my class, says it's not fair that I'm so smart and athletic too. Of course, I'm not the only one. It's too bad you couldn't try out for after-school sports. I know you'd be good. Come spring, I won't join any outdoor stuff because I'd rather practice riding.

Write back to me, April. And tell me what you think of my project. I'm going to work on something about Riel. I need a few more books though. Well, I'll sign off for now. Got a load of homework to do.

Love,
Cheryl

Again, I dutifully read through her essay. Again, she wrote about the Métis with such pride.

. . . The two armed parties met at Seven Oaks. Grant sent an emissary to Semple, demanding his surrender. An argument ensued and a settler fired. The sound of gunfire brought a nearby group of fifty more Métis to the scene. The battle-experienced Métis fired their round of shots and then fell to the ground to reload. The settlers, thinking they had shot these men down, began to cheer. The Métis, with their guns reloaded, charged the settlers. Terrified, most of the settlers turned and ran. The horsemen took over as if running buffalo. They overtook the settlers and shot them. Within fifteen minutes, twenty settlers and two of Grant's men were dead. . .

I thought it just made the Métis look like blood-thirsty savages, but Cheryl went into great detail pointing out all of the 'grievances' of the Métis and why they had fought some of their battles. But when I finished reading, I didn't feel much happier. I hated dates and company names. And how come all this mattered to Cheryl so much? She was going to keep it amoung her papers. Did it help her accept the coloring of her skin? Was that why we thought so differently? That and her superior intelligence? One had to be intelligent to find this kind of thing exciting. Skin coloring didn't matter in this school. Everyone treated me like a full-blooded Indian. "Gramma Squaw!" I hated those DeRosier kids so much. I sure wished I knew what they had been up to this time.

A few months later, I did find out. The Guidance Coun-sellor, Mrs. Wartzman, was waiting for me in the hall one day at lunchtime. She said she wanted to see me in her of-fice. As Mrs. Semple had done, the Counsellor came right out and made her speech. I suppose the speech would have been okay if I had been guilty of any wrongdoing.

"April, I've heard some disturbing things and I feel I should talk this over with you. I know that you're a foster girl and perhaps that's the reason. You feel a psychological need to be loved. Well, what I'm really trying to say is that you shouldn't be letting Raymond and Gilbert fondle you. From what I understand, you've also been trying to flirt with Mr. DeRosier."

I sat in the chair with my mouth open. I felt such humiliation. I was sure my face was red. I thought later that Mrs. Wartzman probably assumed I was embarrassed because the truth was coming out.

"Perhaps it's not my place to be talking to you. But it's such a sensitive issue. I know that you're doing well in your grades and I want to warn you that a pregnancy would disrupt your life. Let's see if we can't get your life on the right track again. And if Mrs. DeRosier has taken this up with your social worker, I can say that we had this little talk. Okay?" Mrs. Watrzman finished it with a smile.

I walked out of her office in a daze. It was a warm spring day so I went outside to eat my lunch. I really wanted to avoid the lunchroom and have some privacy to myself but there were kids outside. When they saw me, some of them snickered. I wanted to die, crawl away into some hole and never be seen again. Instead, I sat and nibbled my sand-wich. If it had been Peter I was accused of fooling with, I would have been embarrassed. But Raymond and Gilbert? Both? At the same time? Not only were they ugly and pimply but they passed their grades only because of their age and their size. I didn't have anything against them but I'd have to be plumb out of my head to even look at them in 'that' way. Well, it was no wonder Jennifer and Peter stayed away from me. But then, how could Jennifer believe that of me? And had Raymond and Gilbert gotten that same kind of speech? Probably not. Only girls got pregnant.

For the rest of that week I walked around thinking of this. On Saturday, I found myself at the riverbank, talking to my old friend, Rebel.

"I know I shouldn't feel so sorry for myself. I know that other kids go through much worse than me. But knowing that doesn't help very much. At least Gilbert and Raymond are getting out of this rathole. I wonder who they're going to accuse me of doing things with next. And if they don't get some other boys, I'll probably have to take the bales off the fields all by myself. How could Jenny believe all those things about me? How could she? I thought she was such a good friend. Maybe she doesn't believe them. Maybe she's just scared to be seen with me. Boy! I'm going to get even with those DeRosiers. I don't know how, but somehow, some way, I'm going to get them. And when I get through with them, they're never going to get another foster kid. Never!"

6

I HAD NO idea how I was going to get even with the DeRosiers for those horrible rumours. It just made me feel a little better to think I could. I would entertain different ideas but I discarded them all. Talking to my social worker was futile because she'd already proven to me that she was on Mrs. DeRosier's side. And the same thing went for the teachers at school.

Since I never saw Jennifer over the summer months, Cheryl and I didn't write to each other. It was when I went into Grade Ten that my opportunity presented itself to do something about the DeRosiers. I didn't recognize it as such. Jennifer came to me with a letter from Cheryl in September. I expected her to walk away but she stayed and finally talked to me.

"April, about last year . . . I guess I should have told you what was going on when I first heard about it. But there are these sayings, you know, about being judged by the company you keep. Well, I didn't want to get the same hassles you were getting. I'm chicken. I couldn't take that kind of thing."

I looked at her and said, "Did you believe any of that?"

"No. I knew you. I knew you wouldn't do anything like what they said. I'd like for us to be friends again."

"I'd like that, too," I said, gratefully.

In October, Mrs. Gauthier, our English teacher told us that the *Southern Journal* was holding a competition for Christmas stories and we'd have two weeks in which to submit entries. At lunchtime, Jennifer and I talked about the competition. English was my strongest subject and compositions were easy for me. It was mostly just a matter of choosing a topic that would attract attention.

"Why don't you write about your life with the DeRosiers?" Jennifer asked with a grin.

I thought it was a great idea. But then I said, "It has to be a Christmas story, and they have a way of destroying Christmas for me."

For a week I pondered over how I could work my life at the DeRosiers into a Christmas story. Finally, the idea came to me and I started on my story at lunchtimes. The title was "What I Want For Christmas" and I ended the story with the sentence: "What I want for Christmas is for somebody to listen to me and to believe in me." I handed it in to Mrs. Gauthier.

The next day, Mrs. Gauthier asked me to stay at lunch. I waited and was surprised when Mrs. Wartzman came into the room with my story in her hand. Mrs. Wartzman said to me, "This is an incredible story, April. Is this really what's been going on?"

I nodded, unable to speak because that lump in my throat was back. I was sure they were going to throw my story in the garbage after giving me a good scolding. Maybe they would even show it to Mrs. DeRosier. Mrs. Gauthier's next words gave me hope. "I believe the story. I've heard the rumours about April and she's never done anything to indicate that they were true. She's a very good student."

"Oh, I'm sure she is. I've checked with Cheryl's former Grade Five teacher and she confirmed what you wrote, April. I can't believe that workers would place children in this kind of home."

"Why didn't you ever tell your social worker or one of us?" Mrs. Gauthier asked.

"We tried. We tried to tell our workers but they would only believe what Mrs. DeRosier told them. And when you said those things to me last year . . ." I looked at Mrs. Wartzman.

"I owe you an apology, April. I'm sorry I jumped to conclusions," Mrs. Wartzman said.

It was decided that my story would not be entered in the competition and they urged me to write another one in its place. From what I understood, Mrs. Wartzman was going to call my social worker herself. That was good enough for me.

I waited impatiently and in November, 1963, something happened in the United States which made me forget my impatience temporarily. The President of the United States, John F. Kennedy, was shot. I was just coming back from lunch when I heard the news. The whole class was subdued and I was shocked. Cheryl and I had talked about him a few times. She admired him for many reasons. In the weeks which followed, I saved clippings from the newspaper on his funeral and his family. I wasn't allowed to watch television so I missed an awful lot, including the death of Lee Harvey Oswald. I planned on giving my clippings to Cheryl. We were supposed to have a visit but for some reason it was put off.

I returned to my impatient waiting. Had the wheels of

motion begun or was nothing going to come of my story, after all? Christmas passed and then it was 1964. The only consolation I had until then was that two grown-ups were aware of my predicament. Then in January, I got a letter from Cheryl.

January 16, 1964

Dear April,

How are you? I got your letter and obviously you didn't know you missed a visit with me. I waited at the Children's Aid office all afternoon December 23rd, then Miss Turner came and told me that Mrs. DeRosier called to say she wasn't able to make it to town because she'd gotten stuck. Did you know about that? Anyways, I'm glad you've gotten through to your teachers. Have you heard anything further? We are getting a new social worker, did you know that? I sure hope she's going to be good for us.

Wasn't it terrible about President Kennedy being assassinated? I wanted to see you so much to talk about it. I cried that night when I was alone. I read a lot of history. All the Kennedys were so interesting and young and vital. I used to collect items on them. I'm sure that Robert Kennedy will get in as President, though. I hope he keeps the same speech writers. Kennedy's speeches were really good.

Anyways, I've enclosed my historical piece on Riel at the Red River Insurrection. You ought to see this load of crap we have to take in History. I don't know if you took the same textbook. It's *Canada: the New Nation*. It makes me mad the way they portray native people. It makes me wish those whitemen had never come here. But then we would not have been born. At least the Indians would have been left in peace. Nothing those tribes ever did to each other matches what the whites have done to them. Whoa, there, Cheryl. You probably don't agree with me, do you, April? But history should be an unbiased representation of the facts. And if they show one side, they ought to show the other side equally. Anyways, that's why I'm writing the

Métis side of things. I don't know what I'm going to do with it but it makes me feel good.

Well, I hope you like my essay. I'll sign off for now. Let me know what happens. Sure is taking a long time.

Love,
Cheryl

When I finished reading her letter, I felt awful about the fact I had missed a visit and had not even known about it. Did Mrs. DeRosier do that because she knew about my own essay? All of a sudden I felt scared. She did know. She had put a stop to everything. I was going to be stuck here until . . . until when? It wasn't fair. It just wasn't fair.

To preoccupy my mind I read Cheryl's essay on Riel and the Red River Insurrection. But reading her essay didn't help. Knowing the other side, the Métis side, didn't make me feel any better. It just reinforced my belief that if I could assimilate myself into white society, I wouldn't have to live like this for the rest of my life.

That afternoon, I didn't pay much attention to classwork. My mind was on my present problem. I believed Mrs. DeRosier knew about my essay. I felt I had been betrayed. What could I do about it? I could think of only one thing. Come summer, I'd take off. But then I had wanted to finish school so bad. I had wanted to be able to get a good job. I wanted to be rich. Oh, to heck with being rich. I'd run away anyway. Maybe to some other city so they wouldn't find me. I'd lie about my age if I had to and I'd get a job. For the moment, being free was more important than anything else in the world.

That night, I lay in bed still thinking about my soon-to-be future. Another problem came up. I had no money at all to even start out. I'd have to get some. But how? Steal it? I'd been accused of stealing already so why not? That would be justice of a sort. Oh, sure, April, and when you run out of money in the city, you can just sell your body. And what else do native girls do? By now, I knew what meant skid row. I bet all those girls who ended up on skid row just wanted freedom and peace in the first place. Just like me. I'd had good intentions about my life. But here I was, forced to go out into that world, unprepared and alone. With only a Grade Ten and no money. No matter, I'd still run away. I felt so, so sorry for myself and what I'd end up being, I started to cry. My life would be hard. But staying here would be harder. I felt I had no choice.

My running away plans were discarded when rescue did come at the beginning of our spring break. It came in the form of Mr. Wendell, my new social worker. When I saw him enter the house and introduce himself, I was downright disappointed. He was just a short little man with a meek demeanor. Glasses and balding. Really! He was no match for Mrs. DeRosier. I studied him as he exchanged preliminaries with the old hag. Suddenly, he said, "I'd like to see where the boys slept."

"The boys?" Mrs. DeRosier asked. She was obviously flustered by his unexpected question. I could tell and I was glad she was off-balance. But the thought that she was going to get more boys must have hit her the same time it hit me. She recovered and my face grew long.

"Oh, yes, Raymond and Gilbert. How are they doing now that they're on their own? I hope they're not getting into any trouble. They were such good boys when they were with us. And such hard workers. You couldn't get any better workers. I believe that hard work is good for the soul, don't you?"

I thought to myself, "So that's why she doesn't make her kids work; they have no souls."

Mrs. DeRosier led the way into the living room towards the stairs, saying, "They used to share my son's room. We moved their bunks into the storage closet for now."

When we were upstairs, Mr. Wendell had a look but didn't say anything. He asked where my room was. Mrs. DeRosier took him down the hall to Maggie's room. I followed them everywhere and when she could, Mrs.

DeRosier scowled at me as if trying to tell me to get back downstairs.

"I can only see one bed, Mrs. DeRosier. I understand you have a daughter. Isn't this her room?" Mr. Wendell said.

"The girls share it. The other bed was old so I've ordered a new one. It should have been here by now." She smiled at him.

This was my chance to prove what a liar Mrs. DeRosier was. I said, "My bedroom's really downstairs, at the back."

Mrs. DeRosier said quickly, "Well, the girls have been having trouble so I moved April there but only temporarily." She glared at me when Mr. Wendell turned to start back down.

"I've been in that room since I first came here. And so was Cheryl." I was beyond caring about the later consequences.

"How about if you show me where your room is, April?" Mr. Wendell said to me when we were back in the kitchen. Mrs. DeRosier said nothing as Mr. Wendell looked at my belongings.

"Well, Mrs. DeRosier, I think that under the circumstances, I can only recommend that April be moved as soon as we find a new foster home for her." He was about to say more but Mrs. DeRosier cut him off.

"And I think you can take her and get out of my house right now," she bellowed.

"Mrs. Semple has had a very heavy case-load, otherwise I'm sure you wouldn't have been able to fool her for so long," Mr. Wendell said to her.

He told me to get my things ready. When we started for the car, Rebel came to me. I stopped to pet him one last time. "Poor old Reb. I wish I could take you with me. Thank you for being my friend here. Bye, Rebel." Rebel wagged his tail and as we drove off, I saw him lay down by the roadside, probably waiting for me to come back.

7

ONCE WE arrived at the Children's Aid Office, arrangements were quickly made for me to attend St. Bernadette's Academy, but they were now on their spring break. I waited that whole morning in the waiting area, not quite sure I wasn't dreaming all this. I would actually be going to an Academy. Rich girls went to Academies. When Mr. Wendell came back late in the afternoon he brought back news that topped my excitement. I was going to the Steindalls to be with Cheryl until the spring break was over. All of this excitement was inside me. Outwardly I might have smiled slightly but I was now used to keeping my feelings to myself.

When we arrived at the Steindall's place, in Birds Hill,

Cheryl was waiting for me on the veranda. When she saw our car pull into the driveway, she bounded off the steps and came running up to greet me. She was practically jumping up and down. I greeted her in a cool, reserved manner and that put an injured look on her face. At the time, only Cheryl and Mrs. Steindall were home. Their own daughter was away in the city for the holidays, visiting an older sister. After Mr. Wendell made sure I was settled in, he left. I had lunch while Cheryl chattered away. Mrs. Steindall seemed nice enough but she didn't attempt to join in Cheryl's questions. Cheryl seemed used to her being quiet because she wasn't the least bit self-conscious about what she said.

After lunch, she was anxious to show me her horse.

"You know what I used to think about doing all the time?" Cheryl asked me as I admired the horse.

"What?"

"I used to think of riding him to the DeRosiers and rescuing you from them. But then I probably would have gotten lost and I couldn't figure out how to feed and water the horse. Anyways, Mr. Steindall only gave me the horse to ride, not for keeps. If I'd taken him, I'd have been a horse thief." While I smiled, Cheryl seemed to ponder for a minute before she spoke again. "April, how come you didn't seem very glad to see me?"

"I was Cheryl, really. It's just that I'm used to keeping the way I feel inside of me. I've been doing that for practically five years now. Maybe even longer. I don't know. It just seems it's safer not to show your feelings. Like, if the Steindalls were mean people, or even Mr. Wendell, and they saw that we liked being together, they might try and keep us apart. Remember, DeRosier did that."

"Yeah, I guess you're right."

After that, Cheryl and I talked every minute that we could, catching up on things we didn't say in letters. I must have made up for all the laughing I didn't do while I was living at the DeRosiers. But too soon I had to leave for school.

I finished my Grade Ten at St. Bernadette's Academy. When I'd been living at the Dions, I had known nuns and they were okay people. I was able to relax at the convent. A daily routine was followed. I made friends with a lot of the boarders. The only thing was that they spoke of their friends and families back home and I had no one to speak of except Cheryl. It wasn't until June that I came up with an outright lie, an excuse for being with the Children's Aid. I told my friends that my parents died in a plane crash. I didn't plan on that lie. It just came out on the spur of the moment, when I was being asked about my family. They were so sympathetic towards me that I knew I would never be able to take those words back. I credited my ability to make friends easily to the fact that none of them knew I was part Indian.

My summer holidays that year were simply wonderful. The Steindalls had agreed to take me for the two months. Mr. Steindall taught me how to ride. Sometimes, we would all go out riding, even Mrs. Steindall, who looked out of place in her pair of jeans and cowboy boots. When I became a good enough rider, Cheryl and I were allowed to go camping overnight by a small creek about four miles away. The first time, Mr. Steindall rode over in the evening and helped us set up the tent.

One night, when we were sitting in front of our small fire, Cheryl told me the things she had dreamt of when we lived together at the DeRosiers.

"Remember how I used to look at your Geography book?"

"Yeah, and daydream."

"Well, I used to think that when Mom and Dad got better and took us back, we could move to the B.C. Rockies and live like olden day Indians. We'd live near a lake and we'd build our own log cabin with a big fireplace. And we wouldn't have electricity probably. We'd have lots and lots of books. We'd have dogs and horses and we'd make friends with the wild animals. We'd go fishing and hunting, grow our own garden and chop our wood for winter. And we wouldn't meet people who were always trying to put us down. We'd be so happy. Do you think that would ever be possible, April?"

"It's a beautiful dream, Cheryl." She was watching me and I didn't want her to know then that I had my own plans. I wanted to be with people, not isolated in the wilderness.

"But do you think it's possible that it could happen?"

"Maybe. Maybe our parents might start coming to see us again. But it all depends on them." I realized that moment that I had stopped thinking of our parents as Mom and Dad and it was hard for me to refer to them as Mom and Dad now.

"I wanted to ask our social workers about them but I was too scared. I don't know why. I still think about us living out there together. When I'm feeling down, that picks me up. Mom and Dad would become real healthy again. I always think of Dad as a strong man. He would have been a chief or a warrior in the olden days, if he had been pure Indian. I'd sure like to know what kind of Indians we are. And Mom was so beautiful to me she was like an Indian princess. The only thing that I couldn't be realistic about in my daydreams was that Rebel would be with us." Cheryl's eyes sparkled. I could tell that this fantasy had meant a lot to her. It had probably helped her get over her loneliness. So I didn't tell her the truth about our parents. I felt that by not telling her I was also betraying her, letting her hang on to impossible dreams. If only Cheryl would forget about them, forget that she was Métis. She was so smart that she could have made it in the white world. White people has a great respect for high intelligence. Again, I wished my parents were dead.

When I first came for the summer, I'd tell Cheryl how great it was to be at the Academy. But by the end of it, when she started talking about going there, too, I changed my tune. I then told her, "You wouldn't want to leave this place and Fastbuck to go to a Convent, would you? I'm sure you wouldn't like it there. There are hours and hours of praying in the Chapel and then there's also the hours of study periods. There's hardly any sports activity. You'd be bored to death." I didn't want Cheryl at the Academy because of the lie I had told about my parents and because I was white as far as the other girls were concerned. I wanted to keep it that way as long as I could.

"Sounds to me as if you don't want me there," Cheryl said, tilting her head to one side.

"You know it's not that. You have it so good here. And I could probably come and visit you for holidays. Besides, I'll be finished school in two years and you still have four years to go. What would you do if you didn't like it? When I graduate, you'd be alone. If you left there, they might put you in another home like the DeRosiers'." Cheryl shrugged and accepted my reasoning. I was very relieved.

Going to St. Bernadette's was good for me. I had many friends and it was easy to study and do well in my school work. On weekends, I was invited to go to other girls' homes, with Mr. Wendell's okay. I never told Cheryl about those weekends, knowing she'd probably feel slighted. Long weekends I always went to the Steindalls. I'd often wish that I had been placed as a boarder at this school long before. There were no hassles about belonging to a family all the time. There was no one who made fun of my parents. Of course, that was due to the lie I had told. I might not have known a family life as I had at the Dions, but I would not have known the cruelty of the DeRosiers either. I spent Christmas with the Steindalls. Perhaps Cheryl had put her family fantasy aside, I thought, because when I went there, she had something new to tell me.

"You know, April, I think that since we have made it or we're going to make it, we ought to help other kids like us make it too. You know what I've been thinking? I'm going

92

to become a social worker when I finish school. And I'm going to be a good social worker, just like Mr. Wendell. What about you? What are you going to be when you grow up?''

"I haven't got a clue what I'm going to be. I used to think of being a lawyer but I'm too shy. All I know for sure is that I don't want to be in anything medical, I don't want to be a teacher or a social worker. I just don't know."

"Well, geez, April, you better start thinking about it because you only got a year and a half to go."

True, I did have only a year and a half to go before I would graduate. But even so, I'd only be seventeen. What I wanted to do was start working and making money.

At the end of my Grade Eleven school year, Mr. Wendell gave me the option of returning to the Steindalls for the summer or going to Winnipeg and finding myself a summer job. He said my room and board would be provided. Not another foster home, but room and board I opted for the city. To ease the guilt I felt for not choosing Cheryl's company, I told myself that I had to start making my life, for me, and that both of us should have friends of our own, not always relying on each other. I wrote Cheryl a hurried letter to tell her all this.

I moved to Spence Street, just off Portage Avenue, near the heart of the city. It didn't take me long to find a job as a waitress and I made new friends among the other boarders. Some of them were natives from northern communities and were there to go to the University of Winnipeg. Others were former foster children who were working at steady jobs, on the verge of going into the world on their own but who still required the security of the Children's Aid to fall back on. I would work from eight in the morning to four-thirty. After supper, I would go with the other girls, down to a coffee shop where a lot of other kids hung out. On Fridays and Saturdays, we would all go to the Hungry Eye, a discotheque on Portage Avenue, near

Carlton.

The people I met at the discotheque were fascinating to me; from the musicians who played in the bands to the individuals with whom I made friends. I liked the way they dressed and I liked the way they danced. They were good and bad at the same time. Good in that native girls I saw were beautiful and sure of themselves. Good in that natives could go with whites and no one laughed. Good in their open acceptance of others. Bad in that they went shoplifting, drank liquor even though they were under-aged and had easy sexual relationships with each other. When the discotheques closed, all-night parties followed. I always went back to my place, though. I felt at home with these new friends but a lot of times, I imagined myself much better than they were. The girls made me think of Mrs. Semple's speech on the syndrome. So, I enjoyed the good things they offered but stayed away from the bad.

I worked hard all that summer and put all my earnings in a savings account. I hadn't bothered to write to Cheryl because I had kept putting it off. When I returned to do my Grade Twelve at St. Bernadette's, I was more aware of what was happening in the world. I was there less than a week when I got a letter from Cheryl.

September 7, 1965

Dear April,

How are you? In case your forgot, it's me, Cheryl, your sister. How come you never came to see me once this past summer and you never even wrote to me? Your last letter made me very sad. It's like you don't want to have anything to do with me anymore. Your pretense about not caring seems to be turning into reality. I was looking forward to our spending the summer holidays together again. Instead, all I get is a short letter. I know we each have to have our own friends and make our own lives. But it was you who said all we've got is each other. We're family, not just friends. Are you coming for Christmas? I hope so.

I finally got another essay done on Riel. I didn't have much time in school with sports and other things going on. I did have a lot of rainy days when I was alone this past summer, though. I'll probably grow up to be a nag, huh? You're so lucky to be in Grade Twelve. They really should have let me skip a grade too. Well, I'm going to sign off now. This was just going to be a short note to let you know how much you hurt my feelings. Hope you like Riel at Batoche.

Your loving sister,
Cheryl

I felt guilty all over again after I had read the letter. She was right. I should have written to her and given her my address in the city. I should have made a special effort to go and see her. I tried to imagine myself in her place. Yes, she must have felt abandoned by me. More than she showed in her letter. I had to write her a long letter to make up for it. I even sent her lavish compliments on her essay. It was quite extraordinary for someone her age. But it had no big effect on me. Riel and Dumont, they were men of the past. Why dwell on it? What concerned me was my future. And this essay proved my point once again. White superiority had conquered in the end.

By Christmas, I had decided what I was going to do. Some of the girls had talked of becoming secretaries. That sounded good enough for me. I would take a secretarial course after I graduated. Over the Christmas holidays, I told Cheryl my plans, she was disappointed. She was sure I could do something better, like become a psychologist or something. She figured I would be wasting my life away. I told her she was beginning to sound like one of those ambitious white mothers she scorned so much. We teased each other back and forth but I knew she was serious. She really did want me to attend university. And, of course, she was still set on becoming a social worker.

After my graduation, I got my old job as a waitress for

the summer months. It was arranged that I would go to the Red River Community College in September. I lived once again on Spence Street, expecting everything to be the same as the previous summer. It wasn't. The Hungry Eye had been closed. I ran into a few of the old crowd. They told me that some of the others had gone to other cities or they were doing time at the Headingley Jail. Another discotheque had opened on Graham Avenue. I went along with them to check it out. One of the girls I had met the last summer now had a baby at home and was living on welfare. That bothered me a lot and somehow the magic of that kind of nightlife was gone for me.

By September, I had over eight hundred dollars in the bank. I thought I was quite wealthy. My first boyfriend wasn't really a boyfriend. He spent most of his time pining away over his old girlfriend. We went to the school dances together but in private we never got real close to each other. If he had tried to kiss me, I would have ended it right there. The thing I liked most about Ted was that he was safe to be with. I turned 18 two months before I finished my course. When I finished the course, I knew I would never see Ted again, except by accident.

Children's Aid assured me they would support me until I found a job. About three weeks later, I became employed as a legal secretary at the law firm of Harbison and Associates. I was thrilled when I found out I'd be making over four times the amount I had as a waitress.

When I had my last talk with Mr. Wendell on what I called my Independence Day, I showed no outward reactions. He gave me the accumulation of my family allowances along with reassurances that if I needed assistance of any kind, I could always come to him. Then I heard myself asking about my parents and what were the chances of finding them. He went off and came back with a list of names and addresses. I thanked him and said goodbye. I'd probably see him again but I would no longer be a foster child. I was free, *free! FREE!*

8

I FOUND FREEDOM rather boring, once I'd settled into my new routine. I'd found an apartment on Cumberland Avenue which was within walking distance of where I worked. Then I furnished it with used furniture. Working was easy, that is after the first couple of weeks when I got over my nervousness. I worked for Mr. Lord, a young lawyer who did real estate work. I was nervous about making mistakes when I typed up all the legal forms, I was nervous answering the phone, I was nervous each time I handed in the letter I had typed for his signature in case I hadn't got my shorthand right. Mr. Lord was generous with his compliments, though, and that soon put me at ease. The other girls in the office were pleasant, several were my age and when I got to know them better, we would go to movies or shopping together.

Evenings and weekends, I spent on the search for my parents. I'd take the list and a map of the city and go to the addresses on the list. Sometimes the addresses would lead to a parking lot or a new building. The house where we had lived on Jarvis had been torn down and replaced by a government building. I would feel a vague kind of relief when this happened because I didn't like the people I'd meet who once knew Henry and Alice Raintree "a long time ago." I found out that both of them had relatives in the North. I wasn't going to go to the northern towns on the slim chance I might find them because I considered it unlikely.

At one address on Charles St., I was practically dragged into the house by a rather large, squat woman. When I asked if she knew the whereabouts of Henry or Alice Raintree and told her who I was, a grin spread on her face from ear to ear. All happy and smiling, she took me by the arm and led me into the house. She hadn't seen my parents for the last couple of years but maybe Jacques had. I figured Jacques to be her husband. I didn't want to stay there but I could think of no polite way of leaving. Besides, she assured me that Jacques would be home in a short while. Meanwhile, she offered me some tea, then a beer, but I refused both. She'd been cooking and she resumed her position at the old stove. I sat at the kitchen table, looking around.

What a horrible place. The linoleum was coming apart at the seams and here and there pieces were missing. I could see why it hadn't been washed. The cupboards had been painted white, maybe twenty years ago. The plaster was also coming off the walls and the ceiling was warped and water-stained. Flies! They were everywhere and reminded me of the book *Lord of the Flies*. One fly landed on the rim of an uncovered lard can which sat on the table with some bread. It rubbed its legs together, as if with glee.

How could anyone eat that food and not be sick? Suddenly it was very important to me that those flies not touch me and I waved them away. Of course the windows couldn't be closed, but hadn't they ever heard of screens? I wondered what they did in wintertime, when the smell of the place must be raunchy. They were probably immune to all the germs in the house, but me, I feared going home, getting sick and missing work.

I stared over at the old woman, her back to me, probably unaware of my presence. From our initial encounter, I thought she would have been the talkative type, but no, she was silently busy filling up a pot with cut up vegetables. I thought she probably used the flies for meat, and then I scolded myself for being so merciless. I couldn't help it, though. I looked down at her feet, stockingless, and stuck into a pair of men's backless slippers. Her legs were lumpy with varicose veins or some other disease. Her heels were dried and scaly. Ugly! Her, this house, this kind of existence. I finally cleared my throat, mostly to remind her that I was still sitting behind her.

"I really have to go now. I'm supposed to meet someone. I could come back another time," I said.

"Oh, I'm sorry, I was sure Jacques would have been back by now," she said, turning to me. "Are you sure you really have to go? You could stay for supper."

"Well, thank you but I really have to go." I turned to leave, knowing I would not return.

Later, as I sat in the bathtub, washing off all those germs I'd probably picked up, I thought about the scene I had witnessed. If I hadn't been brought up in foster homes, I would most likely have been brought up in those slums. I would have been brought up with flies, with mice, and rats, and lice, and germs. I would have been brought up by alcoholic parents and what would I be like now? Would I have any ambitions? Or would I come to live just for today, glad when each day would end? I would not go back to that house on St. Charles. I would not go out of my way for a long, long time to come to try and find the parents who had abandoned Cheryl and me—all for a bottle of booze! When I finished my bath, I put all the papers Mr. Wendell had given me, along with the new addresses I had been given, into a box and stuck the box in the back of the closet, out of sight and out of mind. If I did find my parents, there would be emotional pain for Cheryl and me. It would probably tear me apart once again. That part of my life was now finished for good. I had a plan to follow and from now on I would stick with it, whether Cheryl agreed with it or not. It was my only way to survive.

Mr. Steindall usually came to get me for long weekends so I could spend them with Cheryl. Otherwise, I usually stayed home, watched T.V., read books or magazines and if I wanted to go out and do something, I would go to the movies.

I'd buy magazines that featured beautiful homes and study how they were decorated. Then I would lay back and day-dream of myself being in one of those homes, giving lavish parties and I'd have a lot of friends surrounding me. I also studied fashion magazines and I'd spend hours shopping for just the right thing. I had no idea how I was going to become rich. All I knew was that one day I would have a beautiful home, a big fancy car and the most gorgeous clothing ever. Yes, when fortune kissed me with wealth, I'd be well prepared.

I had been working at Harbison's law firm for almost six months when another lawyer was added to the eleven already there. When I first saw Roger Maddison, I thought to myself, "Now there's a man I wouldn't mind spending the rest of my life with." It wasn't that I was a sucker for all handsome men, just that his rugged kind of handsomeness was the kind I could look at forever. Since some of the other girls openly swooned over him, I figured I'd be cool about my infatuation with him. But then I had to do some work for him because he didn't have his own secretary. My infatuation quickly wore off. He was a perfectionist and when I made my first small mistake, he tore into me. I was so angry that he would criticize me. Or maybe it was that I was hurt that our feelings weren't mutual. I practically yelled right back at him. From then on, we were sarcastic towards each other, made snide remarks, always trying to outdo the other. Even when he did get his own secretary and she began to do all of his work, we still glared at each other whenever it was appropriate. Or he would smile and greet everyone, excluding me. The thing I couldn't figure out was that he seemed to study me an awful lot. I'd be working away, then I'd feel his eyes on me. I'd look up and there he was. But he'd give me a dirty look and turn away.

While I worked, Cheryl was finishing her Grade Twelve. In June she graduated at the top of her class and even won a scholarship to go to the University of Winnipeg. If she hadn't, Children's Aid would have paid for her education anyway. There were some advantages in being a ward of the C.A.S.

In July, Cheryl moved in with me, even though she wouldn't be eighteen until October. Children's Aid agreed to pay all her expenses. The day Cheryl moved in with me, July 6, 1968, was like the real honest Independence Day. The Steindalls brought Cheryl and her belongings to my place that Saturday morning, had lunch with us and then left. Cheryl and I went shopping for a sofa that opened into a bed. Then we went on to other stores. We dropped our purchases off back at the apartment, then went out for supper. That evening, we sat around talking and thinking about the wonderful feeling of being together with no one to control our destinies but us.

I went to work on Monday and Cheryl went to the Winnipeg Native Friendship Centre. She volunteered her services for the rest of July and August, believing the experience would help her in her future career as a social worker.

Cheryl began her first year of university in September. I

began to meet her for lunch in the university cafeteria. She quickly accumulated a number of friends, both white and native. To my biggest surprise, she started going out quite steadily with a white student, Garth Tyndall. I was amazed because the way she had talked in the past she didn't like anything white. I wasn't surprised she could attract the opposite sex because she was very beautiful. She was also outgoing in her new crowd, and stubborn when she made up her mind about anything. When she was home, she'd usually have her friends around. And when she was over at Garth's place in the evenings, I would be alone.

I gave a party for her eighteenth birthday. I could see that night how close she and Garth had become. He seemed to care about her more than she did about him. I was very pleased. If anyone could change a woman's mind about things, it was a man.

But my hopes were dashed when a month later they split up. At first Cheryl wouldn't tell me what happened. One night she was supposed to have been going to dinner with him and then to a movie. They had gone out together, but later in the evening Garth had called for her. When she came in a few minutes later, I said to her, "I thought you two were going out tonight."

"No. Something more important came up. If he calls again, tell him I'm not in. I'm going to take a bath and go to bed." She seemed very depressed.

"Hey, Cheryl, did you two have a fight?"

"No, not a fight. More of an insight." With that she stalked off to the bathroom.

Garth called again and I was tempted to ask him what had happened but I felt I should hear it from Cheryl. The next day was Saturday and Cheryl was still in a state of depression. Finally, I asked her again what had happened. After hesitating, she finally told me.

"We were walking down Portage and Garth saw some of his friends coming toward us. He told me to keep walking and he'd catch up. I pretended that I was window shopping so I could listen to them. You know what he did? You know what that creep did? He left me there and went for a beer with them. He didn't want them to know about me. That goddamned hypocrite. He's ashamed of me.''

I didn't say anything. I didn't say anything because I was guilty of that, too. I had never invited Cheryl to come and meet me for lunch because I didn't want anyone at work to see her, to know she was my sister. Even now, I knew this wouldn't change me. I would continue to walk the five blocks or so at lunchtime, so I could meet her where she was already accepted. That night, Cheryl decided she was going to keep a journal. I smiled and told her she shouldn't start a journal with an unhappy opening.

"Wait until something good happens to you, something special.''

"Well, I haven't got a lifetime. I want to start this thing right now. I have a feeling there will be a lot more of this kind of thing.''

I thought to myself, "Oh, no, I could be in there one day.''

Not long after Cheryl's break-up with Garth, I met someone I thought was very special. I was waiting for Cheryl outside one of her classrooms, when another of Cheryl's professors approached me. We talked until Cheryl came out. His name was Jerry McCallister and whenever he saw me alone after that, he'd stop to chat. One day, he asked me to go out with him. I guess he thought I shared some of the same ideals as Cheryl because he talked about native subjects, like their housing and education. Having heard Cheryl speak about such things often enabled me to carry a reasonable conversation with him. When he dropped me off at my apartment, he asked me to go out with him again, but he didn't try to kiss me. I had gone out with some of the students to plays and concerts but they had only one thing on their minds at the end of the evening. So Jerry's behavior was refreshing to me. We'd go out together frequently after that, even during the week. He was always a perfect gentleman. The more I saw of him the more I appreciated him.

Finally one night when we stayed at my place for dinner and some conversation, he made his first advance. I held back. Good girls didn't do that kind of thing. Furthermore, and more importantly, if things got out of hand and we went all the way, there was the risk of getting pregnant. Maybe that was my worst fear because when Jerry tried to get too close, I would always back off. Jerry's initial amusement and patience waned and one night he was trying to coax me again. Finally, he said, "April, what are you scared of? Are you scared of getting involved with another human being? Or is it sex you're afraid of?"

"I don't know. I never . . . well, I never . . . so how would I know? I can't. That's all." I hadn't wanted to reveal that I was of the stone age. It made me feel so immature.

Jerry smiled and said, "April, if you feel the same way that I feel, then making love is the most natural thing in the world. And if it's respect you're worried about, I'll certainly not respect you any less. We're not teenagers anymore. We're man and woman. Adults, with adult feelings and adult needs." He pulled me close to him and I tensed up.

"I can't."

"Why not? There's nothing wrong with it. Now stop acting so childish." He took his arms from around me and sat up.

"No, I'm sorry, Jerry. I want to but I just can't." I looked to him for some understanding.

He stood up and went to the closet and got his coat out. As he put it on, he said, "I don't like playing silly little games, April. Either you want me or you don't. When you make up your mind which it is, I'll be at the university."

In the following weeks, I agonized over Jerry's absence. I had really liked the intimate suppers, long talks, and having a steady friend to go out with. I had planned to ask him to our social and show him off, especially to Roger Maddison. I didn't attend the law firm's Christmas social after all. I went with Cheryl to spend Christmas with the Steindalls and returned alone because of work. I was so lonely during the holidays that my resolve broke down and I decided to call him. I had never been out to his home and I looked up his name in the phone book. As I dialed the number, I thought of being flippant about the whole thing. I'd say something like, "Hi, Jerry. I was wrong and you were right, so I'm yours for the taking." No, that wasn't my style. I'd just play it by ear.

"Hello?" a small child's voice answered.

"Uh, hello. Is Jerry McCallister there, please?"

"No, Daddy's not home. Do you want to talk to my Mommy?" and before I could say no, I heard the child calling to his mother.

"Hello," came the voice of a woman. I tried to picture what she looked like.

"Oh, hello, Mrs. McCallister? I'm a student from the university and I was working on a project over the holidays but I needed Mr. McCallister's advice on something. I'm sorry to be bothering him at home." My cheeks were flaming hot.

"Oh, that's all right. He should be back any minute now. Could I have him call you back? Oh, just a minute. I think he's at the door now. Hold on."

I thought of hanging up but if I did that it might arouse his wife's suspicions.

"Hello," Jerry's voice came on.

"It's me, April. I guess I made a terrible mistake. I'm sorry." I hung up before he could say anything. I felt incredibly stupid. I had been going around with a married man. Not only that, he had a child, maybe more than one. And I was about to go to bed with him! I shook my head and sat there for a long time.

He came to see me one evening, after the New Year. "April, I'd like to explain."

"There's nothing to explain. You're married! You wanted me to . . . to . . . well, you know. And all the time, you were married. And YOU don't like playing games?" I said sarcastically.

"My wife and I have been talking about getting a divorce. Then I met you and I wanted to get to know you right away. I'm sorry I didn't wait until it was all proper and legal."

"And I'm sorry, too. But I don't go out with married men. That is when I know they're married. It's finished. Over. Just leave me alone." I opened the door for him to go, and then stood back waiting.

"But April, you know how I feel about you. We could have a good future together," Jerry said, stalling.

I gave him the coldest, hardest look I could muster. He had no choice but to give up and leave. He looked dejected and I felt sorry for him. For a second I almost said, "It's okay, we could still be friends, at least." I didn't. I closed the door on my almost first lover.

For the next few months I didn't go out on dates. I just stayed in and moped. When Cheryl brought home another of her strays for supper, I didn't even mind. That's what I called the Métis and Indians girls she befriended from the Friendship Centre. Nancy was a dark-skinned native girl with long, limp black hair. The story of her family life was similar to that of other native girls Cheryl met. Drinking always seemed to be behind it. Nancy had been raped by her drunken father. Cheryl remarked that people called that incest but Nancy insisted it was rape. Everyone in Nancy's family drank, even the younger kids. Or the new rage was sniffing glue. Both Nancy and her mother had prostituted themselves. Sometimes for money, sometimes for a cheap bottle of wine. Nancy was like a wilted flower. She even had a defeatist look to her. What a life to have led. I supposed she had stayed at home because there was nowhere else to go. I was shocked when Cheryl told me Nancy was only seventeen. She looked at least twenty-five.

How Cheryl could stand to hear those kinds of stories all the time was beyond me. That she wanted to make a lifetime career out of it was impossible for me to understand. It was depressing, especially when I knew that Nancy and the other strays came from the same places that we came from.

I'd go out with Cheryl and Nancy to nice restaurants and treat them to suppers. I began to notice what being native was like in middle-class surroundings. Sometimes service was deliberately slow. Sometimes I'd overhear comments like, "Who let the Indians off the reservation?" Or we'd be walking home and guys would make comments to us, as if we were easy pick-ups. None of us would say anything, not even Cheryl who had always been sharp-tongued. Cheryl and I never talked about these things either. Instead of feeling angry at these mouthy people, I just felt embarrassed to be seen with natives, Cheryl included. I gradually began to go out with them less and less. Anyhow, Cheryl was starting to spend more evenings at the Friendship Centre, leaving me alone with my magazines and my daydreams. I was even reading books on proper etiquette, preparing myself for my promising future in white society. If Cheryl had known I was reading that kind of material, she would have laughed or criticized me. It wouldn't have mattered because I began to think I would be dreaming such dreams right into my senility. Oh, well, Cheryl once had a fantasy which comforted her and now I had mine.

The other thing I thought about a great deal was the kind of man I would marry. If my future were to be successful and happy, I'd have to give the man in my life much consideration. I would not be able to afford to let my heart rule my head. I couldn't marry for money or I'd be rich but I wouldn't be happy. So I'd have to find someone who was handsome, witty and charming. He'd be a good, honest person with a strong character but he'd also have a fine sense of humor. He'd be perfection personified. 'Oh, yeah? Dream on, April Raintree. If such a man existed, he'd be surrounded by females. What makes you think you could ever compete?' With all my planning and everything, I'd probably end up falling in love with a poor farmer or something. And I'd have to work for the rest of my life.

But that spring, my Prince Charming did come into my life. I was typing a Mortgage Agreement when he walked into the office. He was to see Mr. Lord and the receptionist sent him to my desk. I let him stand there, without even looking at him, while I finished typing. Then I looked up into his merry, blue eyes. He was one of the smoothly handsome men, the kind I didn't like, the kind that was so polished he just had to be conceited.

He smiled at me as he asked to see Mr. Lord. I told him Mr. Lord had a dentist appointment that morning and had been delayed. I asked him to return at one o'clock.

"Well, I suppose I could be induced to return by your having lunch with me."

I thought of saying, "I'm sorry, I'm busy," because it was obvious he was the conceited type I had thought he was. Instead, I asked, "How do you know I'm not married?"

"I looked for a wedding ring. There's none." He spread his fingers before me to show that he was not wearing a ring, either.

I looked closely at his finger and saw that there were no tell-tale marks. At the same time, I figured he couldn't be so conceited after all, since he didn't wear any flashy rings. I realized some of the other secretaries had stopped to watch. I smiled self-consciously and said, "Well, I don't take lunch until twelve."

"I'll wait."

For the next half hour, I felt him watching me from where he sat. My fingers felt too stiff to do any typing at all, but I made a show of being efficient by finishing page after page, all filled with mistakes.

Over lunch he introduced himself as Bob Radcliff from

Toronto. He had his own wholesale furniture business which he ran with his mother. His father had died when he was in university and he and his mother had taken over the business. He was in Winnipeg to purchase land for expansion. Since I knew his home was in Toronto, I had no intentions of becoming further involved with him. Just this lunch and that would be it. But then on our way back, he asked me out again that evening. Okay, so he must be lonely. But after this one night, that would be it.

It wasn't. For the next month we spent nearly every evening together. He met Cheryl and had shown no negative reaction. They got along quite well, considering Cheryl had resumed her anti-white role. I found Bob was gentle, good natured and very considerate. He was everything I thought a good husband should be. It was just too bad he had to go back to Toronto.

The events of the next several weeks are a blur in my memory. Bob proposed. He asked me, April Raintree, to be his wife. He wanted to get married in a small civil ceremony in Winnipeg. My dreams were coming true and I ecstatically floated on cloud nine. Everything happened so quickly.

The only discord came when I told Cheryl that Bob had proposed to me. I expected her to be as excited and happy as I was.

"What do you want to go and marry this dude for? You're asking for trouble. You don't know anything about him, really."

"I know all I need to know. You're just saying this because of Garth, aren't you?"

"Maybe I am. Even if Bob isn't prejudiced, maybe his friends are. And what will they think when they find out he has married a half-breed? If he had to choose, do you really believe he'd stick with you?"

"Cheryl," I said in a warning, angry tone.

"Or what if you had children and they looked like Indians? Do you want them to go through what we went through? It would be better for you to stick to your own kind. I've always felt so out of place, living with white families, surrounded by whites. You really want that for your children? Oh, of course, you're going to pass yourself off as white, aren't you? You're not going to tell anyone there who and what you are, are you?"

"Well, I'm certainly not going to go around saying, 'Hi, I'm April Radcliff, and I'm a half-breed.' So just knock it off, Cheryl."

I stormed into the bathroom cutting our discussion short. I was angry. Not so much by Cheryl's telling me I shouldn't marry Bob, but by her throwing shame and guilt or whatever it was into my face. We'd never talked about it before. I was sure she had not suspected how I felt. But all this time, she knew. She knew I was ashamed of being a half-breed.

We were married on July 25, 1969, on a Friday afternoon with only Cheryl and a "not anyone special" male friend of Bob's to witness our exchange of vows. I wondered why he hadn't even wanted to invite his mother but he had just said that was the way he wanted it. I accepted it, I was so happy. From that moment, I wouldn't have to worry about changing the spelling of my name because it was now legally April Radcliff.

Cheryl came with us to the airport on the Saturday afternoon when we were to fly to Toronto. I guess Bob knew I wanted some time alone with her because he left to do some last minute things. At first, Cheryl and I let some of our precious minutes slip by, just looking at each other and not saying anything.

Cheryl spoke first. "April, in spite of what I said the other day, I do hope you'll be happy. I really do. I was just mouthing off, you know. I'm sorry."

"Don't be, Cheryl. I guess I got on the defensive because some of the things you said were true. And I've never wanted to admit them. You didn't come right out and say it, but I am ashamed. I can't accept . . . I can't accept being a Métis. That's the hardest thing I've ever said to you, Cheryl. And I'm glad you don't feel the same way I do. I'm so proud of what you're trying to do. But to me, being Métis means I'm one of the have-nots. And I want so much. I'm selfish. I know it, but that's the way I am. I want what white society can give me. Oh, Cheryl, I really believe that's the only way for me to find happiness. I'm different from you. I wish I wasn't but I am. I'm me. You have to do what you believe is right for you and I have to go my way. Remember, though, I'll always be there if you need me."

Cheryl was smiling, but sadly. Finally she said, "April, I have known how you felt for a long time. And I decided that I was going to do what I could to turn the native image around so that one day you could be proud of being Métis." To lighten the mood, she added, "Of course, you may be old and gray when the day does come, but it will come. I guarantee it."

Bob came back and it was time for us to board the plane. And for me to say my goodbye to Cheryl. We hugged each other and said goodbye. I felt good, I felt there was a new kind of honesty between us. I was moving into a new phase of my life with a man I loved and who loved me. And I had just had a good honest talk with the other most important person in my life.

But once we were airborne, I was still thinking of Cheryl. I missed her so much already. For a younger sister, she was a lot wiser than me in some ways. So, she had known about my shame for a long time. And she had never said anything. She had just accepted me the way I was in silence. I wished I could do that whole part of my life over again. She was such a giving, unselfish person. What was it that made her like she was and me like I was?

9

I WAS totally unprepared when we arrived at Bob's home, and now mine. When he had spoken of his business, I assumed it was a small time operation. There had been the land deal in Winnipeg. I had worked on that but I had assumed there would be a large mortgage on it. But from the moment I saw their house, excuse me, mansion, I knew I had badly underestimated the wealth I had married into. The house was huge and was located on a sprawling estate.

I felt Barbara Radcliff's disapproval of me from the very start. I couldn't blame her, though. She had missed out on her son's wedding and that's when I realized why she hadn't been invited. He had, in effect, eloped. She was, however, very polite to me and extended a gracious welcome to their home. Somehow I had the feeling I had landed in another foster home. I was even subtly ordered to call her 'Mother Radcliff', although at times I thought of her as 'Mother Superior' and religion had nothing to do with it.

We entertained a great deal and in turn we were invited to social events and theatres and concerts and dinners and clubs. Because it was all new to me, it was quite thrilling. I had plenty of moments of being nervous and tongue-tied commiting social gaucheries and I was forever wondering what the other women thought of me. In all fairness to Mother Radcliff, I must say she taught me all I hadn't learned from my long-ago books. She took me on shopping excursions and on twice-a-week appointments to hair salons, always giving me advice in a detached way. Although we spent a good deal of time in each other's company, we never did become close, never joking and laughing together. Her laughter seemed reserved only for those on her social level. I used to wonder what Bob's father had been like. He must have been a good-humored man because Bob was so easygoing.

As for Bob, we got along very well. We had none of the problems which face most newlyweds. No hassles over finances or work or even in-laws. I suppose because of my childhood, it was easy enough for me to play second fiddle to a woman like Mother Radcliff, even to the point of allowing her to run our lives.

By November, it occurred to me that it would be nice if Cheryl could see how right I had been in my decision to marry Bob. I checked with Bob to see if it would be okay for her to come for the Christmas holidays. He thought it would be a great idea, and urged me to phone her. I did and was surprised that she accepted, just like that. I found out on the phone that Nancy had moved in with her. I thought once again that Cheryl didn't belong with a bunch of native people. Then the other thought struck me. Not once had nativeness been discussed in this household.

Mother Radcliff had resented me simply because Bob had married me without her approval. What would she think once Cheryl came? And Christmas times were for gatherings. What would all the others think?

I should have thought twice about inviting Cheryl to visit. I wanted to show off to her so much that I had forgotten that, in turn, I would have to show her off to these people. I looked over at Bob who was smiling at me. Well, if it didn't matter to him, why should it matter to me? Still, I felt that perhaps Cheryl's predictions would come true. If Bob were ever forced to make a choice, what would it be? In his mother's hands he was like putty. I was beginning to realize that my Prince Charming had a flaw.

Cheryl came on the Saturday before Christmas. Bob and I went to pick her up at the airport and when we arrived home, I was dismayed to find that Mother Radcliff had some of her friends over for dinner. I watched her face for a reaction when Cheryl was introduced, but there wasn't any. It was the same as when I had been introduced five months earlier, gracious but cool. I showed Cheryl around the 'mansion' after dinner, and although she was complimentary, I could tell she wasn't all that impressed. I was piqued. She was so religiously Métis!

Every minute we were alone, she would talk about the Friendship Centre and the program she and some other counsellors had started for teenage native girls. She loved what she was doing, though, and that was great. It was when she criticized my lifestyle that I got on the offensive.

"What you aim to do is very commendable, Cheryl, but I can't see you changing a whole lot of people. You may turn a few lives around, but they're not the ones who are going to make an impression on the rest of the population. It's the ones who are dirty and unkempt and look like they've just gotten out of bed with a hangover and who go to your neighbourhood department store, they're the ones who make a lasting impression."

"Well, there are just as many white people out there

who are in the same state," Cheryl shot back.

"It's not the same. I don't remember the white ones, I only remember the drunk natives. It seems to me that the majority of natives are gutter-creatures and only a minority of whites are like that. I think that's the difference."

"I still think our project with the native girls is worthwhile. Damn it, April, why do you have to be so prejudiced," she exclaimed.

"I'm not prejudiced, Cheryl. I'm simply trying to point out to you how I see things."

"Through white man's eyes."

"Maybe so, but that should be an advantage to you. How many white people would honestly tell you what they think? I don't want to discourage you completely. Helping some of the teenage girls avoid the native girl syndrome thing is certainly worth the effort. Remember Mrs. Semple telling us about that. First, you do this and then you do that, and next you do this and next you do that and she had our whole lives laid out for us. Well, we fooled her. But the thing is, you'll never change the image of the native people. It would take some kind of miracle," I said, attempting to lighten our conversation.

That's how our private talks went and I was grateful that Cheryl kept the native subject private. As I expected, we had a full social calendar over the Christmas holidays and I tried to coax Cheryl, unsuccessfully, to go shopping with me for evening gowns I was sure she would need. She could not see the sense in spending money on clothing she would never wear again. So, I insisted she wear some of my dresses, since we were the same size. As a matter of fact, we could have been almost identical twins, except for our skin-coloring. No wonder I had always found her so beautiful. My pretentious way of admitting my own beauty.

I had taken it for granted that Cheryl would be able to attend the dinners to which we had been invited but Mother Radcliff took me aside, actually she summoned me to her study, and informed me that it would cause upsets to have an uninvited guest. She also stated that Cheryl would feel out of place and although I agreed and understood, it was unthinkable that I would leave Cheryl alone. Mother Radcliff pointed out that we were giving a New Year's party so Cheryl would not be left out of all the festivities. I left her study wondering how much of this I was going to tell Cheryl. At the same time, I was relieved that Cheryl's debut into my society was to be delayed. When I made my explanations to Cheryl, she made it easier by saying it was all right because she hadn't really wanted to go to the big fancy gatherings anyhow and she was relieved to be able to avoid them.

On New Year's Eve, all the important people I had met over the past months, and many I had never met, gathered in our living room and the adjoining family room. To me, it was the biggest sign of how wealthy and important we Radcliffs were. I guess I was the only one who was so greatly impressed because when I took Cheryl around to introduce her to some of the women I already knew, I got a few surprises. It was worse than I had expected. After praising all these people to Cheryl, some came out with the most patronizing remarks.

"Oh, I've read about Indians. Beautiful people they are. But you're not exactly Indians are you? What is the proper word for people like you?" one asked.

"Women," Cheryl replied instantly.

"No, no, I mean nationality?"

"Oh, I'm sorry. We're Canadians," Cheryl smiled sweetly.

Another woman, after being introduced to Cheryl, said, "Oh, we used to have a very good Indian maid. Such a nice quiet girl and a hard worker, too."

I suppose she meant it as a compliment but I felt like crawling into a hole, I was so embarrassed for Cheryl.

Then two men came over and one asked Cheryl what it was like being an Indian. Before she could reply, the other man voiced his opinion and the two soon walked away, discussing their concepts of native life without having allowed Cheryl to say one thing.

Cheryl and I shrugged to each other and I was wondering how she was taking it. It was the questioning stares that bothered me the most.

About an hour later, my discomforting thoughts of what people must be thinking were interrupted when I noticed the entrance of an actress we had seen recently at a theatre production. As I watched Mother Radcliff greeting her, I remembered her name. Heather Langdon. She seemed to know Mother Radcliff quite well. I saw Heather look around the room in anticipation and I noticed the satisfied look on her face when Bob appeared and kissed her on the cheek. They looked like they knew each other even better. And I felt this twinge of jealousy and worry. Mother Radcliff spotted me just then and indicated I was to come over.

When I reached them, Mother Radcliff said, "April, I would like you to meet Heather Langdon. We saw her play the other night, remember?"

"Yes, I do. I enjoyed your performance," I said as I shook her hand. What was the right thing to say to an actress?

"April, go find your sister. I am sure she would like to be introduced to Heather." I was ordered. I obeyed.

Strange, I thought, that Mother Radcliff would want Cheryl to be introduced to an actress. I found Cheryl and brought her back to be introduced and noticed the exchange of looks between Mother Radcliff and Heather. I couldn't read any meaning into the looks and shrugged it off. Heather seemed to make a point of socializing with me for the rest of that evening and my initial worry and jealousy disappeared.

On Friday, Bob went to his office so Cheryl and I had the whole day to ourselves. It was supposed to be a pleasant day but Cheryl had to get her two cents worth in on what she thought about my lifestyle. I think the only thing that really aroused me in those days was when someone criticized me. So I tore right back into Cheryl, openly angry.

"Cheryl, get off my case, will you? I don't ask you to live my kind of life. I know why you're doing this. You want me to take up your glorious cause. Well, I'm happy here. I love the parties and I love the kind of people I meet. I love this kind of life and I have no intentions of changing it. So, go home. And live by what you believe in. But stop preaching at me. I admire your devotion and your confidence in native people, but to me, they're a lost cause. I can't see what anyone can do for them, except the people themselves. If they want to live in their run-down shacks that are over-ridden with flies and who knows what other kinds of bugs, and that stink of filth and soiled clothing and mattresses, and if they want to drink their lives away while their children go hungry and unclothed, then there's not much that can be done for them except to give them hand-outs and more hand-outs. So don't ask me . . ."

"How the hell would you know how they live? You wouldn't go near them if your life depended on it. Who are you to sit around up here in your fancy surroundings and judge a people you don't even know?" Cheryl cut in, even angrier than I was.

"I know because I looked for our parents in those kinds of places. So, don't tell me that I don't know what I'm talking about. I went . . ." I stopped abruptly as I realized I had just let out my secret search.

Cheryl and I looked at each other for a few silent seconds and our tempers were forgotten. Then she said in a quiet, accusing voice. "You went to look for Mom and Dad? How come you never told me, April?"

I sighed and wondered which way to go. "There was nothing to tell. I never found them. I came to a dead-end. And later, when I thought it over, I figured it was probably just as well. Finding them would most likely have opened old wounds for them and for us."

"What do you mean? It wasn't their fault. The Children's Aid had to take us because they were sick. You told me that. You told me Dad had tuberculosis and Mom just had poor health all the time. Anyhow, you should have told me. How did you know where to start? I thought of looking for them. That's one reason why I spend so much time down at the Friendship Centre and listen for names."

"Cheryl, I still think it's best to leave it alone. Just pretend that we never had parents. Leave all that behind us." I thought that now was the time I should tell Cheryl what I already knew about our parents. They were liars, weaklings, and drunkards. That all the time we were growing up, there was a more important reason for them to live and that was their booze. But no. I couldn't do that to Cheryl. I couldn't tell her that alcohol was more important to our parents than their own daughters. I had given her cherished memories of them. I couldn't take that away now. They were too important for her. Those memories and her too idealistic outlook for the future of native people. Those things helped her and gave her something to live for, I added, "Pretend that we're orphans."

"No! They're our parents, April! And we're not orphans," Cheryl's eyes blazed. "I want to see them again. Please, April. I have the right to make that decision for myself. You have to tell me where to begin. How do I find them? You have to tell me, April."

I silently argued with myself. The information I had was dated. Even the notations I had added were now dated. Chances of Cheryl finding our parents were so slim that I felt she wouldn't find them. And because I felt that way, I relented.

"Okay, I guess you're right. Mr. Wendell is the one who gave me the old addresses and names. I guess they were places where our parents used to stay. A lot of the places have been torn down and I've marked that down so you won't have to go there. But Cheryl, when I went to those places and saw the living conditions, well, I would hold my breath so I wouldn't smell the stink or breathe in the germs. I'd try not to touch anything, everything was so dirty. And if they offered me anything to eat or drink, I'd refuse because I was sure their cupboards were infested with bugs. I'd back away from people so I wouldn't get their lice. I didn't feel sorry for them Cheryl. All I felt was contempt. They are a disgusting people. And maybe, just maybe our parents are part of that. And if that's where we came from, I sure don't want to go back. That's why I'm happy with my life here. Happiness to those people was a bottle of beer in their hands. I vowed to myself then that no way was I ever going to end up like them or live in places like theirs. So, Cheryl, if you want to criticize me for my lifestyle, then go ahead, because if I can help it, I'm not ever going to change it.''

"Oh, April, I didn't know why you felt the way you did. I didn't mean to criticize you. I just wanted to rouse you out of your passive state. I just wanted you to be aware of who we are, what we are and what's been happening to us.''

"If you're referring to all the negative aspects of native life, I think it's because they allow it to happen to them. Life is what you make it. We made our lives good. It wasn't always easy but we did make it. And they are responsible for their lives.''

"I don't agree with you. We had a lot of luck in our lives. We've had opportunities which other native people never had. Just knowing what being independent is like is an opportunity. But that's not the point right now. I still want to look for our parents, okay?''

"I doubt that you'll find them after all this time, but okay,'' I sighed and went over to one of my dressers. As I looked through the dresser drawers, I said, "They usually move from town to town from what I understand. I think it's going to be a waste of your time.''

120

"Well, I've got to give it a try. Need some help looking? What do you need all these clothes for? I bet you don't wear half of them."

"You're criticizing again. Here we are. My shoe box. Now this is classy, isn't it?" I held up an old shoe box where I had hidden my past away.

Cheryl looked through the papers and asked, "How come you kept all this stuff if you weren't planning to ever look for them again?"

"I don't know. Some deep, profound motive, I guess. Maybe my last link with my parents. Who knows?"

We copied the names and addresses down and Cheryl said confidently, "When I find them, I'll let you know. Wouldn't it be great to have a family reunion?"

I smiled. Nothing could be worse.

This time when Cheryl and I parted at the airport, I knew it was more realistic to acknowledge there would never be complete honesty between us. And then again, as long as my mouth kept running over, I just might reveal everything I had tried to protect her from. But knowing Cheryl had not hidden any aspects of her life from me made me feel inferior to her in that way. She was so fearless. Me, I was a coward and I knew it. Cheryl never worried about what other people thought about her. Only what she thought about them mattered. Cheryl was that stalk in the field of grain which never bent to the mighty winds of authority. At the same time, that stalk could bend to the gentle breezes of compassion. That was Cheryl.

10

I WATCHED her plane taxi down the runway and gather speed, until its wheels no longer touched the ground. I watched until I could see it no more. Suddenly, I felt so empty. So alone.

Funny I should have felt that way when Bob was right there beside me. On the drive back home, he was as preoccupied with his thoughts as I was with mine so we didn't say much. Sunday dinner that evening was eaten in silence and not even Bob and his mother made any conversation. The atmosphere reinforced my feeling of loneliness. As usual, Bob and his mother retired to his office to plan the coming week's business strategy. I went upstairs to our room. I was restless and didn't know why. I turned the television set on but there were no programs which interested me. I left it on just for the voices. I looked at a book, then another. That was no good either. It wasn't the first time I had felt this way but it was the worst. This bored restlessness which usually came after big parties or large gatherings. Maybe if I had something of my own to do, something which involved . . . what? Useless. That's what I was. Bob had his business. Mother Radcliff had her social calendar, plus the business. Cheryl had her great cause. I had nothing. I had everything I ever wanted, yet I had nothing.

Mother Radcliff and, therefore, I were on different charitable organizations but none of them grabbed my heart or loyalty. Bob and I had our group of friends but I felt I had access to them only as long as Bob was with me. But I did find our own age group much more interesting than the older ladies with whom Mother Radcliff surrounded herself. Especially after Heather Langdon joined us. I wanted to fashion myself after her so much because she so enjoyed living. She lived by her own approval, not that of others. Just like Cheryl.

Cheryl and I wrote monthly letters to each other but the chasm between us had grown wider and there was less to say in our letters. The only thing she told me that was of great interest was her ongoing search for our parents. Where I had spent about a month of weekends and quit, Cheryl wouldn't quit. I worried. Then in May, I got a letter in which she indicated she had finally given up. I was relieved. I didn't know what she would have done if she had found our parents. I hadn't even wanted to think about that possibility. Now that she had ended her search I no longer worried about how shocked and disillusioned she would have been. My conclusion about alcoholism was that once an alcoholic, always an alcoholic. And if one's own children weren't enough reason for one to recover, then there could be no reason at all.

Her letters started to arrive less and less often. She wrote about her education and her work at the Friendship Centre. I found myself again in the position of envying her. She had a reason for being. She was her own person. I merely existed. Comfortable and surrounded by socially prominent people. But I felt that I really didn't belong. That feeling grew worse as the months went by. I didn't belong because I didn't care. Not the way the others did. I was quite content to let Mother Radcliff and Bob run my social life. I performed all my duties as expected.

That September, I picked out a very expensive IBM Selectric typewriter for Cheryl's birthday. That was something she could appreciate. I even thought it might be nice to go back to Winnipeg to spend some time with Cheryl. I tried phoning but found that the service had been disconnected. I wrote Cheryl immediately, offering financial aid if she needed it. She wrote back that she was hardly ever home and didn't need a phone. As if to emphasize her point, she also told me that she had been invited to Brandon over the Christmas holidays. I felt as if she were abandoning me, because I read between the lines that she didn't want me in Winnipeg.

Christmas passed, New Year's, 1971, came and I still couldn't shake my feeling blue. Actually, I don't know why they say 'blue' when it's more like grey. The year of 1971 was to be a year of many changes for me. My feelings of inadequacy and boredom turned to resentment and jealousy. I came to hate how Heather and Bob could laugh so easily and suspicions set in and I began nagging Bob in private. Meaningful conversation between us had all but disappeared. I guess all he could see was my totally negative side and he couldn't see any reason for it. I couldn't have explained it to him at the time anyway, since I didn't quite know what was going on inside of me. Mother Radcliff even showed an open disgust for me because on different occasions I had rebelled and refused to perform my social duties. But that was okay because I was just as disgusted with her and her snobbish friends and her card games and her charitable works, done only so she would be identified as a philanthropist. All these people lived for one or two things: <u>money and power</u>. They were hypocrites, all of them. <u>Charming to each other when they were face to face, but get them into separate rooms and their tongues could cut like knives. They were such superficial people</u>.

I became quite good at it, seeing all the negative sides and criticizing them to high heaven to myself. It came to me that I had criticized the native people and here I was doing the same thing to white people. <u>Maybe that's what being a half-breed was all about, being a critic-at-large</u>.

I suppose things could have continued like that for a long time, but in August, I overheard a conversation between Mother Radcliff and Heather that roused me out of my passive state and got me fighting mad. Our bedroom had a closed-in balcony which overlooked a private garden. A few days earlier Bob and I had had a big fight. To make up for it, Bob had decided to take the day off work and take me out for the day. We had planned to start out right after breakfast. I was amused at Mother Radcliff's obvious chagrin. But then Bob and I had another difference of opinion in our bedroom that morning and he left in his car without me. I was so embarrassed that I hid myself in my room and planned to stay there until Bob got back.

It was about noon when I heard a car drive up. I looked out and saw Heather walking up to the front door. I wondered what on earth she was doing there. I knew she and Mother Radcliff didn't have that close a friendship that they would have lunch together. I went back to the balcony to return to my book, wondering all the time what was going on downstairs. I didn't have long to wait. They came out into the garden below, presumably to have their lunch there. Their voices drifted up to me and I could hear everything they were saying clearly.

Mother Radcliff was saying, "I'd like to get straight to

the point. Is this affair you're having with Bob serious or are you just toying around with him?''

An affair? With Bob? Serious? I couldn't believe I was hearing right. Not Heather. She was my friend. Bob was my husband.

"Of course it's serious. You knew how we felt about each other when you broke us up. And don't deny it. I'm not as naive as I used to be. No, it won't be long before Bob asks April for a divorce.''

"Well, it doesn't appear it will be all that soon when he starts taking time off work to spend with her,'' Mother Radcliff responded.

I heard Heather scoff at that and say, "Well, he's taken a lot more time off for me, I'm sure. But I can't help wondering how come, now that he's married, you approve of Bob and me? I know you purposely went out of your way to have me at your New Year's party. What do you have against April? She makes a nice obedient wife. Why don't you want her for a daugther-in-law?''

"Didn't you notice her sister? They're Indians, Heather. Well, not Indians but half-breeds, which is almost the same thing. And they're not half-sisters. They have the same father and the same mother. That's the trouble with mixed races, you never know how they're going to turn out. And I would simply dread being grandmother to a bunch of little half-breeds! The only reason I can think of why Bob married her after knowing what she was was simply to get back at me. Well, I had my doubts as to how serious he was with you because of days like today.''

Heather shrugged it off. "Don't worry. Bob's a husband with a guilty conscience. He'll realize the best thing for April is a divorce.''

"Yes, I suppose you're right. Of course, we'll give her a nice large settlement.''

'You are so bloody right,' I almost shouted. Perhaps they said more about me, I don't know. With my face burning hotly and my heart thumping like a war drum, I

headed downstairs to confront them. They were both surprised and off-balance when I stepped out on the terrace to
face them.

I had always treated Heather with a certain amount of
awe and respect and I had also given Mother Radcliff her
due respect. But in that moment I eyed them contemptuously and they realized their secrets were out.

"What are you doing here?" Mother Radcliff asked.

I was still breathing hard. Ignoring her question, I said,
"You two make me sick!"

I looked at Heather. "You, you pretended friendship all
this time and I gave you my trust. Oh sure, I suspected. I'm
not blind. But I really thought it was only my imagination.
Maybe I hoped it was my imagination. That Bob's mother
would rather have a person like you, a hypocrite, an
adultress, as her daughter-in-law, rather than risk a few
grandchildren who would have Indian blood in them, well,
that's beyond my comprehension."

Mother Radcliff started to cut in but I turned on her and
cut her off. "And you! You make everyone that comes
within your reach into puppets. But thank you very much
for cutting my strings. And thank God I didn't become
pregnant by your son. I wouldn't want the seed of your
blood passed on to my children." With that, I turned my
back on them in a deliberate gesture and walked out.

A little while later when I was up in my room I heard
Heather's car start up and she drove away. My heavy
breathing returned to normal. My trembling rage subsided.
I had to figure out what to do. Only one thing was certain.
They were going to give me a large settlement. A very large
settlement!

Well, so I had seen through them, yet didn't even know
it. All my criticisms were justified. My big fight with Bob
had been about Heather. Turned out, he was a liar, too.
Just like my parents had been. Married me only to get back
at his mother. Heather, deceiving me with friendship,
while all the time she only wanted Bob. Mother Radcliff,

making me call her 'mother' when she so detested what I was. And then there was Cheryl. She had told me how it would be but I hadn't believed her. And although I had the same thoughts as Barbara Radcliff about children, it was unforgivable for her to tell them to my rival. I did have a fear of producing brown-skinned babies. How could I give my loving to such children when I still felt self-conscious about Cheryl? Well, this wasn't the real issue. I had to plan a course of action. First thing I'd have to do would be to see a lawyer.

I called Ronald Feldman, who I knew was a divorce lawyer from the conversations at parties. I phoned him and he said he couldn't see me for two weeks, but he suggested that if I were serious about getting a divorce on the grounds of adultery that I should cease living with Bob. I thought that meant I had to move out immediately.

Next, I phoned Bob at work. I wasn't surprised to find him there nor that he sounded cold and distant with me. I demanded that he come home at once as an urgent matter had come up. While I waited for him, I looked through the newspapers and phoned to inquire about different apartments for rent. The thought of living in a huge empty place was depressing. I didn't know anyone who would go out of their way to come and visit me. What I also needed was a job to keep me occupied. Still, I knew from past experience that evenings could be long and lonely. Maybe I would get so lonely I'd join the ranks of women who frequented singles bars. I spotted a column under the heading of 'Shared Accomodation'. That would be better than living alone. I phoned and was able to make some appointments for the following day. For now, I could stay in a hotel. I looked forward to a new life where I wouldn't be controlled by anyone else. I felt as if the sun were coming out from behind the clouds and it was a wonderful relief that there was still a sun. "Oh, I know you didn't mean to, 'Mother' Radcliff, but you've made me a happy woman."

When Bob finally came home, I must have sparkled with

excitement because he said, "I thought something was wrong, the way you sounded on the phone. But you look like the cat that swallowed a mouse."

"Well, Bob, I understand you're about to ask me for a divorce. I'll save you the trouble of having to ask."

"Oh, not that crap about Heather again. Is that what this is all about?"

"Well, sweetheart, if you like, I could call a meeting of all those involved. 'We are gathered here today to establish whether there is or there is not an affair going on between my loving husband, Bob, and my good friend, Heather'. I was planning to be very bitter about it but I've changed my mind. I'm going to be sarcastic." I smiled as I watched Bob sit down and the look on his face acknowledged the affair.

"How did you find out? Did Heather tell you?"

"In a manner of speaking, yes. And your mother told me. And in a lot of different ways, you told me, too," I said. "I'd appreciate it if you took me to a hotel for now. I'll look for an apartment or something and then I'll send for my things."

"Don't you even want to make any explanations to Mother before you leave?"

"I'm sure your mother knows I'm leaving. I've packed a few things and I'd like to go. Now."

In less than a week, I had found a place to my liking. It wasn't far from the subway on Woodbine Avenue so I had easy access to the downtown area where I planned to find a job. The rooms were in a large three-storey house and the kitchen and dining rooms were shared by all the tenants. Most of the men and women who lived there were artistic types and they provided me with long overdue companionship, right from the first day I moved in. Once I was settled, I turned my thoughts to getting myself a job. Money wasn't a problem because Bob had given me more than I'd ever need and that was just for one month. One of the other boarders, Sheila, suggested I do temporary work like she did. I signed up with her agency and was sent to different locations, filling in for absent secretaries. Mr. Feldman, my lawyer, told me in December that the court hearing was to be held on January 26th. He assured me that everything was going extremely well. We were both pleased with the settlement Bob had offered. I remembered the time I was starting at the Red River Community College and I had eight hundred dollars in the bank. I had thought then that I was rich. Now, I knew without doubt that I was rich. And independent.

That same day when the mail came, I found that the letter I had sent to Cheryl in November had been returned. On it was marked: "Moved - no forwarding address." That was funny. Why hadn't she written to me to let me know? Or she could have called. I had given her my new number, my new address, and had told her about my new situation. She should have written or called. After all her thinly disguised refusals and excuses why she couldn't come or why I couldn't visit her, I began to feel like my own sister was giving me the cold shoulder. Did she think I was such a failure? On the other hand, I had always said she ought to go her own way and I'd go mine. Maybe that's what was wrong.

Since Cheryl didn't write to me about any Christmas plans, I spent it with those other boarder who also lacked families to go home to. On Christmas Day, we all went to this Old Folk's Home where Sheila's grandmother was living. That's when I got my first understanding of how Cheryl must have felt when she made somebody's day a little brighter.

One Saturday morning, in early January, I received a phone call at eight o'clock. Thinking it was probably the agency looking for last minute secretarial help, I was tempted to let it ring. But I wasn't one who could ignore a ringing telephone. In a second, I was wide awake. It was a nurse calling from the Health Science Centre in Winnipeg, asking if I were related to a Cheryl Raintree. Then she said that Cheryl had been brought in during the night. I immediately asked how serious it was and the nurse said she was still unconcious so they couldn't be positive. Serious or not, I felt I had to at least be by her side. That afternoon I was on a flight back to Winnipeg.

11

AS SOON AS I arrived at the Winnipeg airport, I rented a car and drove straight to the hospital on William Avenue. There the staff doctors informed me that Cheryl had been found in the early hours of the morning suffering from hypothermia and possible concussions. They were holding her for observation. I thought immediately that she must have been assaulted and I became resentful when the doctor asked me if Cheryl had a drinking problem.

"Why, because she's part-Indian?"

"No, Miss, but when she came in she was highly intoxicated."

"What about the concussions you mentioned?" I demanded.

"It does appear she may have been beaten," he admitted.

I nodded and stalked off towards Cheryl's room. Drinking problem! I was sure it was said because she was part-Indian. I entered the room and Cheryl was at the far end. At first, I wasn't sure it was Cheryl. I mean, I knew it was Cheryl but it didn't look like Cheryl. Her beautiful, strong face was now puffy and bruised and her cheeks were hollow. She had lost so much weight. Under the fluorescent lights, her skin was yellowish. He arms, resting on the white covers, were thin. She really had lost too much weight. And aged! I stared. It had been two years since I had last seen her. Two years. It hadn't seemed that long. It looked to me as if Cheryl had been possessed. A cold chill ran down my back. ". . . highly intoxicated." Oh, God, please don't let her be an alcoholic.

I pulled a chair closer to her bed and sat down. Maybe Cheryl had some kind of disease and she hadn't wanted me to find out about it and that was why she had refused to come to Toronto or had put off my coming to Winnipeg. People did that. They would find out they had a terminal illness and they didn't want to tell anyone until the very end. Knowing Cheryl, that's the kind of thing she would do. She'd try to protect me from that kind of truth. Cheryl stirred and woke up briefly.

"Cheryl, it's me, April. Everything is all right. I love you, Cheryl."

She gave my hand a squeeze and dozed off again. I left when the visiting hours were over and took a room in a hotel on Notre Dame, within easy walking distance of the hospital.

I returned the next day and found Cheryl fully awake. She didn't seem to want to talk about what had happened so I didn't push her for answers. I sat there for the longest time in silence. My mind was on what had happened to her and everything else that might have been said was blanked out. It was Cheryl who started talking.

"I'm sorry your marriage didn't work out, April."

"Well, I've been thinking that maybe it's for the best. Bob and I were never passionately in love or anything. And now I've gotten . . . well, used to the idea." I was almost going to tell her I would be getting a very large settlement but for some unknown reason I decided not to.

"Did you get a full-time job yet?" Cheryl asked.

"No, I decided to work for a temporary agency. I'm not at all sure what I want to do once the divorce goes through. I'm changing my name back to Raintree. I was thinking of returning to Winnipeg for good, though."

Actually, the thought had just come to me. It looked like Cheryl could use any support I could give her by staying. If I missed Toronto, I could always go back once Cheryl got a job as a social worker. In June, she'd be finished university. It wouldn't be that long.

"Well, you're almost finished university, huh? And pretty soon, you're going to be a professional. And then I can brag to everyone, 'My sister's a professional'." I smiled but she didn't smile back.

"April, I quit university. I've got a lot more to tell you, but let's not get into it now, okay? I'm tired."

"Sure, okay, we'll talk about it, maybe tomorrow, if you feel like it."

I was shocked by what I had just learned but I tried to cover it up. I left with a faked understanding smile on my face.

All the way back to the hotel, I thought about Cheryl quitting. Why did she quit? Had she failed or given up? All the letters she had sent me, they were all about her courses and her work at the Friendship Centre. Were they lies? When I got to my hotel room, I took a bath, then got into bed with the television set turned on. But all I could think about was Cheryl. I speculated on different reasons why she may have quit and what other things she had or hadn't done so that when she would tell me, I'd be at least partially prepared. As long as she didn't tell me she was dying of some incurable disease, then I could accept anything. I turned the television off and got back into bed. What if she were an alcoholic? How could I accept that? That was an incurable disease. And one was as good as dead if that were the case.

The next day as Cheryl and I talked we both avoided the issue. When evening came, I figured it might help if we discussed my marriage failure first.

Afterward, Cheryl said to me, "Well, at least you've experienced what you always longed for and now you know that's not for you."

"I know. I could treat the marriage as if it were one long holiday, especially since I haven't been hurt by breaking up with Bob. It's funny that I don't feel more pain. I really thought I loved him when I married him."

"Well, everything happened so fast that you never had time to find out for sure. And maybe you convinced yourself that you loved him."

After she said this Cheryl became thoughtful and I wondered if she had been similarly involved with a man.

"Cheryl, have you ever been in love?"

She looked at me and smiled. She didn't say anything for a few minutes and then she sighed and said, "I lived with a man. I thought in the beginning that I loved him. I know that I wanted him. Before I actually met him, there was this great physical attraction between us. So, we moved in together. His name's Mark DeSoto. I was living with him right up until I landed here. He doesn't even know where I am."

"Do you want him to know where you are? Do you want me to tell him?" I asked.

"Oh, no, I should have left him a long time ago but I didn't. I should have," she seemed to be talking more to herself. "Are you serious about staying in Winnipeg? You're not going to come back on account of me are you?"

"Well, I haven't any close ties in Toronto. And this is

my home town. If you wanted to come to Toronto then I would go back. But I'm not staying here only because of you. Should I try what I've just said in a different way?''

Cheryl laughed and said no, she got the general idea. Since she was in a better mood, I figured it would be as good a time as any to bring up the past. "About those things you didn't want to discuss last night, you feel like talking about them now?''

"I was . . . I wanted to tell you that I've been living with a man who wasn't good for me.''

"Oh.''

"Well, what did you think I was going to tell you? That I was dying or something?''

"As a matter of fact, yes.''

Cheryl started to laugh and I sat there watching her closely, trying to determine whether she was being honest with me. When she realized I wasn't going to join in the laughing, she asked, "What's wrong?''

"It's the letters you've been sending me for the past two years. Why didn't you tell the truth?'' I asked as tactfully as I could.

"Oh, the letters. Sorry about them. I just didn't want you to worry about me. You seemed happy enough out there.''

"But why did you quit university? How come?''

"It wasn't going very well," Cheryl shrugged. "And the stuff I was doing at the Friendship Centre, well, I believed I was accomplishing something at first, but then a lot of girls we were trying to help just kept getting in trouble. In different ways it all boiled down to one thing: as a social worker I don't think I would have made the grade. So I quit and got a job instead.

"That was two years ago. It's funny, you know, I was right about it not working out for you in Toronto and you were right when you said the native people have to be willing to help themselves. It's like trying to swim against a strong current. It's impossible.''

"I thought if anyone could do it, you could."

"You're disappointed that I've given up?"

"After all the griping I did against it, yeah, I suppose I am. I used to envy you for having something so meaningful in your life. I mean, I couldn't do it because I didn't believe it was possible—making a better way of life for native people, giving them a better image. So what kind of job did you get?"

Cheryl made a face and said, "Oh, it doesn't matter because I lost it. Mark and I used to party a lot and I started drinking a bit. Anyway, the day I got fired I had a big row with Mark and then I went out and got all tanked up. So that's how I ended up here. I feel so stupid."

"Well, anyone who drinks goes overboard once in a while. I remember I got fuzzy once at a party and then Bob's mother poured a pot of coffee into me and . . . I bet she thought I was getting to be an alcoholic. Just because she knew I had Indian blood. When I think of it now, a lot of things make sense in the way Mother Radcliff treated me."

Visiting hours ended then so I had to say goodnight to Cheryl. On Tuesday morning, the doctor told Cheryl she would most likely be discharged on Wednesday. When she told me, I asked, "What are you planning to do when you get out?"

"You make it sound like I'm in jail or something. I don't know. I don't want to go back with Mark. I don't even want to go back there to get my things."

"Are you scared or something?"

"Oh, no, it's not that. He might want me to stay and then there'd be a scene, maybe."

"I could go and get your things for you. Just tell me the address and I could go tonight. Then you could come and stay at the hotel for now until you get a permanent place."

"Are you sure you wouldn't mind? It's in a rather run-down section of the city."

"If Mark is there, will he give me any problems?"

"No, just explain that I'm in the hospital and you're going to look after me for a while. He looks tough but he's okay. When he laid into me, he was drunk and I pretty well asked for it. Besides, I'm sure he'll be out. Oh, April . . ." Cheryl's face had a guilty look on it.

"What?"

"You know all the things you left me? Well, I sold them. I'm sorry."

"That's okay, Cheryl. If you needed money, though, you should have asked me. I would have sent you some."

"No, I couldn't do that. You see, I was kind of supporting Mark. He's out of a job. Anyway, it would have just gone to him."

Cheryl was looking down at her hands and nervously twisting her fingers together.

"Two suitcases should do it. All I've got is clothing. Our room is right at the top of the stairs to the left. And there's two boxes under the bed with my papers and books in them. You can just take them."

That night, I had supper before looking for the address on Elgin Avenue. I had a lot to digest about Cheryl's past. I had thought mine was full of turmoil and dark secrets. By the time I got to the address I was thinking of the future. With the money from Bob, I could buy a house in Winnipeg. Maybe we could even rent out some rooms and that way we'd have an income every month. On second thought, Cheryl would probably insist on taking native boarders. Besides, people make up creepy stories about two sisters renting out rooms. That wasn't very classy. Heck, with the money I had now, I could buy two houses and rent one out. No, then I'd be responsible for the taxes and repairs and what if someone couldn't pay their rent? I'd end up letting people stay for free all the time.

I spotted a parking spot not too far from the house. It was too bad I couldn't get a spot right in front of the house. I got out of the car and a cold gust of wind struck me. I shivered. The temperature seemed to have fallen. I looked around. Cheryl hadn't been kidding when she said it was in a run-down section. It was spooky. And dark. I got to the gate and wondered why on earth they would have a gate that closed when most of the fence was down anyway. At the same time, I was wondering if Mark would be home. And what was he like? I had to take my glove off to fiddle with the latch.

Suddenly, a male voice close to me said, "Can I help you with that, baby?"

I jumped. Where had he come from so suddenly? I looked up at him and he seemed to be leering at me. This couldn't be Mark. Maybe I should get back to the car.

Before I had a chance to move, an arm came from behind and grabbed me by the front of the neck. There were two men! I stepped back into the man as hard as I could, ramming my elbow into his side. He released his grip. The other man was now grinning.

"You bitch. Oh, no, you're not going to get away from us."

He grabbed my arm but I twisted loose and pushed against him. We were on a patch of ice and he slipped, lost his balance and fell backward, all the while swearing. This all happened in a couple of seconds and I was able to run back towards my car. I didn't know what their intentions were but it was my intention not to find out. I opened the car door and was about to jump in when one of them reached for me and got ahold of me. They were yelling to someone to bring the car up. Headlights were turned on and I saw the two men clearly. I struggled desperately to free myself. The other man who had fallen reached our side and when the car was beside us, he opened the door and shoved me in the back seat and got in beside me. The other one closed the door on the rented car and got in beside the driver.

Like a helpless animal I was trapped and terrified. They meant to kill. I was sure of it. Otherwise they would have disguised themselves or something. They whooped it up and congratulated each other on their 'catch'. I figured if I was going to die, I was going to go down fighting. But then I thought I'd have a better chance if I watched for a police car. I watched for one at the same time as I kept an eye on the man beside me. They were crazy men and now they were probably aroused from chasing me. Crazy men with crazy grins. The one beside me put his hand on my breast. I hit it away. He hit back much harder as if he had a right to do whatever he pleased.

"So, you're a real fighting squaw, huh? That's good 'cause I like my fucking rough.'' He laughed at that.

The driver said, "Hey, we're only supposed to give her a scare. You're talking rape, man.''

"Shut up, dummy. And slow down. We don't want to get stopped now. You're in this as much as us," growled the man beside me. So he was the leader, I thought.

The other man in the front snickered and turned to eye me. I wondered how he knew I was part-Indian. Just because I had long black hair? I didn't pay too much attention to what the driver had said about just giving me a scare. I figured that this had started as a lark to scare women and now the leader and his accomplice wanted to rape me. Maybe I could count on the driver to help somehow. And maybe they weren't out to do any killing. I just didn't know. I hadn't been in Winnipeg long enough to know whether there had been a rash of rapes and strangulations going on. Maybe that's what was going to happen to me. And if they had knives it would be a whole lot worse. They could torture me to death, cut me to pieces, or beat me up and leave me to die in the cold somewhere, all bloody and broken. 'Oh, God, I want to live. This isn't the way I want to die. This isn't my moment to die.' I couldn't help trembling with fear. Horrible thoughts rushed through my mind.

The night ahead could only be shameful, humiliating and even if they didn't physically wound me, it would be tortuous. I braced myself mentally and physically so I would be able to face up to anything they did. I knew I wouldn't be able to stop them from abusing me physically so I'd try to be like a rag doll. But I'd close my emotions and mind off. Maybe it wouldn't affect me so much.

The leader was groping at me and he grabbed my breast roughly. I grit my teeth and sat rigidly, trying hard to ignore his hand, trying hard to show no reaction. I smelled the liquor on his breath as he leaned toward me. Then his hand slid to the crotch of my jeans and I had to pull his hand away. I was pressed against the side of the car. He was saying vulgar things to me, watching my face at the same time. I guess he wanted to reduce me to nothingness.

"Hey, you guys, we're going to have to teach this little Indian some manners. I'm trying to make her feel good and she pulls away. The ungrateful bitch."

As they laughed, the leader grabbed a handful of my hair and pulled my head back. One minute he was laughing, the next he was saying in a low, frightening voice, "Listen, you little cunt, I know you want it so quit pretending to fight it, okay? Or I'm really going to give it to you."

The man beside the driver was watching and he asked, "Hey, man, could I have a turn with her?"

"Don't worry, you'll get your turn soon enough," the leader said ominously.

We were out in the countryside somewhere. I didn't know where because I had lost all sense of direction. They had turned the interior lights on. The leader moved in on me, trying to take off my jacket. I pushed his hands away and for a few minutes my anger overcame my fear.

"You filthy, rotten freaks!"

I threw myself at the leader, trying to scratch and bite him.

"You keep your filthy, rotten hands off me!" I was panting from a mixture of my anger and exertion.

I could hear them laughing like lunatics. The leader held me away from him with ease but I managed to scratch his face, drawing blood.

"You goddamned cunt!" he yelled in rage. Then he followed that with a hard punch to my midriff. That knocked the wind out of me and sent me flying back against the left side of the car again. My head hit the window. The leader then grabbed the front of my blouse and ripped it open tearing the buttons off. I tore back into him.

"Why you fucking little savage. You're asking for it."

He gave me a back-hand across the side of my head, which made my ears ring. He resumed trying to take my clothes off and I tried my hardest to stop him. That's when he systematically started hammering into me. I could hear the driver making weak protests.

After his merciless onslaught, I was too weak to try to defend myself anymore. I felt him taking off the rest of my clothing and feebly I tried to put my arms across my breasts to cover myself. He shoved them aside.

"All right, you guys, mission accomplished. Hey, dummy, you gonna drive all night? Park this damn thing someplace. Maybe we'll let you join the party," he laughed as he turned his attention back to me.

"Yeah, you little savages like it rough, eh?"

He undid his zipper and pulled down his jeans. Then he forced me to lay the full length of the car seat. When he prepared to come down on me, I shifted myself to the side, blocking him with my leg. Without saying a word, he slammed his fist into my ribs, which I already thought had been broken.

Then he said very softly, "You do that again, you slut, and I'm going to lay you wide open. You understand?"

Defeated, I lay there listlessly, my eyes half-closed because I didn't want to see his face but at the same time, I didn't trust him to close my eyes completely.

Suddenly, he shoved his penis into me so violently that when I felt the pain of his thrust tear into my body, my eyes opened wide with terror. I struggled again to get away

142

from him. Again, he grabbed my hair and yanked my head to the side. "You want me to lay you open?" He could see the terror in my eyes. I think that was what he enjoyed the most.

"What's the matter, she giving you trouble?" the man in the front seat with the driver asked.

"Shut up! I can handle this little whore."

He thrust into me again as if he were stabbing me with a deadly purpose. It was pure agony. Inside my head, I screamed long and loud, trying to block everything out.

"Hey, she likes this, boys. These squaws really dig this kind of action. They play hard to get and all the time they love it. You love this, don't you, you little cocksucker?"

After what seemed an eternity, he withdrew, only to exchange places with the man beside the driver.

I don't think I could have fought anymore, even if my life had depended on it. Besides, I thought, the worst was over. I allowed myself to be handled like a rag-doll. The second rapist made me turn on my stomach but I was beyond caring. He inflicted a whole new pain but of the same intensity. My moans were muffled into the car seat. Every driving movement of his sent new pain searing through my body. And all the while, he giggled wildly.

When he finally withdrew, he said to the driver, "It's your turn, dummy."

"Naw, I don't think so. I don't feel like it," the driver said and I knew he was scared. And the others knew it, too.

"You're going to fuck this bitch, dummy, whether you like it or not. You're in this with us all the way. Now get back there and do it," the leader ordered.

The driver came back, made me turn on my back again and tried. I don't know if he had no intentions of raping me but he pretended to and then he told them he was finished.

"You sure?" the leader asked suspiciously.

"Yeah, I'm sure," the driver answered.

I lay there, not daring to move, lest it drive them back into more activity. But now that they had finished, what would they do with me? Would they kill me or let me go?

To my great dismay, the leader came back into the back seat and pulled his pants down again. He made me sit on the floor of the car and then he shoved his penis in front of my face and ordered, "Suck on it, cocksucker. And don't get any funny ideas about biting it or you'll be sorry. You'll be real sorry."

I didn't move so he yanked my head and pulled me closer.

"I said suck!"

My whole face was sore and my lips were cut. He pressed his penis against my mouth. Sluggishly, I turned my head away and opened my mouth a bit to avoid the pressure against my lips. Suddenly he moved my head back and brought it to him so fast that I almost choked on his penis which now filled my mouth. I opened my mouth as wide as I could in an attempt to avoid touching his penis. It touched the back of my mouth and I gagged.

"Suck on it, you little bitch!" he threatened again.

Then he turned to his two companions and said, "Boy, do I ever feel like taking a piss right now."

I heard the driver say, "You wouldn't, would you? Not right in her mouth? Well, for christsake, don't get the car dirty."

I heard them saying this but my sense of reasoning was numbed and by the time the meaning of it filtered through to me, it was too late. Just at that moment, the leader tightened his grip on me and started peeing. Right into my mouth. I started wretching violently, and I struggled but couldn't move my head because of the viselike grip he had on me. I felt the urine run down my chin, soiling the rest of me as well as him. Thinking I was going to vomit all over him, he let go of me.

The driver was yelling, "You're getting the car all dirty and she's going to fucking puke all over the place. Get her the fuck out of here.''

The leader jumped out of the car and he began putting on what clothing he had taken off. The driver jumped out of the car and reached in the back and dragged me out. Then he grabbed all my clothing and my purse and threw them out after me. I kept wretching, although the intense need to vomit had passed.

When the three of them had straightened their clothing, the man from the front seat beside the driver yelled, ''Fucking squaw!'' I heard the leader laughing as the car doors slammed. I pretended I was still trying to vomit. When the lights came on, I was able to make out the license number just before the car sped off.

12

I WAS FREE and I was alive! As I put on my clothes, I kept looking in every direction, fearful they might return. I would run for safety into the fields, even in the deep snow in my bare feet if I had to. Tears ran down my face but I didn't sob. I was finally dressed and started down the road in the opposite direction which they had taken, praying I wouldn't run into them again. As I walked I repeated the license number. Out in the open with no obstruction to impede it, the winds shrieked with icy glee. But they didn't touch me. It must have been thirty below but I didn't even feel the cold. I was numb and beyond feeling. I strained for any sounds of an approaching vehicle and often turned to look behind me. I had no idea where I was.

Finally, I saw a light in the distance. I felt fear and hope at the same time. When I neared the light, I saw that it was a farm yardlight. Then I heard a dog barking. As I walked down the driveway, a large German shepherd came out to inspect me. It continued its thunderous barking all the way to the porch door. A porch light was turned on and a man looked out cautiously. From the way he looked at me, I'm sure he at first thought I was some drunken squaw who had gotten into a fight and had been thrown out of a car. Begrudgingly, he asked me in only after I told him I had just been raped and would he please call the police. His wife had come out and she offered me a cup of coffee. I asked her where the washroom was while he called the police.

When I came out of the washroom, having washed my mouth out, they asked me what had happened. The chill that hadn't touched me outside caught up with me in the warmth of their kitchen and I began to tremble so violently that the woman went and got a blanket off their bed. Tears streamed down my face and my teeth were chattering, although I still didn't sob.

When the R.C.M.P. came, I expected that they would insinuate I had somehow provoked the rape. But the two officers were soft-spoken and kind. They wanted me to show them where the car had been parked and on the drive there, I had the unreasonable fear that they, too, might turn on me. We soon came to the place where I had walked into the deeper snow to get my purse. When they finished examining the tire tracks and the area, they drove me to the hospital back in Winnipeg. I sat in the back seat, my teeth still clicking together from a coldness that just wouldn't leave me.

They took me to the Emergency of the Health Sciences Centre, where Cheryl had been taken just a few days earlier. The doctor on duty examined me and took all the samples that would be required for court purposes, if they ever caught those rapists. As he was preparing to swab my mouth, I told him I had washed it out. He chided me for doing so, saying they needed all the evidence. I couldn't believe his words. I was supposed to go around with the residue of piss in my mouth for the sake of evidence?! I figured he had enough evidence. Before he sent me for x-rays, he asked me if I was related to Cheryl Raintree. When I told him I was, he informed me that he had been on duty when she came through. The x-rays showed no fractures or broken bones so the police took me to their headquarters to take my statement. They told me to recount everything exactly as I remembered it. The whole thing took a long time and it was taxing. While I talked, tears rolled down my face but again I didn't do any sobbing. It seemed to me my voice droned on and on and on but at last I was finished. They told me they would be talking to Cheryl in the morning to see if she had any ideas on possible motives, since I was initially picked up at her door. When they drove me back to the hotel, they informed me that they would later have me look at some pictures to see if I could make any identifications.

When they drove me back to the hotel, they informed me they would have to take all my clothing for purposes of evidence. They waited outside in the hall while I changed into a nightgown and robe. Once they had gone, I took a long bath. My whole body felt sore and I seemed to ache all over. Although I stayed in the bath for a long, long time, I couldn't get rid of their smell. I tried to fathom why they would do such a thing, but I couldn't. It was beyond reason. Later on, in bed, every once in a while I'd give a shudder when the visions of the night became too clearly realistic. It was a long time before my tensions eased off. I stopped shivering and I finally drifted into sleep.

I was awakened by the sound of someone knocking on my door. It was Cheryl and two officers, although not the same ones as the night before. Apparently, they had picked up Cheryl and brought her to the hotel. Cheryl at first was going to throw her arms around me but as she saw me brace for the pain, she stopped.

"Oh, April, I'm so sorry. It's all my fault you came here in the first place. I'm sorry."

"It's all right, Cheryl. I'm okay. Really."

I looked at the two officers. One of them said they would like me to go with them to look at a car. They said they'd wait for me in the lobby while I got ready.

After they left, Cheryl again said, "This is all my fault."

I was dead tired and I snapped, "Oh, Cheryl, stop it, it's not your fault. It just happened." I felt awful for using such a tone of voice so I added in a lighter tone, "Come, help me get dressed. I can barely move."

She did so in silence.

Before I left, I asked her to wait for me and we would go together to get her things and the rented car. As we were on our way to the Public Safety Building, the R.C.M.P. officer told me they had seized the car and arrested the owner. I would have to identify both the car and its owner. Some of my buttons had been found in the car so my identification was merely routine. But a little while later, I identified the owner as one of the rapists from a line-up. He looked very scared, almost like a little boy. Even though he had taken part in the heinous crime against me, I couldn't help feeling sorry for him. All I really wanted to do was hate him. I remembered that he, Stephen Gurnan, had done nothing to try to stop what had happened. My feeling of sympathy disappeared.

When I returned to the hotel, Cheryl was waiting for me.

"April, you look exhausted. Maybe you should try and get some sleep and I'll go and get the car and that. Do you want something to eat?"

"Yes, I'm starved. And I need some coffee. Are you sure you want to go back alone?"

"Oh, sure. After this, I don't care if Mark does make a scene."

After we had eaten and she made sure I was comfortable, Cheryl left. I got out of bed and ran some water into the tub. I got in and then ran the rest of the water as hot as I could stand it. I lathered myself with lots of soap. I had to get rid of that awful smell on me. I could smell it as if they were in the same room as me. Their dirty, stinking bodies. I could feel their hands all over me. I had to get rid of that feeling, too. I scrubbed wherever I wasn't sore or bruised, sometimes hitting a sore area that brought back new pain. But no matter how much I scrubbed and lathered, I still felt dirty and used. It was no use. I cried, my tears rolling down my cheeks into the water, because it was no use. I couldn't get myself clean. I would never be clean again, free from the awful smells, free from the filthy feelings, free from the awful visions.

In bed, I realized just how much I had learned to hate. It wasn't a natural emotion. I had known deep resentments but if I had been given choices, I would rather have been friends with people like the DeRosiers, Mother Radcliff and Heather. But a real, cold, deep hatred had crept into me and I knew that I wouldn't want to let go of it, not for the rest of my life. I wanted those two men in particular dead. By my hand. Yes, I wished with all my might that I could be the one to kill them and make their deaths prolonged and painful. I knew what I'd do. I'd castrate them. Then I'd watch them bleed to death, in agony. Oh, I wanted them dead! I had been touched by evil and from now on it would always be a part of me. Wanting three men dead was evil in itself, but, nonetheless, I wanted them dead.

Finally, I fell asleep. When I woke up, I saw the suitcases and the keys to the car but Cheryl wasn't there. She must have gone to get something to eat. I got dressed and went to the restaurant. She wasn't there but I had something to eat anyway. It was almost eleven p.m. When I got back to my room, Cheryl still wasn't there. Maybe she had gone for a drink. I looked in the mirror and hoped that most of the bruises would disappear within the week.

Cheryl came back about fifteen minutes later.

"You're awake. How long have you been up?"

"Almost an hour. How did it go?" I asked, purposely not asking where she had just been.

"Mark wasn't even there. He moved out, I guess. I was just down in the lounge. Are you hungry?"

"No, I just had something to eat down in the restaurant. I had a good sleep and I feel much better. I bought a newspaper and I was going to look through it but I wanted to talk to you first."

"About what?" Cheryl asked, in a guarded tone, as if she had read my thoughts.

"Well, I'm supposed to get some money from Bob once the divorce goes through. We could buy ourselves a house. What do you think?"

"You mean you'll get enough money from Bob to buy a house?" she asked, incredulously.

"Well, I'm not exactly sure how much it's going to be but I'm sure there'll be enough for a down payment." I retreated to half-truths. I didn't know yet exactly how much I would be receiving but I was sure I'd be able to afford two average sized homes.

"Why not? Beats renting," Cheryl shrugged.

"Good, we can start looking tomorrow."

I started looking through the ad section of the newspaper while Cheryl turned the television on.

"Do I get a say on where we'll live?" she asked.

"Of course. I haven't any strong preferences. I only know where I don't want to live." I was glad she was interested.

Two weeks later I was enroute to Toronto, a day before my divorce hearing. I went to my place on Woodbine and settled everything with the landlord, telling him that after the twenty-seventh I would no longer be needing the place.

On Wednesday morning, plastered with make-up to cover my bruises, I met with my lawyer, Mr. Feldman, and we went to the courthouse together. Bob, Heather and Barbara Radcliff were all waiting outside the courtroom, so I made a special effort to be busy talking to Mr. Feldman to justify my ignoring them. Inside the courtroom everything went smoothly, although I was nervous when I was on the stand. I also experienced feelings of hurt and regret when a former 'friend' testified about the relationship in which Bob and Heather were involved during our marriage. But when it was over, I felt almost smug since I was more independent, money-wise, than I had ever been before in my life. I wasn't quite as smug as Heather, though. She had a possessive hold on Bob's arm as we left. Remembering the rage I had felt on that day of revelation, I was tempted to go up to them all and say something terribly sarcastic but since I couldn't think of anything, I left quietly with Mr. Feldman. He told me that his fee could come out of the settlement as we had agreed and then I would receive the balance of the money through my bank within three weeks at the latest. Later that evening, I was on a flight back to Winnipeg.

Cheryl had continued looking for a house while I was gone for the few days and when I got back she found a house she liked on Poplar Avenue. It was close to Henderson Highway, Watt Street and the Red River. Come summer, we would be able to take walks and watch the boats. Ever since I had spent those long hours by the river when I was with the DeRosiers, I had found areas by water had a soothing kind of feeling. Sometimes, if I watched the water long enough, I got the feeling that it was I who was moving. I also loved to watch the birds circle overhead, swooping down now and then for a morsel of food. I thought Cheryl's choice was a very good one and I asked the saleslady what the earliest date of possession would be. Unfortunately, she said it wouldn't be until March 1st. That meant another month of living in a hotel room.

That same evening, Cheryl and I both settled in our room to watch television. Things were shaping up.

"I can't wait for March 1st, eh? We'll have to go

shopping for furniture and make sure they can deliver it by March 1st. Let's see, that's a Wednesday. Yeah, there shouldn't be any problems. Are you sure you want to take an upstairs bedroom?"

"I'm sure. That way, you'll be close enough to the kitchen and when I come down in the morning you'll have coffee and breakfast all ready for me."

"Oh, yeah? Thanks a lot," I said as I threw a pillow at her.

Then she looked at her watch and said, "Hey, April, you want to go down to the lounge with me and have a few drinks? To celebrate finding ourselves a new home?"

I had noticed that she had grown fidgety and only then did I suspect why. An instant decision was required.

"Sure, sounds like a good idea."

Later that night when we were both in bed, I was unable to go to sleep. I had no idea on how to deal with Cheryl. It appeared she really needed those drinks. Maybe she was an alcoholic. And what would have happened if I had refused to go along with her? She'd been like a child asking me for a favor. Would she have reacted like a child and thrown a tantrum if I had not gone along? I thought that from now on I would have to be careful with my words and reactions and that was the only way I knew how to deal with Cheryl.

I was also caught up in my own problem and spent hours thinking over the rape and its consequences. What would I and other "squaws" get out of my going to court? Maybe two years of safety from those particular rapists. Probably less because hardly any criminal ever served a full sentence anymore. Rehabilitation, today, meant coddling the prisoners to the point of giving them every down-home comfort. Cheryl had told me of a lot of native men who did something illegal so they would land in jail for the winter months. So what was the big deal about going to prison. I sighed at the hopelessness of so-called justice. Mostly because there was nothing for the victim. Nothing, especially for victims of sexual assaults, except humiliation

153

in and out of the courtrooms. Nothing but more taxes to put more luxuries into the penal institutions. To keep a single prisoner for a year cost more than what a security guard earned in that year. So where was the justice of it? The only consolation I could derive was from killing them over and over again in my mind.

I had an appointment to see Mr. Lord, who was handling the real estate transaction for me, on February 8th. He was very happy to see me and, despite my fears that I would be embarrassed because of my divorce, everything went smoothly. When I came out of his office, it was almost noon. Roger Maddison came out of his office just then and he seemed not at all surprised to see me. I was wondering if he remembered me, his old verbal fencing partner, when he said in a pleasant voice, "Hello, April, how are you?"

"Hello, Mr. Maddison. I'm fine, thank you. What about you?"

"Fine. Alex told me you were coming in today."

"Oh?"

"I was looking forward to seeing you again," he smiled and then asked, "How about lunch?"

"Okay, I'd like that."

I did most of the talking over lunch. He listened and drew more out of me with appropriate questions. He asked me if I would go out with him sometime. This gentle, concerned side of Roger, I hadn't seen before. I wondered why he had never gotten married. Then I wondered if he had gotten married.

"Have you ever been married?" I asked.

"No. I never found the girl I wanted to spend the rest of my life with. Once, I thought I had found her." By the reflective way he looked at me when he said that, I wondered if I could have been that girl. But I didn't have the gumption to ask that question.

"Well, I guess I'd better let you get back to the office. Thank you for the lunch. You can reach me at the

Maryland Hotel. That's where I'll be staying until we move into our house.''

Before I headed back to the hotel, I bought several books for Cheryl and me. There wasn't much that one could do in a hotel room. I picked up a book called, *Bury My Heart at Wounded Knee* by Dee Brown. Cheryl would like that. Maybe it would keep her from going down to the lounge. Like that morning, she said she was going over to visit Nancy but then Nancy was supposed to have a steady job so how come Cheryl was visiting her during the day? Maybe Nancy worked nights. Or maybe Cheryl was out drinking somewhere. No. Although Cheryl had a drink almost every day, she'd never been drunk or even appeared to be close to being drunk. Maybe drinks to her were what coffee was to me. I couldn't get a day started without at least two cups of coffee.

On Thursday, Roger phoned in the morning to ask if Cheryl and I would like to have dinner at his place Friday evening. I told Cheryl about it, excited that he really had called.

"I really didn't think he'd call me.''

"Isn't this the same guy whose guts you used to hate when you worked at the law firm?''

"The same one. Oh, you're not going to tell him that tomorrow night?''

"Don't worry. I'm not even going to be there tomorrow night.''

"Oh, you have to.''

"Oh, but I don't. He really wants you there. I've got things to do. Besides, you don't need me to hold your hand.'' I tried to change her mind but she wouldn't budge.

Friday evening started out with both Roger and I trying to make polite conversation. I guess he was as uncomfortable as I was. After the meal, I was sipping coffee when I asked him, "Roger, how come you were so nasty to me when I worked there?''

"I liked you,'' he smiled.

"Well, that was no way to treat someone you liked."

"Well, I got your attention, didn't I? Until that man came along."

"I did like you, you know," I said. "I hated you, too. I hated liking you. Of course, if I had known you liked me then maybe things would have been different."

"Well, that's what I get for playing games. I've decided not to play games anymore. So, why didn't Cheryl come tonight? Has she no faith in a man's cooking?"

"No, she just figured we ought to be alone, I guess. It was a very good meal. Where did you learn to cook?"

"I've been a bachelor for a long time. You were telling me about your marriage, care to tell me about why the divorce?"

"Well, I divorced Bob on grounds of adultery. But now when I think about it, that's not what bothered me most. My mother-in-law, she was some lady. She didn't want to be grandmother to a 'bunch of little halfbreeds' as she put it."

"Why would she say a thing like that? You're not Indian, are you?"

"No. I'm . . . a Métis." I had to force those words out.

"And from the way you say that, I gather you're not too proud of it." Roger had a hint of an understanding smile on his face, but his eyes were serious.

"I'm not. It would be better to be a full-blooded Indian or full-blooded Caucasian. But being a half-breed, well, there's just nothing there. You can admire Indian people for what they once were. They had a distinct heritage or is it culture? Anyway, you can see how much was taken from them. And white people, well, they've convinced each other they are the superior race and you can see they are responsible for the progress we have today. Cheryl once said, 'The meek shall inherit the Earth. Big deal, because who's going to want it once the whites are through with it?' So the progress is questionable. Even so, what was a luxury yesterday is a necessity today and I enjoy all the necessities. But what have the Métis people got? Nothing. Being a half-breed, you feel only the short-comings of both sides. You feel you're a part of the drunken Indians you see on Main Street. And if you inherit brown skin like Cheryl did, you identify with the Indian people more. In today's society, there isn't anything positive about them that I've seen. And when people say off-handedly, 'Oh, you shouldn't be ashamed of being Métis,' well, generally they haven't a clue as to what it's like being a native person. Oh, I'm sorry. I didn't mean it. I meant the words, I didn't mean for them to come out all at once.''

I was really embarrassed. I had held those words in for such a long time and then I lay them on Roger of all people.

"Well, believe it or not, I understand. There will always be some form of discrimination, whether it is someone discriminating against an Indian on Main Street or your Church telling you you have to teach your children its beliefs because theirs is the only right one. I've got a brother, an adopted brother who's an Ojibway. Joe things it's not important what others think of him. It's what he thinks of himself that counts.''

"Well, Cheryl lives pretty much by that philosophy and even so, she's come down with a drinking problem, I think. I'm not really sure. Anyway, only she has the right to tell me I ought to be proud of what I am because she's worked so hard to do something about the native image.''

"Your sister sounds remarkable. Maybe something is bothering her. It could be she's impatient to see the changes or it could be almost anything.''

"I think my being back in Winnipeg will help a lot. It's funny, you're the last person I thought I'd be able to talk to about these things. Thanks for listening.''

"I found it interesting. I find you interesting. I'm not going to tell you to be proud of what you are. Just don't be so ashamed.''

157

13

ON MARCH 1st, Cheryl and I moved into our very own home. By March 2nd, most of our furniture and appliances had been delivered. The following Saturday, I gave a house-warming party, but only Roger came. Cheryl refused to invite Nancy or any of her other friends.

Next, Cheryl and I went looking for a car. It was wonderful to have money to be able to pay cash for a car. The salesman really catered to us, even offered us a two car deal. But Cheryl absolutely refused my offer to buy her her own car. I really wanted a big expensive luxury car, but because of Cheryl I bought a little Datsun which I never did like very much, not after the Radcliff automobiles. Cheryl asked me again in that accusing manner just how much money I did have. I counter-attacked by saying enough to send her back to finish her university courses if she liked, adding that was about it. Of course, I had no idea how much that would have cost. But it was convincing and made Cheryl change the subject. She insisted she had no intentions of being a social worker.

It was the middle of March and I was half-watching the evening news as usual, when a news story came on which made me sit up and take notice. Actually, it was a picture of a man who'd been shot to death by the police earlier that afternoon. It had something to do with a bank robbery. I wasn't sure because I had also been reading the newspaper. If I hadn't glanced up at that moment, I wouldn't have seen the picture of one of the men who had raped me. It wasn't the leader and it wasn't Stephen Gurnan. It was the one who had helped grab me and had sat beside the driver. I was positive. My heart was beating fast and I paced back and forth in the living room, wondering if I should wait for the late news to come on again or whether I should call the police immediately. Since I was positive, I called the police right away.

I was told someone would be sent down to see me, so while I waited, I thought things over. If only it had been the leader. Maybe the leader had been with him. Maybe they've got the leader. I looked through the paper again but the story wasn't in the paper. I was sure that if they had arrested the other man, I would be asked to go down to police headquarters to identify him. I was sure that those two would hang around together.

Then I hoped Cheryl wouldn't return while the police were there. I had never talked about the rape to her in detail because she had initially blamed herself. So far, I hadn't even told her about Stephen Gurnan. For that matter, she had never told me what questions the police had asked her. I had wished those men dead and now that one was dead, I was glad. But it should have been the other one.

Almost two-and-a-half hours passed before two officers showed up. They had brought some pictures for me to look at and I picked out the dead rapist immediately. They asked if the other rapist was among any of the other pictures, but he wasn't. None even looked like the third man.

On March 23rd, I got a call from the police asking if I could come down to the Public Safety Building immediately. It was in the afternoon and Cheryl was out job hunting. There could only be one reason why they'd want me there. They must have arrested the third man. After I got there, I had to wait for at least forty-five minutes. Then, there in the line-up was the leader! He looked arrogant and unafraid. He looked evil! It gave me great pleasure to be able to pick him out so easily without any fear of being mistaken. At the same time, that cold chill came over me again. From the minute I saw him, I began to tremble, just as I had that night. Not being able to control myself scared me. I really feared the possibility of losing my mind. Going crazy. In that way, rape was a double assault. Rapists abused their victims both physically and mentally. Some victims' minds really did snap after a brutal sexual assault. Maybe it had something to do with what I had tried during the assault. Separate my mind from my body. I didn't know. I wasn't a psychologist. I just knew how I felt. I was driven home in a police car and I was grateful for that. To be out alone, especially in the dark was just too terrifying for me.

Cheryl hadn't yet returned so I again went through my ritual of trying to exorcise the evil within me by bathing. I poured half a bottle of perfumed oil into the hot water and then spent the next hour scrubbing vigorously. When the water would get cold, I would just add more hot water. All the while, I thought of the rapists, laughing crazily, pawing at me, coming down on me, putting their smell on me, putting their dirt on me. And no matter how hard I scrubbed, I couldn't get rid of the smell of their awful slimy bodies, the awful memories. I wanted to scream aloud that long silent scream I kept in my head that night. I wanted them to feel my anguish. I wanted to gouge their eyes out. I wanted to whip the life out of them. Mutilate them. Kill them. Because bathing never worked.

I always got worked up like that whenever I would take a bath, although it had never been with such intensity before. Back in the bedroom I paced the floor back and forth, cursing Fate for having placed them on Elgin Street that night, cursing the judicial system because those two, if they went to jail, they would get out again to rape again. When I had cooled down somewhat, I began wondering for the hundredth time why they had kept on calling me squaw. Was it obvious? That really puzzled me. Except for my long black hair, I really didn't think I could be mistaken as a native person. Mistaken? There's that shame again. Okay, identified.

When Cheryl got home, I hadn't even started supper yet. We decided to order pizza and have it delivered. Cheryl had news that she was quite sure she was going to be hired at a downtown factory where she had put in an application that afternoon. She had to phone back the following Monday. I asked her what she would be doing because I couldn't see her working on an assembly line. She said she'd be doing a lot of different things but wouldn't specify. What a waste, I thought to myself.

That started me thinking of opening our own business, maybe a fashion boutique like the ones I used to visit on Yonge Street and in the Yorkville area of Toronto. From my shopping experiences with Mrs. Radcliff, I'd learned a lot. Could have learned more if I would have paid more attention. But Cheryl was what discouraged me. She would insist on drawing in native women which would drive others away. Moreover, Cheryl's heart wouldn't be in it. She dressed well enough for one of her crowd, but that certainly wasn't the world of high fashion. In the end I thought it would be best not to mention it.

For the time being, I decided that I would go back to

temporary secretarial work because I didn't want to be tied to a job until the whole rape trial ordeal was over.

In April, Roger, Cheryl and I went out to celebrate my birthday. It was only rarely we did anything together. Cheryl still hadn't brought over a single friend to our place. She went out a great deal. She would come home from work, have supper, change and go out again. I spent more and more time with Roger.

In May, I was cleaning the house on a Friday because I didn't have a job for that day. It was when I was collecting the garbage from Cheryl's room that I came across an empty whisky bottle in her garbage container. I was so shocked to see it, the implication of it rushing into my head. Cheryl wouldn't do that. Sneak drinks. So why the bottle? I tried to think of a number of reasons why she'd have a bottle in her room. I had never seen her even slightly drunk. Of course, we hadn't seen much of each other over the past few months. I decided I was making too much of it. We were getting along all right and I didn't want to change that. Cheryl never did say anything to me, although she must have realized I had found the empty bottle when I had done the cleaning.

A few weeks after this, I spotted a promotional piece in the newspaper about an Indian Pow Wow to be held on the July 1st long weekend at Roseau River. It would be good if Cheryl and I attended the festival, I thought. Especially good for Cheryl. Perhaps it would renew an interest in her native cause.

That evening as soon as Cheryl came home from work, I asked, "Hey, Cheryl, what's an Indian Pow Wow?"

"Oh, it's mostly a dancing competition among different tribes who come from all over the place."

"Are they interesting?"

"Oh sure, I've been to several of them. I like going to them."

"Well, there's going to be one in Roseau on the July 1st weekend. I'd like to go to it and see what it's like. How about it? We could buy some camping stuff and make like we were teenagers again. Remember?''

''You really want to go?''

''Yeah, I said I did, didn't I?''

''Okay, I'm glad you want to go. You'll finally rub shoulders with real Indians,'' Cheryl said and I wasn't sure if she was happy or just being sarcastic.

I was quite anxious to go and then I thought of Roger's brother, Joe. Funny that so many Indian boys were called Joe. Probably Catholic mothers naming their sons after Joseph, the foster father of Jesus. I wondered if Joe was married. Roger hadn't said. I thought maybe I should invite Roger to bring his brother and join us for the Pow Wow. I'd have to ask him.

I never did ask him, though. I had supper at his place not long after, and I was wondering about how to broach the subject but Roger had picked that night to decide it was high time we showed our affection for each other. During the past weeks of seeing each other, I had subtly dissuaded him from giving me even a simple goodnight kiss. As far as I knew, Roger was most likely seeing other women, which was fine with me. Men, to my knowledge, did not tend to be celibate for long periods. And Roger and I were just good friends. But on this particular night, he kept getting uncomfortably close. At one point I went over to look out the window but he followed me. He made me turn to face him and was about to kiss me.

''Don't touch me,'' I heard myself say in a cold, icy voice that stopped him dead. He looked at me for a long time before he released me.

''I'm sorry. I wanted for us to be just good friends, that's all, just good friends,'' I said in a whispery voice.

''Well, I wasn't going to rape you, April. I can't figure you out. I thought we had more than just a friendship going for us.'' His voice was neutral and I couldn't tell whether he was angry or hurt. After that, he served me coffee but our conversation was stifled. He saw me out to my car but this time he didn't say he would call me. He just said goodnight.

I had an appointment on June 1st to see the Crown Attorney, Mr. Scott. I had already received a subpoena from an R.C.M.P. officer for the Preliminary Hearing. Mr. Scott's office was in the basement of the Legislative Building. The police had explained some of the general court procedures but Mr. Scott explained things in more detail. For instance, as we went over my statement, he told me I was allowed to say things like 'I smelled liquor on his breath', but not 'he was drunk'. It had to do with hearsay evidence. One could testify to what was directly known. Anyways, it was quite complicated to me and I worried about messing up my testimony. I also worried about the Defense Counsel misconstruing whatever I would say.

On the day of the Hearing, I went early to Mr. Scott's office as we were to meet there. As we went to Stonewall, I reread my statement which Mr. Scott handed me. He reminded me of a few things and before I knew it we were at the Community Hall in Stonewall where the judicial process was carried out. Mr. Scott showed me to a small room where I was to wait until my turn to testify. By lunchtime, I still hadn't been called and I was both bored and apprehensive.

After lunch, I went over my statement again, although I loathed going over those words that told the story of that night. I was finally called to give my testimony and I started shaking as soon as I heard my name. My stomach had been tied up in knots all day but it tightened up even more by the time I was in the witness stand.

Mr. Scott asked me to recount the events of January 11th, 1972. I did but minimized the dirty details as much as I could. On occasion he'd have me go into some of those details, like the rape itself. I couldn't just say I had been raped. I had to describe the act itself. I tried at all times to look only at his eyes or his lips as they moved, pretending I was talking only to him and that no one else was there. Of course, I could feel their eyes buring into me. I knew darn well there were others in that room, listening to what I was saying. When that thought would overwhelm me, my voice would fade out and the court stenographer would ask me to repeat myself. I wondered what those other people were thinking. It wasn't just a simple matter that a horrible degradation had happened to me. The thing was *I had been part of it*. I'm sure that's what they all thought, even if unwillingly. I had been part of that depraved sexual activity. I had known in advance that I would have to use explicit words when referring to private parts of the anatomy. And I had come across those words as well as the slang words in the past. But to me, to say them out loud, in front of all those people, well, I faltered every time I had to say them. In the future I would better understand why some women chose not to seek justice in the courtrooms.

And then I was questioned by the Defense Counsel, Mr. Schneider. He sounded very skeptical, at times even sarcastic. He tried different insinuations which made me feel defensive. I felt like it was me who was on trial by the time he was through with me. He persisted in making me go into depth about some incidents and I really believed it was just to make me say those words I had stuttered on. I understood full well that it was his job to defend his client in any way he could, but I also felt what he did to me was morally wrong.

A recess was called after I was allowed off the stand and I headed straight for the washroom. Once there, I threw up. One woman had been in there when I walked in and she glanced at me. I couldn't interpret what was in her glance but when she expressed sympathy, I broke down and began crying. I wished for the moment that I could stay in the washroom until everyone was gone, but I had to go out to Mr. Scott's car. I fixed my makeup and braced myself and returned to the courtroom, very grateful that at least one person sympathized with me.

The court ruled that there was sufficient evidence to proceed with a trial. That's what the Preliminary Hearing was for. The court also ordered a ban on the publication of evidence for which I was extremely grateful. On our way back to Winnipeg, Mr. Scott was in good spirits because he had been successful. I was just relieved that this portion was over and done with. There was still the trial ahead.

Cheryl and I left early Saturday morning for the Roseau Reservation. There was a camping area set aside for the likes of us. As we made our way to the main area, we noticed license plates from Montana, the Dakotas, Minnesota and even Arizona. Men, women and children were in traditional tribal costumes. Somewhere in the background, drums could be heard, sounding the heartbeat of the people. Teepees had been set up and Indian women in buckskin dresses now tended to fires, making bannock for curious onlookers.

The main event, as Cheryl had said, was the dancing competition. During the intervals, everyone was invited to participate in the dancing. Cheryl joined in but I stayed on the sidelines. That night, we sat, Indian style, around a bonfire, listening to the chanting and tales of Indian singers. Cheryl told me that was probably how it had felt on those long-ago buffalo hunts. I was impressed by all the sights and sounds. It went deeper than just hearing and seeing. I felt good. I felt alive. There were stirrings of pride, regret and even an inner peace. For the first time in my life, I felt as if all of that was part of me, as if I was a part of it. It was curious to feel that way. I had gone expecting to feel embarrassment, maybe even contempt. I looked over at Cheryl. She, too, seemed so relaxed.

She was deep in conversation with some people on the other side of her. I didn't attempt to join their conversation. I was occupied with enjoying my own realizations. I also noted with satisfaction the old animation on Cheryl's face as she gestured and talked with her companions. Earlier that evening an Indian family had set up their tent next to ours and had come over to offer help. At the end of the ceremonies, Cheryl and I returned to our tent.

"Well, did you enjoy yourself?" Cheryl asked.

"Oh, I don't know. In this atmosphere everything is staged. It's romanticized. On Monday we'll all go home and to what? I'll go back to see the drunken Indians on Main Street and I'll feel the same old shame. It's like having two worlds in my life that can't be mixed. And I've made my choice on how I want to live my everyday life."

"Yeah, but the Indian blood runs through your veins, April. To deny that, you deny a basic part of yourself. You'll never be satisfied until you can accept that fact."

"How do you do it, Cheryl? How is it that you're so proud when there's so much against being a native person?"

"For one thing, I don't see it that way. Maybe I have put too much faith in my dreams. But if alcohol didn't have such a destructive force on us, we'd be a fabulous people. And that's what I see. I see all the possibilities that we have. Nancy, for instance, you never did think much of her when I was attending university, did you? Well, she does drink and does other things that you would never dream of doing. But she also holds a steady job and she's been at the minimum wage for a long time. They use her and she knows it. And she gets depressed about it. But with her education and the way things are, she knows she doesn't have many choices. She helps support her mother and her sister and a brother. The reason why she left home in the first place was her father. He was an alcoholic who beat her mother up and raped Nancy. Okay, she doesn't have much, maybe she never will have much, but what she's got she shares with her family. And she's not an exception."

"I didn't know that," I said. We sat for a time in silence before I spoke again.

"When we lived with our parents, I used to take you to the park. The white kids would call the native kids all sorts of names. If they had let us, I would have played with the white kids. Never the native kids. To me, the white kids were the winners all the way. I guess what I feel today started back then. It would take an awful lot for me to be able to change what I've felt for a lifetime. Shame doesn't dissolve overnight.''

"I can understand that. Me, I've been identifying with the Indian people ever since I was a kid. The Métis people share more of the same problems with the Indian people. I guess that's why Riel was leader to both. I wrote this one piece in university but they wouldn't publish it because they said it was too controversial. I still know it be heart. Want to hear it?''

"Sure," I said. There was little in our conversation we hadn't discussed before, but sitting there in our tent, surrounded by proud Indians, everything seemed different.

White Man, to you my voice is like the unheard call in the wilderness. It is there, though you do not hear. But, this once, take the time to listen to what I have to say.

Your history is highlighted by your wars. Why is it all right for your nations to conquer each other in your attempts at dominion? When you sailed to our lands, you came with your advanced weapons. You claimed you were a progressive, civilized people. And today, White Man, you have the ultimate weapons. Warfare which could destroy all men, all creation. And you allow such power to be in the hands of those few who have such little value in true wisdom.

White Man, when you first came, most of our tribes began with peace and trust in dealing with you, strange white intruders. We showed you how to survive in our homelands. We were willing to share with you our vast wealth. Instead of repaying us with gratitude, you, White Man, turned on us, your friends. You turned on us with your advanced weapons and your cunning trickery.

When we, the Indian people, realized your intentions, we rose to do battle, to defend our nations, our homes, our food, our lives. And for our efforts we are labelled savages and our battles are called massacres.

And when our primitive weapons could not match those which you had perfected through centuries of wars, we realized that peace could not be won, unless our mass destruction took place. And so we turned to treaties. And this time, we ran into your cunning trickery. And we lost our lands, our freedom and were confined to reservations. And we are held in contempt.

"As long as the Sun shall rise . . ." For you, White Man, these are words without meaning.

White Man, there is much in the deep, simple wisdom of our forefathers. We were here for centuries. We kept the land, the waters, the air clean and pure, for our children and for our children's children.

Now that you are here, White Man, the rivers bleed with contamination. The winds moan with the heavy weight of pollution in the air. The land vomits up the poisons which have been fed into it. Our Mother Earth is no longer clean and healthy. She is dying.

White Man, in your greedy rush for money and power, you are destroying. Why must you have power over everything? Why can't you live in peace and harmony? Why can't you share the beauty and the wealth which Mother Earth has given us?

You do not stop at confining us to small pieces of rock and muskeg. Where are the animals of the wilderness to go when there is no more wilderness? Why are the birds of the skies falling to their extinction? Is there joy for you when you bring down the mighty trees of our forests? No living thing seems sacred to you. In the name of progress, everything is cut down. And progress means only profits.

White Man, you say that we are a people without dignity. But when we are sick, weak, hungry, poor, when there is nothing for us but death, what are we to do? We cannot accept a life which has been imposed on us.

You say that we are drunkards, that we live for drinking. But drinking is a way of dying. Dying without enjoying

*life. You have given us many diseases. It is true that you
have found immunizations for many of these diseases. But
this was done more for your own benefit. The worst
disease, for which there is no immunity, is the disease of
alcoholism. And you condemn us for being its easy victims. And those who do not condemn us weep for us and
pity us.*

*So, we the Indian people, we are still dying. The land we
lost is dying, too.*

White Man, you have our land now.

Respect it. As we once did.

Take care of it. As we once did.

Love it. As we once did.

*White Man, our wisdom is dying. As we are. But take
heed, if Indian wisdom dies, you, White Man, will not be
far behind.*

So weep not for us.

Weep for yourselves.

And for your children.

And for their children.

Because you are taking everything today.

And tomorrow, there will be nothing left for them.

Cheryl had become more and more emotional as she
went on. When she finished, we sat in silence. The only
sounds were those of the crickets. Somewhere in the
distance, a child was crying.

Finally I said, "I can see why they said it was controversial. I think it's powerful." We sat in silence for a few
more minutes. "At the same time, though, I think you put
too much blame on white men for everything. The Indian
people did allow themselves to be treated like children.
They should have stood up for their rights instead of letting themselves be walked on. You know what I mean?"

"Yeah?" Cheryl shot back in a challenging voice.
"Where did it get the Métis?"

"But what exactly is it the Métis want? To live like Indians on reservations? To be dependent of the governments and therefore the white people? You once said the Métis people were an independent breed, freedom lovers.''

I still maintain that. But we don't have that kind of life.'' Cheryl added as an afterthought, ''because we don't have very many choices.

"Besides, that piece was mostly to warn those in control that they are going too fast. I'd like them to slow down. Let's enjoy life, give our children hope for tomorrow and get rid of those bloody clouds of bombs hanging over us all.''

14

AFTER THAT long weekend, I tried to keep the feeling I had alive even though I was back in the city. I noticed Cheryl had gotten some good out of it, too, because she made more appearances around the house. She also seemed more relaxed, more willing to discuss events concerning native people that appeared in the newspaper and on television. No matter what the issues were, she always found some way to defend the native side of the question. Now when she began telling me that she was going to the Friendship Centre, I knew without doubt that she was indeed going there. The old fire had been rekindled. Cheryl began tearing clippings out of the paper, presumably to act on them, if possible. For Cheryl, I knew it was probable.

I returned to working part-time but the scenes I saw on my way to and from work on Main St. gradually made that weekend's emotions disappear. I remembered my original evaluation of these people. Everyone always said, "Those Indians on Main Street", but there were a lot of Métis there, too. No, I felt no affection towards any of the native peoples there. But for Cheryl I faked interest. So when Cheryl asked me to go down to the Friendship Centre with her one evening, I agreed.

We decided to walk or rather Cheryl decided to walk. Walking was Cheryl's chief mode of transportation, even in winter. I suspected she was also snubbing my little car. However, it was a beautiful evening to be out, the kind where you could breathe deeply and smell the delicious night air. It made one feel giddy, as in giddy-up-go, the kind of evening that if I were a horse, I'd be kicking up my heels and running like crazy.

Cheryl and I talked about the Steindalls kind of longingly. We admitted that we both felt too embarrased to go back and see them, having been out of touch with them for so long. And perhaps our main desire would have been just to see and ride the horses. Cheryl and I decided we would go horsebackriding a lot more often than we had been doing. It was one way for me of getting her into my car. Our car.

When we got to the Friendship Centre, we entered a large recreation room. I saw a a lot of elderly native people and Cheryl mixed among them immediately with me tagging along behind her. While she conversed with them, I could only smile patronizingly, and nod when it was expected. I knew that Cheryl saw their quiet beauty, their simple wisdom. All I could see were watery eyes, leathery brown skin — uneducated natives.

Cheryl explained that many of the people were in the city for either medical reasons or they were visiting relatives. When they returned north to their homes, they would resume fishing, trapping and committing themselves to crafts.

"One thing you wouldn't like is the way they live in winter," Cheryl said to me. "Some of them have to walk miles and miles just for their water. They roll up newspapers inside their jackets for extra warmth. Cardboards and plastics replace broken window panes. Their furniture is wooden crates and blankets on the floor. Well, you've seen the pictures in some of the books I've given you."

"Sure, but I thought that was in the olden days. I thought they had new houses now."

"New houses, yeah, but cheaply made, no plumbing, no sewer system. Besides, those housing programs were thought up by Indian Affairs, which means only Treaty Indians get any of the supposed benefit out of them. Non-status Indians and Métis get welfare and that's it."

I didn't know what to say. I felt it was good that they didn't have the federal government to rely on, that it would help them be independent to a certain point. But I also knew what Cheryl said was true about non-status Indians and Métis and employment was hard for them to come by.

Just then, an older woman came up to Cheryl. Thinking that she wanted a private word with Cheryl, I moved away a bit and occupied myself by studying some Indian art hanging on the wall. Then Cheryl and the old woman approached me. The old woman suddenly reached towards me and put her hand on mine. I glanced down at her hand. It looked rusted and old. Her fingers were swollen at the joints, disfigured, the veins stood out and it took everything I had not to remove my hand away from hers.

Her hand felt so warm, so dry, so old. I'm sure my smile froze and then faded. I waited for her to take her hand away. I looked at her questioningly but she didn't say anything. Her gaze held mine for I saw in her eyes that deep simple wisdom of which Cheryl had spoken. And I no longer found her touch distasteful. Without speaking a word to me, the woman imparted her message with her eyes. She had seen something in me that was special, something that was deserving of her respect. I wondered what she could possibly have found in me that could have warranted her respect. I just stood there, humbled. At the same time I had this overwhelming feeling that a mystical spiritual occurence had just taken place.

Sheepishly, I told Cheryl how I had felt as we walked home. Cheryl smiled and said, "Well, you should be honored. White Thunderbird Woman is an Elder. I told her that you were my sister but in blood only. I told her your vision was clouded but that when your vision cleared, you would be a good person for the Métis people."

"You do have a unique way of putting things."

"Comes from reading so many Indian books. Actually, most Indians today don't talk like that at all."

"It's a pity. It sounds so poetic."

When my vision cleared . . . Would it ever? And would it mean that someday I would come to accept those Main Street people?

I gave that incident a lot of thought over the following weeks. If I'd had such a grandmother when I was growing up, maybe I wouldn't have been so mixed up. My emotions were getting the better of me. Finally, I put it all down to the fact that it was a very emotional time of my life with the divorce and rape and all. Still, I continued to waver back and forth as to just how I felt about being a Métis. It *was* a part of me. I *was* part-Indian. But so what?

In September, Roger came over to my place on a Saturday morning. It had been two months since I had last seen him. I had missed him of course and I had found it lonely without his company. But then I had Cheryl's company and that made up for it, a little. I had consoled myself by thinking that with me, no deep relationship would ever be possible and therefore it was better for Roger to stay away. When the doorbell sounded, I wondered who it could be because Cheryl and I had virtually no one to call on us.

Even though she had returned to her former self, Cheryl still had invited no one to our house. It was probably an Avon lady.

"Hello, April."

"Roger! What are you doing here?" I was surprised and pleased to see him and a smile came to my face instantly.

"Oh, I was in the neighbourhood, thought I'd drop by for a cup of coffee and see how you were," he smiled.

"In the neighbourhood, huh?" I smiled back, and led him into the kitchen. When I had gotten the coffee, we sat at the table, but didn't say anything.

Finally, he said, "Look before . . ."

At the same time, I said, "I missed you."

"Well, I missed you, too. I was hoping and waiting for you to call me. But then, that's like playing a game, isn't it? And I said I wasn't going to play games anymore. If you don't want to see me, then I want you to tell me now, and I want you to tell me why. Is it because of your marriage? Did you get hurt by it? Is that why you've always held me at arm's length?"

"No. No, it has nothing to do with my marriage. I do like you, Roger. I just don't want you wasting your time with me, especially if you want more than just being friends. I can't give you more than that. And I can't tell you why. I won't tell you why." I sighed and put my cup down, emphasizing how hopeless the situation was.

Roger looked at me. I didn't look at him, but I knew he was looking at me. I could feel it. After a while he said, "Well, I'd rather for us to be friends than nothing at all. So we'll continue seeing each other, all right? And if you ever feel like telling me exactly what is bothering you, then don't hold back, okay?" He reached out and put his hand under my chin and made me look at him.

"Okay. But just don't count on it."

Roger had some things to do but we made plans to go out later that evening. When Cheryl came down later, I told her Roger had been there. Then I wondered if my going out with him again would have an adverse effect on her.

"You don't mind me going out with him, do you, Cheryl?" I asked after much hesitation.

"Of course not. I think he's a heck of a lot better than Bob. I'm glad. You need a strong man to take care of you. You know what I mean? I'm the kind of woman who might feel smothered by a man after a while. But you, well, it's not that I think you're weak or anything. Just that I see you with a husband and kids and still doing what you have to."

I liked Cheryl telling me that. It wasn't quite the way things were between Roger and I but if I hadn't been deranged by those rapists, that's probably how things would have been.

In the middle of September, a police officer came to my place to serve me with a subpoena to appear in court in the trial of 'The Queen vs. Donnelly' on October 10, 1972.

On October 3, I had to return to that basement office in the Legislative Building to see Mr. Scott, the Crown Attorney. He explained that Oliver Donnelly was going on trial only for the charges of unlawful confinement and rape. If a verdict of Not Guilty were reached, then he would proceed with the other charges of indecent assault, gross indecency and assault causing bodily harm. If the verdict was Guilty then the lesser charges would be stayed. When I left, I was well aware that the trial was less than a week away.

I told Cheryl about the trial and she said she was going to attend. I told her I'd rather she didn't, but she was insistent.

"Look, April, you've changed a lot and I want to know why. You've never told me exactly what happened. You smile, you laugh, but I can see in your eyes there's no joy. I want to help you in any way I can."

"Cheryl, you blamed yourself in the first place and it's not your fault. What happened to me was Fate. But I know you, you're going to start blaming yourself when you had absolutely nothing to do with it. Some terrible things did happen to me and I don't want you to know about them. So please stay away, okay?"

"I won't make any promises," Cheryl said. "If I can take time off work, I still might come."

On Tuesday morning, I was at the Mr. Scott's office by nine a.m. in case I had to go over any last minute details. Then I was secluded in a witness room while the jury selection took place and the professionals like the doctors had their turns to testify first so they could get back to their jobs. Lunch came and went and it was two-thirty before I was called.

I could feel everybody's eyes on me as I walked to the witness stand. My insides were twisted into a knot. Nervously, I listened to the clerk ask me if I would swear to tell the truth, the whole truth, nothing but the truth so help me God. I said, "I do."

I was already trembling and I hadn't said but those two words. While the Crown Attorney shuffled through some papers on his table, I looked around, not moving my head. On my left were the jurists. On my right and higher up was the Honorable Mr. Justice Saul. There in front of me, enclosed in the prison dock, was Oliver Donelly, staring up at me. I quickly averted my eyes.

Mr. Scott was quite different in his role before the jurists. He was very sympathetic and seemed thoroughly offended by what he knew had happened to me. Again I had to tell of the night of the rape. I answered in as much detail as I thought he wanted. I faltered at times, turned red, looked at the floor. It was a horrible experience saying in front of all those people what had actually happened to me. I had to fight to control my trembling and shaky voice. I had to pretend it wasn't as bad as all that. I was asked to describe the man who had raped me. I did so.

"Is that person whom you are describing present in the courtroom today?"

"Yes, he is."

"Could you point that person out?"

"He's over there," I said, pointing at Donnelly as I had been previously instructed to do.

Mr. Scott said, "Let the record show that the accused, Oliver Donnelly, has been identified by April Raintree, the Complainant."

When Mr. Scott finished with me, it was Mr. Schneider's turn. He was the defendant's lawyer. I expected him to be aggressive as he had been at the Preliminary Hearing but he wasn't.

After going over my identification of Oliver Donelly, he asked, "All right, you were in the car. What did you do while you were still in the city limits?"

"I sat in the corner of the back seat."

"Did you fight or plead with them to let you go?"

"No, I was . . ."

"So, you didn't do anything at all?"

"No."

"Now would you say the defendent was intoxicated?"

"I don't know."

"Didn't you state that you smelled liquor on his breath?"

"Yes, I did."

"You did what, Miss Raintree?"

"I did smell liquor on his breath."

"You stated that you were going to your sister's place to pick up her effects. Is that correct, Miss Raintree?"

"Yes."

"Do you know how your sister earned her living at that time?"

I answered "No" at the same moment Mr. Scott raised his voice, objecting that the question wasn't relevant to the case. The judge intervened to say he didn't have to make a ruling because I had already answered.

After I had completed my testimony, the Crown Attorney called Stephen Gurnan to the stand. He was sworn in but the judge called a recess until the following day.

That night, I wondered why the the Defense Counsel had asked me what Cheryl did for a living. She seemed distracted but I didn't think it was important enough to ask her. She said she was going to go out for a while. I took the opportunity to take my ritual bath. Maybe tonight I would be able to get rid of that awful stench, forever. But instead, everything was more intensified. The smell became stronger as if the perfumed oil had somehow turned into their bodily scents. I again had the visions of their lunatic faces, laughing, sneering. I hadn't been able to say that in court! Franctically, I scrubbed and lathered and scrubbed some more. Finally I broke down and started crying. I dried myself off, roughly. Then I put my night gown on and methodically began to brush my hair.

Suddenly, I could stand it no longer. I threw the brush down and it hit the bath tub with a resounding clang. Then I snatched the bar of soap and the bath brush and threw them on the floor. With my arm, I swept all the perfume jars and other containers off the vanity. All I felt was a frenzied frustration. My sobbing had grown louder and louder and I finally screamed.

"You bastards! You lousy dirty bastards. I wish you were all dead! Do you hear me? I wish you goddamned bastards were dead!"

I slumped to the floor and pounded the ceramic tiling as hard as I could. I wanted to transfer the pain from inside to my fist. I cried until I had no more tears.

I stayed there for a while, not thinking of anything. Gradually, some of my humor returned and I chided myself for making such a mess because it was me who had to clean it up in the end. But first I'd have a coffee. I went to the kitchen, made myself a cup and sat down at the table to smoke a cigarette. It sure felt good after all the crying I'd just done.

The second day of the trial started with the Crown Attorney having Stephen Gurnan tell everything that had occurred that night, and they went over the identification of the rapist. There was no doubt that the Crown Attorney had the identification area well covered. As far as I was concerned, the defendent didn't have a leg to stand on in the way of defense.

The Defense Counsel then got up to question Gurnan. As expected, he asked him what he had originally been charged with. He noted to the jury that Gurnan had gotten the charge reduced to forcible confinement. Mr. Schneider's tone when he questioned Stephen Gurnan showed his open contempt. The Defense Counsel brought out the fact that Stephen Gurnan had told Donelly that the intended victim was a known prostitute.

"How did you know that this certain girl you were supposed to scare was a prostitute?"

"Objection! That's hearsay evidence. Mr. Gurnan could not know that for a fact since he didn't know the complainant."

"It is hearsay evidence, My Lord, but we believe this evidence is important not to prove that the girl was a prostitute but that the witness believed her to be a prostitute."

Mr. Justice Saul said to Mr. Scott, "He does appear to have a point. Overruled."

The defense lawyer repeated his question, to which Stephen Gurnan answered, "My sister told me."

"And what is your sister's name?"

"Sylvia. Sylvia Gurnan."

I was indignant that I could be mistaken as a prostitute. If Mr. Schneider intended to prove that I was or had ever been a prostitute, he'd better forget it. I could prove beyond a doubt that I was a decent citizen.

It was after the lunch recess when Cheryl showed up.

"I lied at work and told them I was sick. I would have come a lot earlier but I was stuck at something I had to finish. Anyways, how's it going? And how do you feel?"

"Well, I'd like to say I'm happy you see you, but you shouldn't have bothered coming."

"That's gratitude. How's the case going?"

"I think it's almost over, but I'm not sure. I think, too, that the Defense Counsel is trying to prove I behaved like a prostitute or something. They'll try anything."

Cheryl and I entered the courtroom together and sat near the front. A little later in the afternoon, Sylvia Gurnan was called to the stand. She testified that she had asked her brother, Stephen, to scare a certain prostitute. I presummed her testimony was to corroborate what Stephen Gurnan had said, thus making him a credible witness in the eyes of the jurists.   "You specifically told your brother, Stephen Gurnan, that this certain girl was a prostitute?" Mr. Schneider asked.

"Yes. We all knew she was a prostitute. It wasn't a secret," Sylvia replied.

"Did you know this girl's name?"

"Yes. Her name's Cheryl Raintree."

Shock waves went through me. I looked sideways at Cheryl. She didn't move at all. It was as if she had been expecting it. I sat there shivering. My own sister? Champion of native causes. A whore?

"Cheryl, say this isn't so," I whispered to her in a hoarse whisper, begging her to deny it. But she didn't. She just sat there looking at the floor.

What happened after that I'm not really sure. My mind was in a whirl. I know the jurists left the room but it didn't have anything to do with this recent exposé. A police officer testified as to how Oliver Donelly's statement had been obtained. Then I remembered that Mr. Scott had told me about this *voir-dire*. When the judge was satisfied that the statement had been given voluntarily, he ruled that the evidence could be submitted and the jury was called back. Then Oliver Donelly's statement was read to the court.

He said he had been first approached by Jason Steeps to help Stephen Gurnan put a scare into some hooker. "Jason and I had been drinking heavily, most of the afternoon prior to that evening. We sat in Stephen Gurnan's car which was parked where the hooker was supposed to be living. When the girl came, Stephen Gurnan told us she was the one, so we grabbed her and got her into the car. We drove around for a while and the girl never said anything so I figured it would be all right to have sex with her. I believed she was a prostitute. When she did object, I thought it was because I hadn't paid her. I had never paid before and I wasn't going to start then. The liquor made me lose control and I hit her a few times. If I hadn't been drunk, I wouldn't have hit her. I believed at the time when I had sex with her, it was with her consent.''

There were no further witnesses so court was adjourned until the next day for the summations by the lawyers. Because it seemed Cheryl wasn't going to budge from her chair even though the courtrom was almost empty, I said, ''We'd better go now.'' My voice sounded cold, even harsh.

Cheryl stood up then and looked right at me. I saw her face in that split second before I looked away from her. I just couldn't look her straight in the face, not at that moment. I didn't even know how I felt towards her. She followed me to the bus stop. All the way home, we were silent. I then understood that she really had been to blame. I blamed her. At the same time, I didn't blame her. Or didn't I want to hold her responsible? I waited for her explanations, her excuses but she didn't make any. When we had eaten supper, she went out.

I again checked the newspaper and was relieved to find they hadn't printed my name. I was simply referred to as the complainant. What a way to get into the papers, as a victim. A victim of my own sister's folly. A victim of Sylvia's revenge. Another victim of being native. No matter how hard I tried, I would always be forced into the silly petty things that concerned native life. All because Cheryl insisted in going out of her way to screw up her own life. And, thus, screwing up mine.

For some reason, I didn't feel the urgent need for the

ritual bath that night. I turned on the television to get my mind off Cheryl. It didn't help much. I kept thinking of the look she had given me that afternoon. The look I had so coldly turned away from. As if I had judged her guilty. Still, she was my sister, my flesh and blood and when she returned I would tell her everything was okay. It really wouldn't be okay but I decided I would try my best to forgive and forget. The late show came on and Cheryl still hadn't come home. I fell asleep and woke up about three-thirty. The movie was over and there was still no sign that Cheryl had returned. I went up to her room to make sure. Afterward, I went to bed disappointed and worried.

The next morning I went to the trial alone. The Crown Attorney made his summation to the jury. He went over all the testimony of the witnesses emphasizing that the element of corroboration and legal principle had been met by both my testimony and that of Stephen Gurnan. Then he pointed me out and said, "Ladies and gentlemen of the jury, look at the poor victim, the victim of this deplorable crime. How she has suffered, not only from the physical and mental anguish, but also the emotional pain of the whole onslaught. Whether she was a prostitute or not, and I stress to you that she is not and never has been, is not the question at hand. The fact is, ladies and gentlemen of the jury, that she suffered at the hands of Oliver Donelly. She will never forget the torment of that winter night. Remember how she gave her account of what happened that night of January 11, 1972. Trembling, but honest. Not once did she change any of her testimony. Not once did she waver between truth and fiction. Ladies and gentlemen of the jury, there is one thing we can do on behalf of the girl, April Raintree. That is to find this man, the defendent, Oliver Donelly, guilty of rape. To give her justice."

I had to squirm under everyone's scrutiny. I objected to being pointed out like that, and being called that "poor girl". It sounded overly dramatic. It sounded like he wanted them to say the defendent was guilty on the grounds that I was such a pitiful creature. I wanted him found guilty because of what he had done. I was glad when he concluded his summation. I took the opportunity to look behind me to see if Cheryl had come. All I saw were strange faces, staring at me.

Next, Mr. Schneider, the Defense Counsel, went to work on the jury to try and convince them that his client was innocent. He emphasized that Donelly had been drinking heavily, that Donelly honestly believed that the girl was a prostitute, but more importantly, had consented by her own silence to have sexual intercourse. The accused further believed that the objections by the complainant were made only because she had not received compensation for her services. I sat there thinking of only one thing. That man, the accused, that bastard, Donelly, had raped me. He had done more than rape me. He deserved to be found guilty and nothing else. By the end of the Defense Counsel's speech, I began to worry that there was a possibility that the jurists would find him innocent. The judge called a lunch recess.

I walked down the corridor, then the stairs, wondering why Cheryl hadn't come and feeling lonely for her company. I also wondered if Donelly was going to get off, scott-free. But then how could he get off when Gurnan had already pleaded guilty to one charge? Wouldn't that be ironic?

I was on my way out the front doors when I heard Roger's voice.

"April, what are you doing here?"

I looked at him, dismayed. I thought of lying but I couldn't think of any good lies. "I'm attending a trial."

"Oh? What trial? You didn't tell me about it."

"It's the Queen vs. Donelly. It's a rape trial. I'm a witness. Or is complainant the proper word?" I said, looking straight at him.

Roger looked at me for a minute, a long minute. "You should have told me about it. I'm sorry. It must be rough on you. How is it going?"

"It's almost over, I think. I don't know how it's going to end. What are you doing here?"

"Oh, I had a few things to do and I was going to do some searches at Land Titles for Alex. But it can wait. How about I take you for lunch right now? Is Cheryl here?" he asked, looking around.

"No. She didn't come today. She was with me Tuesday and yesterday," I answered, not mentioning her involvement.

We had lunch and afterwards, he said that he'd come back to the courtroom, later in the afternoon, when he had finished his work. I talked with Mr. Scott in the hall and he took time to explain what was going to be happening next. He also assured me that things looked good.

I felt slightly better when I took my seat back in the courtroom. The Honorable Mr. Justice Saul gave his charge to the jury, summarizing once again the evidence given, explaining the law pertaining to the charges. It strained my patience to have to listen to him. I began thinking of what I should tell Roger. No doubt if he hadn't read last evening's paper, he would read about the trial now. So far I had been able to talk to him on just about anything. He had listened and given me good advice on occasion and, all in all, he had been comforting. It was almost three-thirty when the jury filed out of the courtroom to consider its verdict.

The courtroom emptied and I walked out into the corridor, hoping to find Roger. He was coming toward me from the other end of the hallway. We waited together, not saying anything about the trial. He asked me again about Cheryl.

"I'd rather not talk about Cheryl right now, Roger. I just hope she's fine but I'm worried because she didn't come home last night. But I'll tell you about it later. Right now, I'm just waiting to see what the jury decides."

It was a little over an hour later when we were

summoned back to the courtroom. I was impatient because it took everyone such a long time to get back in their places, especially the judge. I sat there, scarcely breathing, waiting for that one word: Guilty. The jury filed back into the courtroom and there was more legal footwork as I waited for that word. I looked at a distant point in front of me, not daring to look at the faces of the members of the jury. I heard the Foreman of the jury respond affirmatively to the question of whether they had reached a verdict. And then I heard it: "We find the Defendent guilty as charged." I sighed with relief. Justice to a certain point had been done.

15

BEFORE ROGER and I returned to my place, we went out for supper. When we did get home, I looked for signs of Cheryl but it appeared she hadn't bothered eating or anything, if she had been home. Cheryl usually piled her coffee cups and dishes in the sink and there were none. I made coffee, knowing Roger was waiting for me to talk. As we were drinking coffee, I did.

"Well, you found out what my big secret was. Do you understand why I felt the way I did?"

"Of course. I don't know why you didn't say something, though."

"Rape isn't something you talk about, Roger. I never even discussed it with Cheryl. Cheryl . . . she blamed herself, you know. She blamed herself because she was in the hospital and I came to Winnipeg to be with her. It was when I was going to her place that I was raped. That was why she had blamed herself. And then in court, we both found out that those men were after her. It wasn't just my bad luck. She caused them to be there at that time. She apparently had angered some woman and that woman wanted her to pay for it. And instead, I paid for it.

"How do you feel about Cheryl?"

"I don't know. They said she was a prostitute. I can't resolve how I feel about her. I just don't know. One minute, I want to hug her and tell her it doesn't matter. And the next, I just want to give her hell. I feel like her baby-sitter. As soon as I leave her alone, she goes out and does all these incredibly stupid things. And I always thought she had it all together, more so than me. What is the matter with her?"

"Maybe you feel that way about her because what you went through is a very traumatic experience."

"You're right. It's not as if she made me lose all my money. Funny, that doesn't even seem so important any more. Once, all I wanted was money, lots of it. And now, what I did lose was much more precious than money. I'll never be the same as I once was. You know, when I was married, I didn't want children because I thought they might turn out looking a little native. Lately, now that I can't have children, I would really like to be able to. Settle down and raise a dozen kids."

"Why can't you have any children?"

I looked at him. Couldn't he figure that out?

"Because I was raped. I'd be scared to . . . to ever let a man get close to me."

"And how long are you going to feel that way, April?"

"I don't know. I suppose I'll always feel that way."

"Do you like feeling sorry for yourself?"

"I don't feel sorry for myself," I said indignantly. "I just know how I feel inside. I feel dirty and rotten and

189

used. I'll never be what I was before. I'll never be the same. Can't you understand that?''

''From what I understand, you're keeping what you feel inside of you alive. You're not even trying to let go. Now that the trial is over, let it go, April. Let time do its healing. The big tragedy now is not that you've been raped. It's that you refuse to let yourself heal.''

''You men! You haven't a clue as to what a rape does to a woman. It kills something inside. That's what it does.''

I was angry with Roger. Perhaps what he was saying had some truth in it, but I felt he was being very insensitive to my feelings on that day.

In my anger, perhaps because of the emotional roller-coaster I'd been on, I ordered him to get out of my house. I wanted someone to comfort me, not make me feel that I was wrong in my reaction.

''I'm sorry, April. Maybe I shouldn't have said what I did, but I really believe you're going to have to let go of your hatred and resentment sooner or later. I'll call you tomorrow.''

My anger continued to burn after he left. Who was he to tell me my reactions were wrong? What did he know about rape? I stormed into the bathroom and began to run the water for my ritual bath. Then I realized Roger would think I was just wallowing in my self-pity so I shut off the tap and stormed back into the kitchen and poured myself another cup of coffee. It was cold and I slammed the cup back down on the table and sat there, staring at nothing in particular. What could any man ever understand about rape? They just had no comprehension!

But as I sat there, I began to think about what he had said. It was true that I had come to look forward to those ritual baths. I enjoyed killing them over and over again in my mind. But, really, who was I hurting by it? I had wanted Roger to comfort me, but maybe what I really wanted was his sympathy, maybe even pity. It was something he hadn't given me and I resented it. How was I supposed to just 'let go', as he said? It simply wasn't possible.

When I finally tired of waiting for Cheryl, I went to bed, my mind still in a muddle about my feelings. I was still full of hatred but I was also beginning to realize that probably Roger was right and I should try and let go. The same feelings were with me when I awoke the next morning. I spent the day wandering aimlessly around the house trying to read a book or watch television. I was making supper when Cheryl walked in.

"Cheryl, where have you been?"

"That's none of your bloody business."

I was taken aback by the bluntness of her answer.

"Sorry. I was just worried. There's no need to snap at me."

"Oh? You think things should return to normal, do you? Well, good luck! I've got to go up and change." With that she quickly went upstairs, not giving me a chance to say more.

I walked back to the kitchen. Then I went back to the foot of the stairs and called up, "Hey, Cheryl, supper's almost ready. Are you going to come down soon?"

"I'm not hungry," she called back.

While I was washing the dishes, I heard Cheryl coming down the stairs. I was glad. Maybe we could talk. But she called, "I'm going out. See you later."

"Cheryl, wait . . ."

But the front door slammed. It was no use. I could just see myself scurrying down the street, pleading for her to come back so we could talk.

Roger called a little later and asked if I wanted to go out to a movie or something. I agreed, thinking it would take my mind off Cheryl.

I didn't go to court the day Donelly was sentenced, but I learned on the news that he had been sentenced to five years at Stony Mountain. I wondered if those five years—he'd probably be out on parole after three—would leave as deep a mark on his life as he had left on mine?

In the following weeks, Cheryl absolutely refused to talk to me unless it was in little biting sentences. At first I was patient but then I started loosing my patience with her and my sympathy. Sometimes I'd come home from a date with Roger and she'd go upstairs, leaving me in mid-sentence. Sometimes she'd come home, drunk. That really upset me. Then she'd say all kinds of nasty things about me that weren't true or were only half true. Those things would hurt me the most and once she saw the hurt in my eyes, she'd seem satisfied and would leave me alone.

One Saturday afternoon, she came in the front door. She looked in pretty rough shape, her hair was dishevelled and her eyes were reddish, dopey looking. She immediately went upstairs as I expected. But a few minutes later she came down, carrying one of her whiskey bottles.

"Thought I'd keep you company today. I haven't seen my big sister in such a long time. I'll watch you clean up the place. It's like an Indian having a white maid. Well, go ahead, don't let me stop you. I'll just go and get me a glass. I can drink this stuff straight, you know. Want to see?" She took a swig from the bottle, then smacked her lips.

"Well, I'm sorry to disappoint you Cheryl, but I've already done the cleaning. And while you're getting a glass get me one, too, will you. There's Coke in the fridge. I'm not up to drinking it straight."

Cheryl looked at me suspiciously. "Oh, I get it, if you can't beat 'em, join 'em, eh? And what is poor, sweet Roger going to think?"

"Doesn't matter. Once I told you that *we* were going to make it. Well, if you're not going to try, then why should I?"

"Oh, no. Don't lay that crap on me, big sister. You turned your back on me a long time ago. You think I don't know why you married Bob? It was to get away from me, that's why. I'll bet you wished you were an only child. I bet you wished I was dead."

"You know that's not true!"

"And now you're back here, right in there, with another white man. Half-breeds aren't good enough for you. You're a bigot against your own people. You want to know something else, April? I'm ashamed of you. Yeah, ashamed. You're not my sister. You're my keeper, buying this house, paying for my keep. That's all you are, just my keeper. You're disgusting. And you have the nerve to look down on me?"

"I've never looked down on you, Cheryl. Never. Just on what you do. What you're doing to yourself. I don't understand why."

"Don't give me that bull. You heard what they said in court and I saw what you felt when you avoided looking me in the eye. You think you're better than me. You've always thought you were better than me. And you'll never understand me. You'll never understand me." Cheryl repeated the last line more to herself than to me. Then in a louder, more aggressive tone, she said, "You know, April, you sure have lied to me a lot. You tell me one thing when you know it's a bloody lie. It's pretty bad in this stinking world when you can't even trust your own sister."

Cheryl never did pour me a drink. She went back upstairs, I assumed to sleep it off. I felt as if I had been in a physical fight with her. I was breathing hard. I lit up a cigarette. It was unreasonable of Cheryl to accuse me of all she accused me. She wasn't faultless. So why, why, why, did she tear into me all the time? I thought of Alcoholics Annonymous. Cheryl would never go there, not in a hundred years. Cheryl was an out-and-out drunkard. In the previous several months I hadn't seen her sober because when she was sober, she avoided me like I was the plague.

In December, Roger invited me to go to Killarney with him to meet his parents. They lived on a farm and Roger went out to visit them as often as he could. I felt I couldn't leave Cheryl alone and Roger said I was to invite her, too. I knew Cheryl wouldn't go and in the end, Roger decided he would remain in the city for Christmas and spend it with me. I protested, of course, but he remained firm in his decision.

We waited most of Christmas Day for Cheryl to return so we could open our presents together. Cheryl didn't come. I was embarrassed. Roger had forsaken Christmas with his family to be with Cheryl and me. I had forsaken a Christmas with his family for Cheryl. And Cheryl didn't even do us the honor of staying home.

We spent New Year's with his parents. I also met his brother, Joe, who wasn't Indian at all. When we were by ourselves, I said, "You lied to me, Roger Maddison. You said your brother Joe was an Ojibway."

"Well, I figured that would help you open up a little," Roger grinned. "I thought it would make you feel like we had something in common. Actually, the guy I was talking about was a good friend in school. Heck, for that matter, I was going to tell you I had a sister who had been raped. So I could say I did understand how you felt, even though I was a man."

"Were you really? You don't have any scruples, do you? And here I was going to ask if Cheryl could meet Joe and you know, maybe get together," I squeezed his arm and shook it, pretending anger. It was the first time I had voluntarily touched him . . .

It was almost a full year after the rape. Roger had succeeded in making me feel good about myself again. I'd have moments when I'd remember but they weren't all-consuming. It would take a long time before I would heal completely. But Roger was right. Time was the best medicine.

Still, I couldn't get through to Cheryl. There was no communication between us. I had resumed my part-time job but one day at the end of February I didn't have anywhere to go. I sat around for most of the day, bored.

Late in the afternoon, I decided to do some baking. It was already dark by the time I put the muffins in the oven. That's when Cheryl came home. I heard her as she came down the hall and into the kitchen. She still had her jacket on but she took it off and placed it over the seat behind her.

"Aren't we domestic today," she said in sneering voice. "Practicing up, are you?"

"No, I just thought it would be nice to have some home baking. It's a little early but do you want supper?"

"If I wanted something to eat, I'd fix it myself. After all, I do live here, don't I?" Cheryl said.

"Well, excuse me, I was just offering."

Cheryl got up and went upstairs. I figured tonight if she wanted to grind away at me, I was going to give her some of her own medicine. Sure enough, a few minutes later, she came downstairs again with a full bottle of whiskey. She set it on the counter, got herself a glass, poured some Coke in after the whiskey. It was about half and half.

I watched her do all this and then I said, "Is this private property or can I have some, too?"

"Go ahead, help yourself. Don't expect me to serve you." She went back to sit at the dining room table.

I decided to join her with my drink.

"So, are the three of us going to have a nice cozy little chat?" Cheryl asked, looking at me. Her eyes were glassy and she had to focus to look straight at me.

"What do you mean, the three of us?" I said, looking at her stomach area, avoiding her eyes.

Cheryl laughed and said, "You, me, and my good friend there," she said pointing back at the bottle of whiskey. "He's going to keep us company. Yes, sir, the family that drinks together, stays together," Cheryl laughed again.

"Well, do take off your boots and stay awhile," I said sarcastically. I had washed and waxed the floor the day before and I noticed then that Cheryl had tracked watery marks on it. Cheryl ignored me and took a long sip of her drink.

"Cheryl, I wish you'd tell me what's been bugging you these past months. Ever since that day in court you've been treating me as if I'd done something wrong."

Cheryl looked at me but didn't say anything.

"I wish we could get everything out in the open. I wish there were no secrets between us. I want to help you, Cheryl, that's all I want to do. Put that away for tonight. Go to bed and tomorrow we can have a really frank discussion, okay?"

"Quit it, April. All you ever do is nag at me. Nag, nag, nag. Is that how you drove Bob away? And how long is this new one going to last, eh? How long is Roger going to last before you try to run his life? Ex-Mrs. Radcliff. Socialite of the East. Big-shot. You're such a phoney. Couldn't manage her own life but she wants to manage mine." Cheryl finished her drink and got up to pour herself another one. She brought the bottle with her and set it down beside her glass.

I sighed and said, "Cheryl, don't . . ."

Cheryl cut me off and mimicked my plea, "Cheryl, don't, Cheryl, don't. Don't do this, don't do that. You're only hurting yourself, poor, dear Cheryl. Well, I know damn well what I'm hurting. Because of me you don't bring any of your white friends here, do you? And with Roger, you had to explain all about your poor, drunken sister, didn't you? So he would understand about me. And pity me? Same way you pity me. Well, I don't need your goddamned pity."

I studied Cheryl. This was far worse than it had ever been before. I didn't know what to do. Should I try to appease her or provoke her into talking to me about what was making her say these things?

"You're ashamed of me," she continued. "You're ashamed of what I do. If you were ever proud of me, you'd be proud to be a half-breed. Proud, I tell you." Cheryl glared at me, daring me to say differently. She was swaying from side to side as she again refilled her glass.

I said in a quiet voice, "Go look in the mirror and tell me what I've got to be proud of."

"Oh, so the truth comes out. As long as I act like a proper whitey, I'm something, eh? But a few drinks and I'm a stinking, drunken Indian."

"You're doing all this to hurt me, right? Why? Do you hate me, Cheryl?"

"Hate you? No, I don't hate you. I hate a lot of things about you. You're a snob. You have double standards. You were so shocked when they said I was a hooker. Well, look at you. How did you buy this house, April? How did you buy that car out there? How, April? You prostituted yourself when you took Bob's money, that's how. You never loved that man. You loved his money. You figured you were going to be Miss High Society. But you figured wrong. But you still came out of it with your pay. A nice big fat roll for a high-classed call-girl. Yeah, your kind makes me sick. Big white snobs who think they're the superior race. Your white governments, your white churches, sitting back in idle, rich comfort, preaching what ought to be, but making sure it isn't. Well, Miss Know-It-All, I know something you don't. And you won't feel so goddamned superior once I tell you what I know."

Cheryl put her finger across her lips as if to warn herself to keep silent.

"Shh, I'm not supposed to tell her," she said to herself.

She smiled a silly, secretive smile, then frowned to herself, questioningly. It looked as if she were wondering why she had to keep this secret.

I was waiting, hoping she would continue. I felt that what she was on the verge of saying would help solve the mystery of what had made her give up on everything. I felt it wasn't just that she blamed herself for the rape. Something had happened before that. She had started drinking before that. Maybe it was something I had done. Whatever it was, I wanted to know. To goad her into more angry outbursts, I said in a cold voice, "Cheryl, you've had enough. Come on, I'll help you to bed."

I got up and put my hands on her arm to help her.

Cheryl shook them off viciously. "You take your bloody hands off me. I'm gonna have another drink and no one's gonna stop me. Especially not a superior white bitch. I can take care of myself. I don't need anyone. Not anyone."

I recoiled at her loud outburst and sat down again. I watched the liquid in Cheryl's glass go down once again. The bottle beside her was half-empty.

"I don't need anyone," Cheryl repeated to herself. Then she looked at me and said maliciously, "Especially not you. I couldn't give a shit about your fancy ways. You're just a social climber who didn't make it."

Cheryl was slurring her words badly and when she saw that I winced every time she used a vulgar word, I could see that she was delighted.

"So, April Raintree, you think you got all the answers, eh? But you can't tell me a goddamned thing, can you? Because in reality, you know fuck-all. I'm the one who knows what life is really all about. Me. That's who. I got the answers. I found the answers all by myself. You lied to me and I lied to you. I did find our precious dear ol' Dad. He's a gutter-creature, April. A gutter-creature! All the tricks I turned, well, that helped him, you know? That kept him in booze. Not only that, I joined him, too. Ah, but that's not all. The best part is still to come."

She smiled a lop-sided smile, as if she had lost control of her facial muscles.

"Mother, you know what happend to our poor, dear Mother? She jumped off the Louise Bridge, is what she did. Committed suicide. You know why she stopped seeing us? Because she couldn't bear the pain. Yup, she committed suicide. They were bums, you know. Both of them. Bums. Boozers. Gutter-creatures. Dad took all that money from me. He didn't know where it came from. He didn't care where it came from. Mark DeSoto. Jack-of-all-trades. Drug pusher, bootlegger, stealing, breaking and entering, pimping, if it was illegal, he was in it. And guess who was right there in it with him? Your little sister, Cheryl Raintree. Your baby sister. Pardon me. There was another one after me. Baby Anna. Did you know about her? Well, she died when she was still a baby. She was the luckiest one of us.''

Cheryl leaned her head on her arms which were crossed in front of her on the table. She was weeping to herself, repeating the last sentence, ''She was the luckiest one.''

I was shocked by her revelations. I didn't believe them. Cheryl was only trying to shock me. Except she wasn't watching me for the desired effect. She wasn't lying. I stood up, taking the bottle with me to the kitchen sink. I was going to make coffee for us. Then I was going to see Cheryl to her bed. Tomorrow we were going to talk together. Now that I knew the reason behind her actions, I knew I could do something about it. I was also relieved that it wasn't because of me that Cheryl had given up. Absentmindedly, I began pouring the liquid from the whiskey bottle down the sink.

''WHAT THE HELL DO YOU THINK YOU'RE DOING?'' Cheryl screamed at the top of her lungs. She startled me so much that I dropped the bottle into the sink as I jumped. For all of Cheryl's drunkenness, she moved as swiftly as a mother cat coming to the rescue of her endangered kittens.

''Give me that, that's mine, you bitch!''

I had a hold of the bottle again and Cheryl lunged for it. We both struggled for control of it. I guess all Cheryl could see was that her precious liquid was seeping down the drain. All I wanted was for her to quit drinking for the night. When the last drop was gone, I let go of the bottle. I started turning toward Cheryl. She was enraged. She glared at me furiously and before I could speak to her, she brought her hand up and struck me as hard as she could across the face. I was already off-balance and the blow sent me reeling backward across the kitchen. I hit the refrigerator hard with my back and shoulders. I put my hand to my head where Cheryl had struck me and looked at her unbelievingly.

Cheryl, momentarily horrified by what she had just done to me, seemed to come out of her drunken stupor.

"Well, you shouldn't have done that." Then she grabbed her jacket and I heard her go down the hall. The front door slammed.

16

I SHOOK MY head to clear it. This was all too much. I returned to the sink and put the empty bottle into the garbage container. My mind started activating again and I realized I should have gone after Cheryl. I went to get my jacket and boots and then I had to look for the house keys. They weren't in my purse and I couldn't remember where I had put them. It was stupid to think of such things but my mind was still in a muddle. The closest bus stop was at Watt Street so I walked in that direction. I reached the bus stop but there was no sign of Cheryl. I went back towards Henderson. I was sure that if Cheryl had intended to take a bus, she would have gotten one by now. Just in case, I waited at the bus stop for the next Downtown bus and got on. I tried looking out both sides of the window but with it being dark outside and lighted inside, plus the condensation on the windows, I couldn't see the sidewalks very well. I got off in front of the City Hall and decided to walk back home, over the Nairn Bridge and all.

That meant the Main Street strip. I walked on the north side because there were more people on that side. If Cheryl were among these people, I could spot her. But I walked all the way home without running into her.

I couldn't sleep at all that night. The wind had picked up outside and I was sure there was a blizzard going on out there. Mixed in were the noises of the house, all those creakings one doesn't notice during the day. I listened to them, deciphering what made them and several times I thought Cheryl had returned. I got up more than once and went upstairs to check her room. The next morning, I got up, tired. I thought perhaps I had made too big a deal the night before when I worried about never seeing Cheryl again. Nonetheless, I called where she worked and found out that she had quit a few months back. I called the Friendship Centre but the person who answered didn't know Cheryl. I made coffee. I spent most of the day waiting and worrying. When my employer from the agency called asking if I wanted to start a job Monday, I said no, that I'd be taking some time off again.

At four-thirty, Roger phoned to say he was going to pick me up in an hour. We were supposed to go out for supper but I had forgotten.

"Oh, Roger, I can't go. Cheryl left last night. I don't know where she is. She's not going to come back."

"Well, April, Cheryl has been away overnight before. Why are you so worried?"

"We quarreled. She was drinking heavily. She told me everything, Roger, all the things that have been bothering her. I have to find her."

"Okay. We'll have supper and then we'll go and look for her, all right?"

"You don't have to come with me. I don't even know where to begin."

"I'll come with you. Don't worry, April, we'll find her."

While I waited for Roger, I decided we could go down to the Friendship Centre and talk to anyone who might know where Cheryl would be. I tried to remember places Cheryl had mentioned in the past. Was it Carlos or was that the name of a beer? I got my coat and boots on and waited for Roger. I went back to the kitchen and looked in the phone book. There was a place called DeCarlos. That was it. I noted the address. Since it was a Friday night, I thought we might even find Nancy. I cursed myself for not taking more interest in Cheryl's friends. I didn't even know Nancy's last name.

After we had a quick supper, we went to the Centre. A few people said they knew Cheryl but that they hadn't seen her for the past couple of months. From there we drove down Main Street over to DeCarlos which was on Carlton. There was a line-up of people waiting to get in, different types of people and it reminded me of the Hungry Eye. My crowd once. When Roger and I got in we looked over the crowd. Already there was a smoky haze hanging over everyone's heads. Music was blasting from the amplifiers. The way we were dressed, Roger and I were obviously out of place. We ordered a drink but were barely able to talk because of the noise. I looked for Cheryl or Nancy. I even felt I'd be able to tell who Mark was if I saw him. I wondered if this was where they all still hung out. On the other side of the room, there was a girl who reminded me of Sylvia Gurnan. I couldn't see clearly because of the dimly-lit, smoky atmosphere. People kept passing between us and sometimes I was sure it was Sylvia and then I wasn't sure. I studied the other people at her table. They were all white. Mark, as far as I knew, was Métis. When the band took a break, Roger asked me if I recognized any of Cheryl's friends. I said I didn't and we might as well leave.

We drove around for a while, up and down the downtown streets, as we searched the faces for Cheryl's. We were unsuccessful. We returned to my place and I went upstairs to see if she had returned but she hadn't. We took our coffee into the living room and I turned the television set on.

"You know, Roger, I'm to blame. No, I'm not going into a self-blaming thing. It's just that I wanted her to have all these good memories of our parents. I always told her only the good things that happened when we lived with them. I knew that they had drinking problems. That's why we were taken away. I should have told her when I gave her those names. I should have told her then that our parents were alcoholics. But I didn't. I just gave her the stuff and hoped that her search would come to an end. And she went out and found our father and found that he was an old drunk. I'm sure she never told me all of the things she discovered because she felt she had to protect me from the truth. She carried that around with her all alone, not wanting to share her problems. And I knew about it! Well, not the part about our mother committing suicide. So many lies to protect. And in the end, they destroy anyway. I just can't understand why all that would have such an adverse effect on her. Unless . . ."

"Unless what?"

"Well, maybe she just used these things as an excuse to start drinking. Maybe she was an alcoholic all along and she just needed some real good reason to start into it. Do you think that's possible?"

"I guess anything is possible but Cheryl doesn't sound like the type of person who would use that as an excuse. The reasons for drinking can be very complicated."

"Sometimes I think if we really were white, we wouldn't have all these complications in our lives. I'd just be a wife, maybe a working mother, just an ordinary person. You know what I mean? There probably wouldn't be any problem with alcoholism. Our lives would be so different. But as it is, I lie to protect her and she lies to protect me, and we both lose out. I don't know. If I was more like her or she was more like me, maybe we wouldn't have pulled apart."

"Maybe that's what's been wrong. You've both pulled in different directions. Cheryl has identified with the Indian people and all the wrongs that have been done to them. And you, having identified with the white people, well, she's taken everything she's felt out on you. Earlier when you told me the things she used to say when she was drunk, well, she wouldn't believe them herself when she was sober. Being drunk gives one false courage."

"Cheryl never needed false courage. She was always spunky enough. She had courage."

"I think, from what you've told me, Cheryl saw you in a superior white role. You supplied her with all her needs. You stayed in Winnipeg to help her, to be by her side. You've stressed that she can depend on you, right?"

"Well, I am her big sister."

"Maybe you could have told her that you needed her help from her. Or at least, not have made it so clear that you were in charge. People need to feel that they are needed and worthwhile. I'd say Cheryl has a very low self-image right now. Drinking helps wipe out that image. And she can't let herself become sober because it hurts when she's sober. So she drinks again."

"I kind of figured something like that. I wanted her to go to bed and sleep off the alcohol. I wanted for us to really talk when she was completely sober."

The weeks passed and Roger and I continued to look for Cheryl. She had never come back to the house. Every day when I'd get home, I'd look in her room and everything was always just as it had been that first night. We returned to DeCarlos regularly but always without any luck. Sometimes, we'd drive around and I'd spot someone who I was sure was Cheryl. I'd get Roger to park the car and I would jump out and go after that person. But when the woman would turn to me, my excitement would turn to disappointment because it was never Cheryl.

The month of April brought erratic temperatures. Some days were warm enough to tempt impatient women into their shorts. The nights brought back the cold temperatures, though, sometimes even below freezing. April 18, 1973, was a cold rainy day. My birthday. I stayed home, hoping Cheryl would remember and come home. But she didn't. Roger and I celebrated alone.

Ten days later, it was the same kind of dismal day. The winds started early in the afternoon, first in short bursts as if gathering momentum for the gales that would follow. It had drizzled off and on for the previous several days. Since it was a Saturday, Roger and I had been out combing the city, more specifically, the hotels. We'd even gone to all the hotels along Main Street. The rain began to fall more and more heavily as the day wore on and the wind had also picked up. Late in the afternoon we decided to call it quits after I had rushed out into the rain, thinking a stranger had been Cheryl.

When we got to my place, I was still soaked to the bone. I felt so discouraged. While I changed, Roger made us coffee. Then we sat silently in the living room, just listening to the steady pelting of the rain against the windows. I wondered what Roger was thinking. Maybe he thought I wasn't worth all the trouble and aggravation. Maybe he wanted to call it quits with me but not at this time, because of Cheryl. I sighed.

"What's the matter?" he asked.

"Oh nothing. Just wondering about all the trouble I've put you to, and how much gas you have used up."

"Well, it's not enough and won't be until we find Cheryl."

"You really and truly don't mind?"

"In spite of her current problems, I think Cheryl is quite a person and she is your sister."

I laid my head on his lap, reassured. It felt so good to be

near Roger. It seemed hard to believe I had held him away for so long. I would have been completely content, except for Cheryl.

Suddenly, the phone rang, exploding into the stillness of the house. I jumped. By the second ring, I got there and picked up the receiver.

"Hello?"

"Is this April?"

"Yes."

"I don't know if you remember me. It's Nancy. Cheryl has been staying with me."

Nancy's voice sounded shaky.

"I remember you. What about Cheryl? Is she okay?" I said anxiously, shooting out the questions.

"She just left here. I didn't want her to go. She seems okay but in a funny way. I wanted her to stay here. But she said she had to go. She said goodbye to me as if she wasn't going to see me again." Nancy sniffled.

"Do you know where she was going?"

"No. And I couldn't go after her because I've been sick the past couple of days and I'm not dressed. My Mom thinks she's going to do something terrible. My Mom's the one who told me to call you. Maybe you can do something. I'm so worried."

"Oh no."

I leaned against the wall, my voice was barely a whisper. Roger was at my side and then he took the receiver from me.

"What's going on," he asked Nancy. He listened to her for a few minutes and then asked for her address. Then he asked some questions about what Cheryl was wearing. When he hung up, he immediately called the police. He explained the situation and gave them Nancy's address and told them we'd meet them there.

It was still raining but not as heavily as we drove to the address on Henry Avenue. There were a number of look-alike, run-down shacks and we found Nancy's house among them. Nancy opened the door before we could knock.

"Anything new?" Roger asked immediately.

"No. I didn't know how to stop her. I just didn't know how to stop her," Nancy sobbed.

"It's all right, Nancy, don't worry. We called the police and I'm sure everything is going to be okay. Thank you for calling me." What I really wanted to say to her was that she should have called me a lot earlier. But she looked so sorrowful.

"Let's drive around and see if we can spot her," Roger suggested.

We had pulled away when Roger noticed a police car arrive and stop in front of Nancy's house. He braked and put the car in reverse. We both got out and walked back to the car. I was so hopeful they had found her. I looked in the back of the car for Cheryl but there was no Cheryl. Roger exchanged some words with the officer, who then turned and asked me if I had even the vaguest idea where she might have gone.

"No, I don't. We've been looking for her and looking for her and all this time she was here. If only Nancy had called us before this. Now I just don't know where she could be."

" . . . and you know what our poor, dear mother did? She jumped off the Louise Bridge, is what she did. She committed suicide . . . " Cheryl's words flashed across my mind.

"She jumped off the Louise Bridge . . . ," I said out loud.

"What's that?" Roger asked.

"Our mother. Our mother killed herself by jumping off the Louise Bridge. Didn't I tell you that?"

"No, you just said that she did it, you didn't say . . . never mind, let's go over there."

Roger briefly explained the situation to the officer and he agreed to drive over to the bridge to check it out. Roger and I jumped in the car and followed the police cruiser. It was only a few minutes ride but it seemed to take a lifetime.

"Why doesn't he put his flashers and siren on, for crying out loud?" I said impatiently as we stopped at a red light on Main Street. My eyes were still combing the sidewalks. Maybe she had stopped for a drink someplace. Maybe she had gone back home. Maybe her goodbye to Nancy meant she was going to move back home. Oh, I'd give her such a big hug if that's what she had done.

Finally, we reached the Louise Bridge. I could see some figures on the bridge waving toward the police car. Roger parked behind the cruiser. I jumped out into the rain, now coming down in torrents, and ran to where the police officer was talking to the two strangers on the bridge.

" . . . not five minutes ago," one of the was saying, "she just stood up on the railing, I tell you, and jumped off. Ask Stan here. He was with me. We both saw it. We tried to stop it, officer. We slammed on the brakes but we couldn't get there in time. Christ, one minute she was standing there, balancing, and the next, nothing. Why would she want to do a thing like that? Those Indians are always killing themselves. If they aren't shooting each other on the reserves, it's this. Holy jumpin' Jesus Christ. What a night this has been. And now this. I tell you it's unbelievable."

I was looking down at the waters, looking for the body. It was too dark to see anything, too murky. The man's word rung in my ears. "She was my sister, mister," I said. What did he know? Someday, maybe, I could explain to people like him why they did it. Roger had placed his arm around me. The man mumbled an apology, said he didn't know. I was crying. My tears were mixed with the rain and they dropped down to where Cheryl was, in that murky water I had once loved to watch. Now I watched, hoping that Cheryl was somewhere down there, alive. But I knew there was no hope. Not for Cheryl. Not anymore. I ached inside. I wanted to let loose with my tears. I felt like sobbing, screaming, wailing. But I just stood there, using the railing for support. Hiding the agony I felt. The agony of being too late, always too late.

After answering some questions for the police officer, Roger and I drove back to Nancy's house. When she opened the door, she saw right away from my expression that the worst had happened. She burst into tears. Her mother saw Nancy begin to cry and walked over and put her arms around her and hugged her. Then she came over to me, a complete stranger, and also gave me a comforting hug. Roger quickly and briefly explained what had happened.

While Nancy's mother busied herself making tea, she said, "Cheryl was like a daughter, you know? She was such a good person. She helped Nancy, you know."

"Yeah, whenever I needed help, she was there." Nancy started sobbing again, but between sobs she continued. "Sometimes, when we needed money, Cheryl would give it to us. She never made us feel like we owed her, you know? When I would get depressed, Cheryl would cheer me up, make me laugh."

"Cheryl would buy groceries," Nancy's mother said, "and she would always joke that they ate them all up anyways."

Nancy and her mother exchanged looks.

Then Nancy said, "I'm not the only one Cheryl helped. She did a lot for other girls, too. Especially at the Centre. She had these big plans, you know. And she used to organize lots of things at the Centre for young people. Then she quit. She changed real sudden but I never knew why. Oh, she'd still help people but she wouldn't go out of her way anymore. And then she met that creep and he moved in with us so I moved back home 'cause Dad left."

I appreciated them comforting me. I sat in silence because I could think of nothing to say to comfort them in return. We sat in silence for a while before Nancy's mother said, "Well, enough for tonight. You're probably tired. You go home and get yourself some sleep."

"Thanks for coming back to tell us about Cheryl," Nancy came over to where I was standing and hugged me. Then she said, "Cheryl left some things for us to take care of. Like the typewriter you sent for one of her birthdays. She didn't want Mark selling it on her. And the other is, well, you come back when you're feeling better. Tonight is not the right time. You will come back?"

It seemed very important to Nancy that I return so I promised I would.

When we were back in the car, I said to Roger, "Imagine that, they're so poor and yet they kept that typewriter for Cheryl all that time, when they could have sold it. And the way they talked about her, like they really did love her. They give out such a family feeling. Cheryl must have liked that a lot. No wonder she felt more at home with them than she did with me."

"I think you should come over to my place tonight, all right?"

"All right. I'd like that. Cheryl hasn't been home for a long time but somehow the house would feel much more empty tonight."

When I finally got to sleep it was past midnight. I dreamt of Cheryl. I could hear her laughter, but I couldn't find her. I looked and looked but all I could hear was Cheryl laughing. When I did find her, she was in some kind of quicksand. I put my arm out to reach her, to help her but she wouldn't take my hand. She just kept laughing and sinking down, deeper and deeper. I begged her and begged her to take my hand and I began crying uncontrollably. When I woke up, I was still crying and Roger was hugging me. When I had quieted down, I lay my head on his chest and listened to his heartbeat. A couple of times, the left over sobs would shake my whole body and Roger would hold me a little tighter. Gradually, I went back to sleep.

The next morning, the police called and asked if we could identify the body they had pulled out of the river. When we returned a few hours later, I was in more of a daze than I had been before. It was final. It had been Cheryl.

Roger did almost everything for me the next few days. I was mostly silent, pondering the why of Cheryl's death. Once in a while I would talk about Cheryl to Roger. Roger helped me with the funeral arrangements. Actually, he did almost everything. After some hesitation, I phoned the Steindalls. I had a long talk with Mrs. Steindall, telling her of Cheryl's death and explaining the absence of our visits. She was very understanding, very sympathetic. That same evening, the night before the funeral, they came to Roger's place to see me.

The funeral service was small and simple. Most of the people who came were Indian or Métis. They had heard about Cheryl's death through Nancy and her mother. They gave me an insight into Cheryl's past by the glowing remarks they made about her. Again, I wanted to cry for the waste of such a beautiful life. But I didn't. I remained outwardly emotionless. Nancy asked me again to come over to their place in the near future and I promised I would.

When it was all over, and Cheryl was buried, I knew it was time to return to the house, alone. Roger seemed to understand my need and drove me back. He didn't come in with me. Before he left, he said, "Take as much time as you need, April. Then call me. I'll be waiting for you."

"Roger, thank you for everything. I love you."

Roger smiled, "I love you too, April."

17

I WALKED INTO the house which now seemed so empty, so cold. I decided I would pack all of Cheryl's things away in a big trunk, even her clothes. That way I'd always have a part of her. And being able to touch her belongings would strengthen that feeling.

I opened the door to Cheryl's room and the first thing I noticed was that empty whiskey bottle. I hadn't really noticed it before when I had gone into her room. But there it stood on Cheryl's dresser, mocking me. Suddenly, I was filled with a deep hatred of what it had once contained. I grabbed it by the neck, raised it high and brought it down and smashed it against the edge of the dresser. Again and again, I brought it down, until it was smashed into a million pieces. I was screaming, "I HATE YOU! I HATE YOU! I HATE YOU!

My tears came flooding out and I continued screaming, "I hate you for what you've done to my sister! I hate you for what you've done to my parents! I hate you for what you've done to my people!"

I threw myself on Cheryl's bed, letting all my pent-up tears pour out. I pounded my fists into the bed, allowing my emotions to tumble out. I felt a frenzied rage at how alcohol had torn our lives apart, had torn apart the lives of our people. I felt angry for having done so many wrong things at so many wrong times. And I felt self-pity because I would no longer have Cheryl with me.

"Oh, Cheryl, why did you have to go and kill yourself? All those people at the funeral, they loved you so much. Didn't that count? I loved you so much. Didn't that count? Didn't it matter to you? You had so much going for you. You didn't have to kill yourself, Cheryl! Why? Why?"

I writhed on the bed as if I was in physical pain. I was. At times I would become still, but not for long. Stronger emotions would come crashing down on me and I would toss and turn again, trying to exorcise the painful anguish from within. I pounded my fists into the bed, again and again, in frustration. "If only . . ." Those words repeated themselves over and over in my head. But it was too late. Cheryl's death was final.

When I had spent the last of my tears, I sat on the edge of the bed and surveyed the mess I had made in the room. The floor had scattered fragments of the whiskey bottle all over it. Cheryl's pillow was soaked with my tears. I looked again at the floor. If only I could smash the problem of alcoholism as easily as I had that bottle.

Temporarily void of all emotion, I systematically began to clean the room. I put the Kleenex tissues into the garbage container. I began picking up the larger pieces of glass. I grabbed one piece a little too savagely and it cut my hand. I looked at the blood oozing out in a thin red line. "Still after more blood, are you? Well, you cut down my sister, my parents, my people. But no more. I'll see to to it. Somehow. Some way."

When I had finished cleaning Cheryl's room, I sat down again on Cheryl's bed. I wondered where to start, not wanting to start. Then I remembered all of Cheryl's papers, the journals she had kept. There were two boxes under her bed and I began going through them. The first was full of newspaper clippings, but I wanted her journals. They were in the other box.

I began looking through them. The last entry she had made was in January 1972. That was the month I had been raped. I looked for a 1970 journal. It was this one that I was most interested in because that was when I had first lost touch with Cheryl.

The entries for January indicated she had started the search for our parents. February had occasional references to her continued search. There was more in March.

I see more and more of what April sees, broken people with broken houses and broken furniture. The ones I see on Main Street, the ones who give us our public image, the ones I see puking all over public sidewalks, battling it out with each other, their blood smearing up city-owned property, women selling what's left of themselves for a cheap bottle of wine. No wonder April ran. She was horrified that this was her legacy. She disowned it and now she's trapped in that life of glitter and tinsel, still going nowhere. Charitable organizations! What a load of crap. Surrounded by a lot of people, business-wise but empty. Just like the Main Street bums.

The more I see of these streets, the more I wonder if April isn't right. Just maybe. Better to live that empty life than live out on the streets. What if I do find our parents? Sometimes I can't help it, I feel like April does, I despise these people, these gutter-creatures. They are losers. But

215

there is a reason why they are the way they are. Everything they once had has been taken from them. And the white bureaucracy has helped create the image of parasitic natives. But sometimes I do wonder if these people don't accept defeat too easily, like a dog with his tail between his legs, on his back, his throat forever exposed.

Happy Birthday, April. What do you give the person who has everything? I can give peace of mind with a few lies.

May, 1970 Struck paydirt with a new address on Austin. The place is rented by a woman named Josie Pohequitas. I knock on the door and it is opened by this little, bent, old woman who is stoned out of her mind. But happy as hell. I have figured out now it's better to see these people at certain times of day. You have to be late enough so they can start getting over last night's drunk and early enough so they're not whacked out of it yet. I ask if she knows Henry or Alice Raintree.

"Henri, Henri Raintree?" she says in a French-type accent.

"Yes, I'm his daughter and I've been looking for him," I say in a pleasant voice. What else can I say?

"Ah, yeah, mais oui, we're good friends, you know. Come in. Here, sit down, here. He comes to our place when the snows are gone. He goes north for winters. He is welcome here. He stays. Sometimes, we have big party. Sometimes, we have big fight. Then he goes. But he always come back, Henri does. He will come back. You come back in couple of weeks. You will see. He will be here then."

I'm tickled a deeper shade of brown, you might say. I tell the toothless woman with her toothless smile that I will be back.

June, 1970 I knock at this door again, having been here a few times with no luck and expecting none this time.

"Ah, Cheryl, it's you again. Come in, come in," her face lights up into a big grin, still toothless.

"Henri, Henri, come out here and see the surprise that is here for you. Hurry up, Henri," her voice is high-pitched and squeaky.

An old, grey-haired man comes walking out of the kitchen. He is trying to keep his balance, curiosity is piercing through his drunken haze. I assume that Josie has told him about me but still it's a few minutes before he realizes it's me.

My smile disappears but a smile slowly appears on that leathery, unshaven face.

"No, no, it can't be. Not my little daughter, Cheryl. My little baby. You're all grown up now."

He chuckles and staggers a little closer to me. He makes a visible effort to draw himself up, but he has drunk too much already and the feat is beyond him. His clothes are worn, dirty and dishevelled. Tears of happiness and perhaps awakened guilt pour from his watery eyes.

The woman, Josie, is beaming with pride as if this "joyful" reunion were all her doing.

"It's like a miracle. It is like a miracle," she cackles over and over again, watching father and daughter facing each other. I am rooted to the very spot, absorbing the true picture of my father. I make no effort to move towards him. This goes unnoticed and the old man approaches me.*

"I cannot believe that we are standing here, face to face, at long last. At long, long last," the decrepit, old man says.*

I stand quietly, hiding the horror which is boiling inside of me. I hadn't known what to expect. But it wasn't this, this bent, wasted human form in front of me. My father! I am horrified and repulsed; by him; by the cackling, prune-faced woman; by the others who have crawled out of the kitchen to watch all this "happiness," all of them with stupid grins on their faces; by the surrounding decay; by the hopelessness. The cancer from the houses I've been to has spread into this house, too. To destroy.

All my dreams to rebuild the spirit of a once proud

nation are destroyed in this instant. I study the pitiful creature in front of me. My father! A gutter-creature!

The imagination of my childhood has played a horrible, rotten trick on me. All these years, until this very moment, I envisioned him as a tall, straight, handsome man. In the olden days he would have been a warrior if he had been all Indian. I had made something out of him that he wasn't, never was. Now I just want to turn and run away, pretend this isn't happening, that I had never laid eyes on him. Pretend I was an orphan. I should have listened to April.

Awkwardly he hugs me. I smell the foul stink of liquor on him. Hell, he probably sweats liquor out of his pores. I close my eyes so no one will see what's in them. I hold my breath against the gutter smell. Seems like ages before he releases me. When he does, he turns to the others and says, "Don't just stand there, bring her a drink. Now we have something to celebrate. I found my little girl after all these years. Tell me, Cheryl, where is your sister? Where is April? I missed you both so much. Ah, here we are."

He hands me a beer and wipes his tears and runny nose on the sleeve of his shirt. I don't answer. I just think, "April is far away from you and she'll never know what you are, you gutter-creature!"

Gratefully, I swallow some beer. Disgust, hatred, shame . . . yes, for the first time in my life, I feel shame. How do I describe the feeling? I swallow more beer.

I stay for the rest of the day in spite of my desire to flee. I stay because I want to know about Mom. But I want Dad sober when I ask him about Mom. Funny, I can still refer to him as Dad. I drink away the hours and pass the dizzy, nauseous, sensations, laughing stupidly with them. Josie puts me to bed, just in time, on the battered couch in the living room.

Next morning. I wait patiently for Dad to get up. It is almost noon. He comes into the kitchen. He looked in rough shape last night but now he looks worse, with his weak, flabby arms showing because he's in a torn, greyish *undershirt. His dark-colored baggy pants are held up by suspenders that are frayed to the breaking point and all twisted. I get coffee for Dad. Josie is busy puttering around the kitchen. No one talks, the only noises come from Dad slurping his coffee.*

Finally, I ask him, "Dad, could we talk?" Sounds like I'm shouting. I lower my voice. "I want to know about Mom. How is she? Do you see her?"

Dad makes a gesture as if he doesn't want to talk about her right now but I persist. "Please, Dad. Tell me about Mom. Where is she?"

Tears come to his eyes again. He says simply, "She died last July."

"Died? Mom died?" I ask, not believing. I then figure out that Mom was in poor health when we were kids and that's why she died. I wish I could have seen her. Poor, dear mother. Maybe that's why Dad turned to booze. He misses her so much he can't live without her. I can forgive that, retract all the bad thoughts about him.

But Dad speaks again. "I may as well tell you everything." He sighs and lapses into another long silence.

I try to make it shorter by telling him to continue. "Tell me what, Dad?"

"Your mother took her own life. She killed herself," he says at last. "She left a letter for me but I had gone up north early that year. I have a nephew in Dauphin. I stop in there sometimes. They sent the letter there. She jumped off the Louise Bridge last July. I took the letter to the RCMP and they checked with the Winnipeg police. They had found a body and everything matched your Mama. She was not happy with her life. Once she lost you girls and Anna died, she knew she would never get you girls back again. Those visits were the hardest on her. So she stopped going. She tried to kill herself before, once a long time ago."

I digest what he says. " . . . too hard on her?" What about April and me? In those foster homes? Okay, only one was real bad and April suffered most of that one. But I suffered for April. And the other ones? Those people weren't our flesh and blood. They weren't even our race. I remember now, those promises you made us, promises we believed, all the waiting for you to take us back home, all the loyalty we gave you—all for nothing.

"Who's Anna?" I'm angry but I don't want to fight. I want information.

"Dad looks at me, surprised. "You don't know about Anna? Oh, of course not, you were just a baby yourself when she died. April must remember her. Maybe not. She was just little, too, and Anna wasn't with us very long. She was your baby sister. But she was a sick baby. They should have kept her in the hospital longer, but, no, they sent her home too early and she died. They blamed your Mama and me. That was their excuse for taking you girls away from us. No, my girl, your Mama was not a happy woman."

"Why didn't you come to see us when we were kids?" I ask in a soft voice, afraid of an honest answer.

There is another long pause. "I went up north for a long time. I was never here to visit you again," he says as if that's a good enough reason. "No, your Mama did not want you girls to see the way she was. She was too ashamed. She couldn't face you again. They shouldn't have taken you away from us. The baby was just sick, that's all." Dad drifts off in silence again.

Dad asks me to come back and see him tomorrow. I say I will. I do. Josie says Dad left that morning to see some friends of his for a few days. Here I thought he would be patiently waiting for me. Ha! What a joke!

I sat back on the bed with the journal clutched to me. This was the second mention of Anna. I'd been thinking of Anna after Cheryl had told me about her. Baby Anna. I remembered that's what I had called her. Recollections of my mother rocking a baby had come back, much clearer. I'd always had vague pictures in mind but I'd never realized the baby was our own sister. Baby Anna. She'd been with us for just a fraction of our lives. But she was sick and had to go to the hospital. And now, here, in Cheryl's journal, were Dad's words saying the same thing. Baby Anna. Such a small part of our lives. Yet she had changed our lives the most.

This was exactly how Cheryl felt when she found Dad. After all that he told her, she still went back to see him the next day, she was still loyal to him. How was it she had the natural family instinct? I had instincts only for self-preservation, pushing anyone away from me who might hurt me. I was a loner. Only lately had I let Roger in. Then Nancy and her mother, hugging me that night, giving me all that they had felt for Cheryl. Before Roger, who else besides Cheryl had hugged me and meant it? Well, maybe Mrs. Dion. I remembered wishing many times that I could be as affectionate as Cheryl. That meeting with Dad, maybe it destroyed her self-image. Funny, though, since she had seen that side of native life before. I wondered what sort of image she had built up about our parents? Was it that image of long ago that had sustained her, given her hope?

February 18, 1971 So. A son is born to me. It should have been a very special day for him. A day when his aunt, his grandparents and all his relatives rejoiced. Instead, it's just him and me. What's that joke I read? If he had known what was going to be in store for him, he would have cried a whole lot louder?

February 22, 1971 Having pondered over what to call you, my sweet child, I've decided on Henry Liberty Raintree. May you grow up to be all your grandfather is not.

March 10, 1971 Nance is babysitting and I'm free for a while. Feels great to be let out. Henry Lee's been so cranky lately. Hell, we've got to move out cause kids aren't allowed. Landlord's just a prejudiced bastard. I thought Henry Lee would change my life for the better but I can see

I thought wrong. Must say I do feel good about this place. Don't think Nance will mind my coming home late. She'll understand.

April 8, 1971 Sure am glad Nancy's Mom is letting Henry Lee stay at her place. I'm not so tied down anymore. She sure gives him some good mothering. I don't think motherhood was meant for me. I'd rather be out partying than sitting at home changing dirty diapers.

June 1971 Nancy's Mom is keeping Henry Lee for me for good now. Do I feel guilty? Only when I'm sober. And I try very hard to see that doesn't happen. I give her money all the time, so I'm sure she doesn't mind. Wish I had a mother like that.

October, 1971 Today Dad says he doesn't know where he is going to stay because he can't pay his rent. I know what he wants so I give him forty bucks. His eyes bulge. Usually I only give him ten or twenty.

At DeCarlos with Nance. The gang is all here, too. Already we got suckers to pay for our drinks. It's cheap coming here. I give my money to Dad so he can go get tanked and I come here and get mine free. I have to laugh at dumb jokes, let these guys run their hands up my legs. They think they're going to get more later, but I can avoid that.

Mark DeSoto. Now if all these guys were like Mark . . . but they're not. Nance says Mark's ol' lady, Sylvia, is going to have it in for me if I hang around with Mark. He's over there at another table. He comes to say hello. I ignore him. He was supposed to call during the weekend and didn't. The suckers at my table are really playing up to me tonight. Got to go to the john.

I'm walking back to my table and I hear this shrill voice. "Hey, squaw, I don't share my man with no one. You hear me, bitch? Especially no squaw."

Sylvia comes into my path and stops. I stop. I look her in the eye. "If I'm a squaw, honey, what's Mark? He's as much an Indian as I am." I feel ridiculous and powerful at *the same time. I know what I'm capable of. I give her my coldest stare. I know I've won this round. She can't match my gaze. The 'blond bomb-shell' jabs a finger into my shoulder, telling me what she's going to do to me. I twist around slightly and bring my fist into the side of her face, not real hard but hard enough to back her off. The dumb broad trips over a chair and sprawls on the floor. Everyone laughs, hoping for a fight. I step over her and continue on my way.*

"You're going to pay for this, Cheryl Raintree."

"Yeah? Well you better give it your best shot, Sylvia."

Mark struts over to my table. My precious companions scatter. He sits down and grins. "So you're my prize," I say to him sarcastically. But the evening ends with Mark in my bed.

Mark moves in. Nance moves out. Landlord requests that we remove ourselves after the first party. I find a cheap place on Elgin.

November, 1971 I'm working. Mark is working the streets. We're always broke. I sell all the furniture, except the typewriter. I wonder why April gave it to me? She's the one with the writing talent. I give it to Nance for safe keeping so Mark won't sell it.

We're stone broke. Mark owes everyone so we can't hit anyone up for a loan. Mark says to me, "You know that guy who comes to Neptune's and he always looks the chicks over. Well he's loaded and sometimes I sit and talk to him."

"I know who you mean. What about him? You're going to borrow some money from him?"

"He never lends money. But sometimes he sees a chick he likes and asks me if I can arrange a meeting. So, I go to her and if she's interested we share the money he pays, see?"

"You mean you're some kind of pimp?"

"Not a pimp, Cheryl. I just do two people a favor and I get some money out of it. We need money now, bad, and I

223

know he's got the hots for you. I just thought you might consider it, just this once.''

"You're asking me to go to bed with another man?''

"Well, it's not like there's any feelings between you. Just think of it as a business transaction. I told him you were a very special girl and he's willing to pay more for you. Come on, Cheryl, one hour's work and you could make fifty bucks. I'll try to get more.''

"Forget it.'' I'm bloody mad.

"I'm no fucking prostitute.'' I storm out of the house.

A week later. We're still broke. I'm drinking at Neptune's. I'm almost drunk. Mark comes over. This sucker who's been buying me drinks leaves quickly. Funny the power Mark has. "Cheryl, please, we gotta get some money. The landlord today said he'd give us another 24 hours and no more.''

"Is he kinky?'' I'm just dirt. Who cares if he's kinky.

Later. I'm back at Neptune's. I have a drink. Another one. Another one. My parents deserted me, April has left me, Mark . . . is a-no-goddamned-good-fucking-son-of-a-bitch. I have another drink. And another one. Let Mark use me. I don't care. Let April sit in her fancy white palace. I just don't give a damn!

January, 1972 I'm an old pro now. I'm working the streets full time. I avoid the pigs by picking johns that are obviously not pigs. Well, pigs in another way. Mark arranges a lot of meetings, too. I've gotten into other things I bet Mrs. Semple never even heard of in her old 'syndrome speech.' I'm still broke. First thing I see Dad, he says, "Cheryl, I need a twenty for groceries.''

"I don't have any.''

He goes into a rage. "What do ya mean, you don't have any? You got enough to go drinking but you can't spare your poor Pa any? Did that bum you're shacked up with tell you not to give me anymore? You're just as bad as your ol' lady was, you know that? A lazy no good for nothing. Running around all the time, living with bums. I need some money. I need groceries and I got to pay the rent. Now I got nothing, just cause you couldn't hang onto a simple job."

I tell him he's worse. I swear at him. I tell him what I think of him, that he's a parasite, a gutter-creature. I tell him it's his fault Mom killed herself. The tears spring to his eyes. I leave him. Let him stew in his guilt. I sure as hell stew in mine.

At home. Mark comes in. I'm angry and still brooding. Mark is angry. I'm supposed to be at Neptune's. We need money real bad. He yells. I yell. He beats me. I'm used to it. He avoids hitting my face. He has learned it's not good for business. He leaves.

I walk along Main Street. This is where I belong. With the other gutter-creatures. I'm my father's daughter. My body aches. I enter a hotel. I don't know which one. The word 'Beverage' is all I see. I need a drink. A couple of drinks. The depression is bitterly deep. The booze doesn't help this time. I'm back on the street. I'm drunk. I want to run in front of a car. The guy who was buying my drinks comes with me. What a creep. We head to my place on Elgin. We take a short-cut down a lane. The creep wants to fondle me and kiss me. He can't wait. "Back off, you ugly old man. I'm no whore, you know?" I don't know why I say that, but I repeat it. I can scarcely keep my balance. It's like there's two of me, one watching, one doing. "I wanna kiss you. I know what you are. So don't pretend with me. I paid for you."

"You stink. Leave me alone, you filthy pig!" I slur the words. He gives me a push. I slam into the wall and fall into a sitting position. My legs have given out. I close my eyes. I like the sensation of everything spinning around at full speed. I open my eyes. I smile dumbly up at the man. He slams his fist into my face.

I wake up. I'm lying on the sidewalk. My legs are sprawled out in front of me. I notice the garbage cans and garbage bags on either side of me. "Hello there!" I says to

them. "I've come home at long, long last." I chuckle to
myself. I think in the morning the garbage men will take us
all away, me and my friends. I giggle. I try to get up. I
can't. So I stay put. Every once in a while I chuckle to
myself. I hum a tuneless song.

I wake up. April holding my hand. I can't see her but it's
April. I squeeze her hand.

I felt anger and bewilderment. Not at Cheryl or anyone
else. Mostly I guess the anger was for me. For being the
way I was. Because it had caused Cheryl to feel so
alienated from me that she couldn't share the most important event in her life with me. Cheryl's baby. Henry Liberty Raintree. Then I smiled. A part of Cheryl still lived. I
looked at my watch. And sighed. It was four a.m. I'd have
to wait until morning. I paced around the room and finally
returned to the journals. I put them back in the box and set
them on the floor. Then I laid on Cheryl's bed, on top of
the covers, still fully clothed. With my hands under my
head, I stared up at the ceiling. The clock downstairs was
abnormally loud and so, so slow. A few hours more and I
could be on my way to Nancy's place to Henry Lee.

For the moment, I thought of Cheryl. The memories of
her voice, the memory of her reciting her powerful message
at the Pow Wow. Why, oh why didn't she talk to me? Why
couldn't we have talked to each other? And would it have
helped? At times I was overwhelmed with her memories
and tears would trickle down the sides of my face.

The next morning I woke up, dismayed that I had fallen
asleep. Then I was dismayed to find it was still too early to
go to Nancy's place. The sun was just beginning to rise. A
golden orange ball of fire in the east. I went downstairs to
make coffee and freshen up. My eyes felt swollen. Again
the house seemed so empty, cold, lifeless. With my cup of
coffee in hand, I opened the front door and stood looking
out at the still empty street. The birds were just beginning
to sing their morning praises to their Creator. It had rained

during the night. Everything was wet. The smell of wet earth was invigorating. So clean. I stood there breathing deeply when I noticed there was a letter in the mailbox. I thought of leaving it for the moment, but didn't. The moment I saw it was Cheryl's handwriting, my heart started to pound. I tore it open and sat down, heedless of the damp step.

Dear April,

By the time you get this, I will have done what I had to do. I have said my goodbye to my son, Henry Liberty. I couldn't bring myself to tell you about him before. Now I know you will do what is right where he is concerned. I also know that Mary and Nancy will do as you wish. They're taking care of Henry Lee. All my life, I wanted for us to be a real family, together, normal. I couldn't even mother my own baby!

Do not feel sorrow or guilt over my death. Man thinks he can control nature. Man is wrong. The Great Spirit has made nature stronger than man by putting into each of us a part of Nature. We all have the instinct to survive. If that instinct is gone, then we die.

April, there should be at least a little joy in living and when there is no joy, then we become the living dead. And I can't live this living death any longer. To drink myself to sleep day in and day out.

April, you have strength. Dream my dreams for me. Make them come true for me. Be proud of what you are, of what you and Henry Lee are. I belong with our Mother.

Love to you and Henry Lee,
Cheryl

An hour later I was at Nancy's place once again. She opened the door for me as if she had been expecting me right at that particular moment. I followed her down the hall to the kitchen. Sitting at the table was a small boy eating some cereal. He looked up at me as I walked into the room. He smiled, the same kind of smile I had seen a long time before on his mother's face when she was that age, the age of innocence.

Nancy began explaining but I stopped her. I told her I understood everything. As I stared at Henry Lee, I remembered that during the night I had used the words "MY PEOPLE, OUR PEOPLE" and meant them. The denial had been lifted from my spirit. It was tragic that it had taken Cheryl's death to bring me to accept my identity. But no, Cheryl had once said, "All life dies to give new life." Cheryl had died. But for Henry Lee and me, there would be a tomorrow. And it would be better. I would strive for it. For my sister and her son. For my parents. For my people.

BEATRICE CULLETON was born on August 27, 1949, in the St. Boniface Hospital in Winnipeg. She was the youngest of four children of Louis and Mary Clara Mosionier. At the age of three, Beatrice became a ward of the Children's Aid Society of Winnipeg. She grew up in foster homes away from her real family and her people, with the exception of several years when she lived in a foster home with one of her older sisters. However, unlike the April Raintree of this story, her experience in foster homes was generally positive, most of it spent with one family. Both of Beatrice's older sisters committed suicide. She has one brother still living in British Columbia. Her real parents currently live in Winnipeg. The characters in this story are fictional and any resemblance to people living or dead is purely coincidental.